THE DIVINELY INSP

D1128912

JAMES CHAMBERS

JOHN L. FRENCH

ROBERT E. WATERS

JENIFER PURCELL ROSENBERG

CHRISTOPHER J. BURKE

MICHELLE D. SONNIER

DANIELLE ACKLEY-MCPHAIL

KEITH R.A. DECANDIDO

RUSS COLCHAMIRO

MICHAEL A. BLACK

PATRICK THOMAS

HILDY SILVERMAN

JOHN G. HARTNESS

Other Anthologies by eSpec Books

DEVILISH & DIVINE

EDITED BY
JOHN L. FRENCH &
DANIELLE ACKLEY-McPHAIL

NEOPARADOXA

Pennsville, NJ

PUBLISHED BY
NeoParadoxa
an imprint of eSpec Books LLC
Danielle McPhail, Publisher
PO Box 242,
Pennsville, New Jersey 08070
www.especbooks.com

Copyright ©2021 eSpec Books
Copyright for the individual stories remains with the authors.

ISBN: 978-1-949691-47-4
ISBN (ebook): 978-1-949691-46-7

All rights reserved. No part of the contents of this book may be repro-
duced or transmitted in any form or by any means without the written
permission of the publisher.

All persons, places, and events in this book are fictitious and any re-
semblance to actual persons, places, or events is purely coincidental.

Cover and Interior Design: Danielle McPhail, McP Digital Graphics
Copy Editing: Greg Schauer

Art Credits - www.fotolia.com
Wings tattoo © silverlily
buffalo abstract skull tattoo on the white background. © photochatree
Firewall Tattoo Tribal Pattern © Diverser

DEDICATION

In loving memory of
our dear friend

DON SAKERS
June 16, 1958 - May 17, 2021

CONTENTS

FAR FROM THE KNOWING PLACE

James Chambers

THE SEARCH PARTY FOUND THE BOY ASLEEP UNDER A FALLEN TREE TRUNK six miles outside Cisqua on the bluffs above the Mattegticos River. At first, the river's roar drowned out the shouts of the rescuers, but then their voices carried, and Betsy Carpenter dashed through the woods, her skirt clutched high to keep the hem from snagging on the brush. Morris Garvey raced after her.

"Careful, now, Betsy," he called. "It won't help Thomas if you sprain your ankle."

"Don't worry about me, Morris," Betsy said. "Worry about keeping up."

"Damn, that woman is fast," Morris muttered.

He leapt over a fallen branch and pushed himself faster, but Betsy vanished among the trees. He followed the voices of the search party until he saw her kneeling with her arms around six-year-old Thomas Yates. Betsy ignored the dirt and leaves that covered the boy and embraced him tight. Relief painted the faces of the men and women from Cisqua who formed the search party.

"A few cuts and scratches, but the boy looks all right otherwise, Mr. Garvey," said one.

"Though I'll wager he needs some hearty food and hot drink," said another.

"Well, that's excellent news," Morris said.

Betsy released Thomas, but the boy clutched her hand and refused to let go. Tears drew glistening paths through the grime on his face. As Morris approached, he sniffled and straightened his posture, falling back on his manners even after all that had happened. Twigs poked out from his hair, and a rip in his pants leg showed a bloody scrape above his left knee.

Betsy beamed with a bittersweet smile. "Morris, I'd like you to meet Master Thomas Yates, my cousin's son."

Morris extended his hand, which, after a moment's hesitation, Thomas shook.

"Pleasure to meet you," Morris said. "You gave us all quite a fright these past two days, but I'm happy to see you looking so well after your ordeal."

"I'm sorry, sir," said the boy. "I didn't mean to scare anyone."

"Hush, now, Thomas," Betsy said. "You've no need to apologize. It's understandable you ran. You must've been terrified. God knows what might've happened if you hadn't. We're only glad to see you in one piece."

"I do hope, though," Inspector Daniel Matheson said, as he crunched through the brush to join the conversation, "you'll tell us all that occurred before you fled the ole homestead."

Fresh tears welled in Thomas's eyes. He held Betsy's hand tight to his chest.

"Easy now, Inspector," Betsy said. "Give him time to recover before the interrogation."

"No interrogation, ma'am. Just a few questions. The sooner we rustle up some answers, the sooner we can reckon what happened to the boy's family and where his father is. You take your time, young Thomas. You've been through an ordeal. When you're ready to speak, we're ready to listen."

The full search party of twenty men and women from Cisqua, plus Morris, Betsy, and Matheson, who'd taken the train up from the sprawling metropolis of New Alexandria some fifty miles south, now surrounded Thomas. Twenty-three sets of eyes studied the boy, most sympathetic, others fearful, and a few angry. Their gazes seemed to stiffen his resolve, and the child stepped away from Betsy, took three deep breaths, and then said, "I'm ready now, sir. My papa killed Momma and my sisters with his axe. When he came to kill me, I ran out of the house. An angel told him we should die and that he should kill a lot of other people too. I saw him with the axe with blood all over it. I saw Momma too and more blood than I ever seen before. My littlest sister, Rachel, she screamed as I ran away. I wanted to go back and help her, I swear I did, but my legs wouldn't listen. They kept me running until I reached the woods. Then I figured it was too late."

After the words rushed from his mouth, Thomas's tenuous composure disintegrated. He pressed his face against Betsy's skirt and sobbed into it. Betsy glared at Matheson.

"Are you satisfied, Inspector?" she said.

"I do apologize, ma'am, but better we know what kind of snake is slithering through the grass. If the boy's telling us the truth, ain't no search party we need to find Mr. Yates. It's a posse."

Murmurs raced through the group, the gist of them hostile toward Arlen Yates, who'd never quite fit into the local community. Morris sensed their outrage growing. Eying the horizon through the trees as it transformed from clear blue to blazing orange, he approached them.

"It's a horrifying, worrying thing, what the boy said." The murmurs silenced. All the searchers stared at Morris. "You're afraid for your families, for your town, and if what the boy told us is true, you ought to be. Getting angry won't help. The sun's going down. We don't need to thrash around in the woods after dark. We must make smart choices. Return to town. Check on your families. Make plans to keep everyone safe until the boy's father is brought to justice. Take the night to secure your homes. We can hunt him by daylight in the morning."

"Yeah? What if he rabbits overnight, and we never see him again?" one said.

"All the better for Cisqua then, no? I promise you, Inspector Matheson and I will spread word of Mr. Yates far and wide to ensure that wherever he might run, he will be caught."

"I don't like it. He might be right around here where we can grab him," another man said.

One of the women said, "Don't be dense. Mr. Garvey is right. First, we must protect our families and organize a town watch. Then we hunt down that murdering heathen."

Chatter among the group indicated majority agreement.

"Excellent. Now, which of you kind people can lead a few city slickers back to home and hearth?" Morris said.

At Cisqua's one inn, The Bald Mountain House, where Morris, Betsy, and Matheson had taken rooms, Betsy cleaned Thomas of filth and debris and changed him into clean clothes she'd brought from her cousin's house. She and the boy joined Morris and Matheson in the inn's dining room for supper. The boy looked quite healthy with the mess scraped off, and a ruddy color returned to his washed-out face as he gulped down food and drink. The adults made small talk while he ate a full meal, after which he set to work on a large slice of cherry pie.

"Now that's a delicious looking slice of pie." Dave Jackson, Cisqua's mayor, placed a hand on Morris's shoulder, startling him. "Remember to chew, young Master Yates. And if you don't mind, I'd like to borrow Mr. Garvey for a bit. That okay with you, Mr. Garvey?"

"Fine with me, Mr. Mayor." His curiosity piqued, Morris pushed his chair back and rose. "Dan, Betsy, I'll be back shortly."

Morris followed Jackson into the barroom. The Mayor knocked twice on the bar, and the bartender hurried over.

"Evening, Nick."

"Evening, Mr. Mayor. What'll it be?"

"Two scotches from my select bottle, please."

Nick nodded and rushed off to pour their drinks, returning soon with two glasses.

"To the health and safety of young Thomas Yates," Jackson said.

He and Morris touched glasses and drank to the sentiment.

"That is an excellent scotch, Mr. Mayor. Thank you."

"My pleasure. You've done our town a huge favor today."

"One of your searchers found the boy, not me," Morris said.

"Oh, I know, but the talk is you're the one who suggested everyone head back to town instead of rushing off blind to find the elder Yates and dump him in the Mattegticos."

"Is that what they had in mind? Can't say I blame them."

"Me neither, but people go off angry like that, sometimes the wrong folks wind up dead or injured. While I don't doubt what the boy has told us, I'm not ready to pass sentence on a man on nothing more than the word of a scared child."

"The corpses of that boy's mother and sisters offer their own silent testimony."

"That they do. If any of those searchers out there today saw the state of those ladies, I doubt even the great Morris Garvey could've persuaded them to stay calm. Your reputation reaches far outside New Alexandria. They respect you, so they listened to you and did the right thing. I'm grateful you were there to help."

"I only spoke plain sense. Surely, New Alexandria has no monopoly on that."

"No, sir, but it can be damnably hard to find among a group of armed, tired folks who fear a madman is roaming their town."

"Is Yates a madman?"

Jackson sipped his scotch while he pondered the question. "What do you a call a man who starts up his own religion and then claims its angels tell him what to do?"

"There are many names for a man like that. As a person of faith, you must know them."

"You religious, Mr. Garvey? I mean, I know you're a scientist, built up your fortune on those steam-powered chimney sweeping machines and other inventions, Machinations Sundry, and all, and you science types don't go in for faith, superstition, and whatnot, but folks in Cisqua are church-going and god-fearing. They don't love the idea of the Yates worshipping a different god than theirs, but they aren't the kind to make trouble for a peaceful family. Folks around here take their beliefs to heart. They're not prone to judgment. Let the one without sin cast the first stone and all that. They treated the Yates like part of the community. This horrible turn of events has shaken some to their core."

"What are you getting at, Mayor?"

"I'd like to know if you think it might be true what the boy said."

"That his father is a murderer? Yes, that's likely true."

"Not that part, I'm right there with you on that. Do you think an angel told him to kill?"

"Are you asking me, Mayor, if I believe he believes it? Or if I believe a literal angel told him to go out and kill? The former, yes. I'd wager Mr. Yates suffers from dementia praecox. The latter, no, but I've seen enough of magic and the preternatural to leave the door open a crack on that."

"A madman, that's all?"

"Isn't that enough?" Morris finished the last of his drink. "Thank you for the fine scotch."

Morris returned to the dining room to find Thomas's pie plate clean to crumbs, and the boy sound asleep on Betsy's lap.

"Behold the power of good cherry pie," Matheson said as Morris took his seat.

"Thomas will stay with me tonight," Betsy said.

"He does appear to have become quite attached to you," said Morris.

"Thomas and I have always gotten on well. I was the only grown-up who'd play hide-and-seek with him at last summer's family reunion."

"What's your opinion of Arlen Yates?" Morris asked.

"Arlen's head has always been in the clouds. Up till now, though, he's been one of the finest men I know. A faithful husband and a doting father. A hard-working farmer. He's always provided a good life for my cousin and her children," Betsy said.

"Then he decided to take it all away." The words left Matheson's mouth as if he spoke to himself, thinking out loud, but the crushed expression they summoned to Betsy's face filled him with regret. "I'm sorry, Betsy. I should keep it to myself."

"What of Arlen's beliefs?" Morris said.

Betsy's hard stare lingered on Matheson another second before she answered. "Arlen's religion was his own, and he indoctrinated his family into it. My cousin, dear as she was to me, was no deep thinker. The faith Arlen created did not offend her, so she accepted it, but she was never devout—in it, or the faith she abandoned to adopt it. She lived for her children, and I think she enjoyed the company of Arlen's many followers. They came from neighboring towns, even other states, and visited for theological discussions. Dottie loved entertaining. Liveliness suited her. I found Arlen's ideas odd but harmless. I see now that I was grievously mistaken. I promise you, no one in the family saw this coming. He was joyous and kind when I was with them a year ago. What altered his mental state so disastrously in that time?"

"With a little luck we'll get the answer to that soon enough," Morris said.

"I hope so," Betsy said. "Morris, Dan, I can't thank you enough for coming here with me, for all your help. With most of my family out west now, Thomas has no one else. You have my deepest gratitude."

"Don't mention it," Morris said. "You're the best designer ever to grace Machinations Sundry's laboratories. I wouldn't dream of leaving you to face this on your own."

"I only came to keep Morris out of trouble," Matheson said, with a wink.

With that, they left the table. Matheson hefted Thomas from Betsy's lap and carried him to her second-floor room. After they tucked the boy into bed, Morris and Matheson retired. Two days of thrashing around the woods had left both men too tired for talk. They fell sound asleep fully dressed, barely loosening their collars and kicking off their shoes as their bodies hit their mattresses.

Later, the crash of breaking glass snapped Morris awake.

He sat up in total darkness, no sense of the time, and shook off the cottony weight of sleep. A muffled voice sounded outside the door. Footsteps. The door handle jiggled as someone tried it from the other side, but the lock held. The voice spoke again. Morris couldn't discern the words. Footsteps moved down the hall in the direction of Betsy's room.

Morris jumped from his bed and shook Matheson awake.

"Get up, Dan, there's trouble," he said.

"Tarnation," Matheson muttered as he pulled himself upright.

After tugging on his shoes, Morris unlocked the door and eased it open. A gelid white light spilled through for a moment then winked out.

He poked his head into the corridor and saw the shadow-shape of a man at Betsy's door. With the click of its latch, the door opened, and the man entered the room. Morris covered the distance in three steps then shoved the door open wide, and yelled, "Betsy! Wake up."

The man, still hidden in shadow, cried out: "Deva, protect me. Stay your burning hands. Let me do thy work and please our Lord."

With a gasp, Betsy stirred and lit the oil lamp on her bedside table. Thomas Yates popped up beside her. The lamplight dispelled the shadows around and revealed the man's face, crisscrossed with scratches, eyes watery and wide, lips trembling, and hair disheveled and wild. Blood dappled the collar of his ragged coat. The man's empty, determined expression made him look as if he acted outside his control, a marionette on strings with a hatchet clutched in his right hand.

"Papa?" said Thomas Yates.

The man's gaze focused on the boy. "Time for you to be with your family, son. The Lord calls us to him through his messenger."

Betsy shoved Thomas behind her. "Don't you dare touch him."

"I know you. My wife's cousin. You're family too. You can be with us. *Should* be with us. Our whole family, together in the Devachan. We'll be pure and full of grace and bask in his fiery touch."

Yates raised his hatchet and stepped toward the bed.

Morris barreled into him, crushing him against a chest of drawers, and grabbing his right arm to deflect the hatchet. The two men struggled, Morris trying to seize the weapon, Yates attempting to free himself. He punched Morris twice in the stomach with his left hand, the blows powered by the strength of a man who spent his days working the land, and knocked the wind out of him. Yates pressed his advantage to flip Morris onto his back and wrench his right arm free. He lifted the hatchet to strike.

A gunshot filled the room with a thunderous crack.

Yates wailed as the bullet struck his left shoulder. He changed his target from Morris on the floor to Matheson in the door with a smoking revolver in hand and threw the hatchet before the Inspector could fire another shot. The Inspector dropped to his knees. The weapon whirled over him and landed in the corridor. Yates leapt by Morris, then thumped Matheson on the side of his head. He raced from the room, retrieving his weapon, and vanished into the darkness. Morris and Matheson caught up as he scrambled out through a broken window at the end of the corridor. They followed, jumping onto the roof of the inn's porch outside the window, dropping to the ground, ready to pursue—but they saw no sign of Yates, no hint of where he'd run.

"Damnation," Matheson said.

Morris stared into the night dark that surrounded them.

"He won't get far with that bullet you put in him. Sun will be up in a couple of hours. We'll find him then," he said.

They reentered Bald Mountain House by the front door and found the proprietor and several guests milling around in the lobby, roused by the commotion. Morris gave them a quick explanation, allowing Matheson to check on Betsy and Thomas upstairs. No one went back to sleep. The innkeeper roused his kitchen crew and set them to brewing coffee and cooking an early breakfast. Word traveled fast. As the sun rose, townspeople drifted in and ate while a posse gathered. By the time Mayor Jackson arrived, thirty people, with rifles and revolvers, milled around in the lobby and outside the inn.

Jackson sought out Morris, who'd straightened his clothes and downed three cups of coffee in preparation for the day.

"Are you hurt, Mr. Garvey? Are the boy and Ms. Carpenter all right?" he asked.

Morris nodded. "Shaken up but fine. Me, too, and the same for Inspector Matheson."

"Thank God. I'm appalled by Arlen Yates' behavior."

"On that we can agree."

"I'd like to ask you a favor, a big one." The Mayor gestured at the growing crowd. "We haven't had a formal sheriff in Cisqua for almost a year since Sheriff Oster died. We haven't had any need 'til now. I'm frightened of what this posse might do unchecked. You handled them well yesterday. I'd be grateful if you led the search for Arlen Yates today."

Morris nodded. "You're wise to be concerned, but I'm not the man for the job."

"Please, Mr. Garvey, I ask you to reconsider."

"Don't worry, Mr. Mayor. The right man is here. Inspector Matheson will turn that mob into an organized party and keep them in check, and he'll do a better job than I would. I'll introduce him to the crowd. His accent will do the rest, I promise. You ever want to intimidate someone, speak like a Texan. I've got other work ahead of me. I'm going to the Yates' house. I've got a hunch there's more method to Arlen Yates's madness than we realize."

The mayor nodded. "All right, I'll go with you. It'd be best to have me there in an official capacity should you find any evidence. It's not wise for you to go off on your own anyway."

"Fair enough," Morris said.

Its pastoral appearance deceptive, the Yates farm stood on the edge of Cisqua. Men had moved the bodies of Mrs. Yates and her daughters to the town icehouse, but no one had yet cleaned the house, and the stale odor of death lingered there. Unpleasant clouds of flies buzzed around it, hungry, agitated, and persistent in contrast to the honeybees in the clover lawn going about their business, same as always. *Outside of storybooks*, Morris thought, *nature ignores human tragedies except to feed on them.*

The house's interior trapped rank, stuffy air within its walls.

Jackson gagged and waved a hand across his face. "We've got to open some windows, let in some fresh air."

"No." Morris held a handkerchief over his mouth and nose. "You'll only let in flies."

Blood stained the floor, some of it so thick it shone, still wet or tacky. Rust-brown streaks ran along the walls, showing where Arlen Yates had raised his gory axe and sent crimson streams into the air. Mrs. Yates had died in the kitchen. The blood of her daughters lay spilled in their room at the back of the house.

"Me and some men from town picked through here with ardent thoroughness before you arrived. What exactly are you looking for?"

"Mr. Mayor, I'll let you know once I find it."

Morris completed a walk-through of the first floor. The sight of so much innocent blood broke his heart, and he wondered if, as it often seemed, all religions truly demanded such bloodshed. He ascended to the second floor, which contained only the master bedroom and a small office where Arlen pursued his religious studies. Two dozen books filled a single shelf mounted on the wall above a writing desk. Morris eyed the titles. Theological and occult works, some he knew and some he didn't, but all related to the spiritualist and theosophist movements birthed in Europe and arrived on North American shores some years ago. A copy of the Bible lay open on the desk, its pages annotated, Morris presumed, by Yates himself. Beside it, several pages of hand-written notes presented a jumble of scribblings. Morris sat at the desk and read through them. Written in crude code, they defied easy interpretation, but Morris cracked enough to see how Yates had attempted to syncretize various doctrines and mesh Biblical quotes with his own ideas about spirituality and the afterlife—which existed not in Heaven but a place called Devachan. On that higher plane of existence one's soul recharged before it returned to the world, reincarnated, striving for a pinnacle of enlightenment that some called Summerland, but which Arlen had named the Knowing Place, because those who resided there gained the full sum of all experience and knowledge, both human and divine, and never returned to earthly life.

"A wondrous place, indeed," Morris said. "Except for all the dying required to reach it."

As if in response, a voice whispered from a corner of the room, setting Morris's hairs on end. He jerked around in his chair but saw no one.

The whisper repeated the sound of almost words, like an infant mimicking speech.

"Jackson?" Morris hollered.

Footsteps pounded downstairs. Jackson rushed up the steps. "What is it, Mr. Garvey?"

"You were downstairs," Morris said.

Jackson nodded as he entered the room. Morris gestured for him to stay silent.

More whispers came. The voice spoke indecipherable words from the corner shadows.

Morris crept from the chair to the corner. The voice grew louder but no clearer. Whatever it said, it used no language he'd ever heard. *Or,* Morris thought, *no language at all.*

"A palimpsest of language," Morris said.

"Huh? A what now?" Jackson said.

"Do you hear that, Mr. Jackson?"

Jackson crouched with an ear directed at the corner. "I do."

"Can you make it out?"

Jackson frowned and his brow wrinkled. "Almost, but its meaning eludes me."

"Quite right. When one who deeply desires understanding comes so close to meaning but falls short, the mind may imprint meaning where none exists. Fill the blank slate, so to speak."

"You mean like how one sees shapes in the clouds?"

"Precisely." Morris opened the room's single window, poked out his head, and looked around. A drainpipe ran along the corner edge of the exterior wall and emptied into a rain barrel on the ground. "Stay here and monitor that voice. I'm going to investigate."

Morris exited the house and walked around it to the barrel. A stiff wind blew from across the open meadow where Yates' livestock grazed in the sun. Beside the barrel, Morris heard the hollow sound of air rushing across an open container. *Like blowing across the top of a jug.* The barrel produced a warbling hiss when the wind hit it right. Morris leaned over and spoke into the open end of the drainpipe: "If you hear me, Mr. Jackson, come to the window and look outside."

Jackson appeared in the open window. "Well, I'll be, it works like a speaking tube."

"I believe we've found our angel," Morris called.

"I'll be right down."

By the time Jackson reached the open yard, two men arrived at the house, shouting that the posse had found Arlen Yates and surrounded him. While the men offered details, Morris gazed up the length of the drainpipe to the window, where a white glow flickered like light reflected off water. Morris squinted then surveyed the surrounding area for its source. The morning sun hung low in the sky on the other side of the house, casting the back in shadow. Morris spied no water or other reflective surface within his line of sight. He looked back to the window. For a moment, the illumination brightened, and he discerned a shape forming in it, but then it faded and vanished, like an oil lamp snuffed out.

Jackson and the men, following Morris's gaze, saw it too.

"That light," Jackson said. "Someone else is here."

"Search the house," Morris said.

The four men rushed inside and moved through the house from bottom to top and back again but found no one. In Yates's office, Morris pressed the back of his hand against the oil lamp on the desk. Cold.

"If anyone was here, they're gone now," Jackson said.

"All right, then, let's go, see if we can get some answers out of Yates," Morris said.

"Assuming he's still alive when we get there," one of the men said.

Morris scowled. "I trust Inspector Matheson will see to that."

The messengers' wagon soon carried them to the entrance of an old estate, then wheeled up to a large house uninhabited for many years and slouched in ruin. Men from Cisqua spread out on the grounds. Jackson rushed off to coordinate with the searchers while Morris leapt from the wagon to meet Matheson by the front door, which hung askew on busted hinges.

"Yates is inside," Matheson said.

"Be cautious, Dan." Morris eyed the decrepit house. White light flickered in one of the upper windows then vanished. "There's more to this than we realized."

"How's that?"

Morris explained what he'd discovered at the Yates house.

"He killed his wife and daughters because of an echoing drainpipe?" Matheson took off his hat, rubbed his hand through his hair, and shook his head. "Maybe someone played a prank on him."

"How so?" Morris said.

"Betsy told us people were always coming and going from the Yates house. What if one noticed that drain and spoke into it, pretending to be the voice of God?"

"The voice of a deva."

"A what?"

"In Arlen's beliefs, devas are enlightened spirits that guide us. We each have our own."

"Guardian angel."

"Something like that. God stays aloof, and they act on his behalf. They're less concerned about protecting us or saving our souls, though, than increasing our spiritual wisdom. Sometimes that means doing hard or terrible things for the greater good, or so Arlen believed. Like in the Bible, when God asked Abraham to sacrifice his son, Isaac." The white light returned in another window. Morris pointed at it. "What do you make of that light, Dan?"

Matheson's eyes narrowed. The glow brightened for several seconds, churning like water in a storm, then smoothing into a fluid circle that rotated behind a cluster of light and shadow. It verged on forming a face, but then winked out, leaving darkness behind the cracked glass.

"Never seen anything like it," Matheson said.

"I saw it last night in the corridor outside our room before Arlen attacked Betsy and again this morning in a window at the Yates' house," Morris said.

"A trick," Matheson said. "Someone's sold Yates a bum steer. Now he's trying to sell it to us too and cover his tracks."

"How'd he get here from the Yates house so fast and slip by you all into this house?"

"Easy. He didn't. There's more'n one of them then, I bet," Matheson said.

"All right, let's assume so for now."

"Assume?"

"You and I have both seen more than enough to know better than to dismiss the idea that some magical force is directing Mr. Yates."

Matheson sighed. "Dammit, Morris, can't we just catch an outlaw for once?"

"I'll be as relieved as you if it turns out like that," Morris said. "You have a plan?"

"I do."

Matheson shouted instructions for the posse to surround the house with three men on every door, warned them they might find others besides Arlen hiding in the house. He recruited four men to go in with him and flush Yates out. Morris and Jackson stationed themselves near the house's rear door, figuring anyone who fled would head for the cover of the woods, not the open road. Long, torturous minutes of quiet passed before a gunshot sounded from inside the house. Shouts followed. The men watching the doors readied their rifles and revolvers. Sounds of a scuffle came from inside. The tinkle of breaking glass. A first-floor corner window opened, and a man leapt out and bolted into the space left unguarded by searchers who'd closed in on the doorways.

"He's running," shouted Jackson.

Morris and the Mayor dashed after him down a footpath into the near woods.

"It's Yates," Jackson said.

They crashed through overgrowth and gained on their fugitive.

Yates dropped an object to the dirt, the hatchet he'd wielded last night. The path took a steep incline. Yates stumbled ascending, and Jackson almost reached him, but he scrambled back to his feet with a spray of dirt and stones that caught the mayor in the face. Morris rushed past Jackson. At the hilltop stood a marble gazebo. Vines twined around its columns, and trees shaded it so deeply it resembled a natural outcropping. Dirt stains and cracks marred its once beautiful appearance. Yates bolted into it and fell to his knees. Blood from his shoulder wound slicked half his shirt dark red and black.

"My Deva, protect and guide me. My time is here," he said. "Is all that I've sacrificed not enough to cool the heat of your wrath? Is it insufficient for forgiveness?"

Morris stepped into the gazebo. A wall of blinding white light flared in front of him and stunned him so abruptly he fell and landed on his back on the path. Jackson helped him back to his feet. The men stood on the edge of the brilliance that filled the gazebo and shielded their eyes with their hands. Light swirled around Yates. The face Morris had almost seen twice before emerged again in the chiaroscuro yet avoided absolute coherence. A melodic hum came with it. The earth vibrated. Wind swept out from the gazebo, stirring leaves. A sweet flowery scent filled the air.

"Why?" Yates cried out. "Why did you not reveal the truth before I acted if you wished otherwise from me? Why did you let me hurt my beloved family so?" Tears streamed from Yates's eyes. All color fled his face, except his cheeks, which flushed crimson from crying. He trembled, head to toe, hands pressed together in prayer, head lowered, supplicating. "I was wrong, oh, Lord, how wrong, but I believed, and I still believe. I can't live with this, can't bear this burden. In my sin and ignorance, I yet place myself before you. I only wanted to bring my family closer to our Lord. I'm yours to deliver unto mercy or punishment. Please, do not forsake me to face this alone."

Yates' words devolved into sobs that wracked his entire body.

The white light deepened and clouded Yates in a glittering haze.

Morris and Jackson squinted against its intensity.

For less than a second, the light appeared to take more definite shape, a semi-human form with an ovoid head that brimmed with shards of light like antlers. It reached for Yates with hands that burned like the sun and wrapped its fingers around his head. Then it flashed once, vanished, and left behind the heat of an open furnace as numinous flames consumed Yates down from his scalp to his feet. Morris and Jackson leapt back to avoid a scorching. The flames lasted seconds, then subsided. Yates, burned beyond recognition, collapsed dead to the unmarked floor of the gazebo.

"My dear God," said Jackson. "What did we just witness?"

"Any answer I give would be a guess," Morris said.

They stood outside the gazebo, awestruck by Yates' smoking corpse, until Matheson and several searchers arrived. Everyone gazed at the charred remains.

"Is that... Yates?" Matheson said. "What the hell happened to him?"

"It appears to be a case of spontaneous combustion," Morris said.

"Are you yanking my chain?" Matheson said.

Morris looked him in the eye and shook his head.

"It's true," Jackson said. "We caught up to him here, then he burst into flames."

"We heard the scuffle in the house, Dan," Morris said. "Who else was there?"

"One of Yates' former followers. Once we, uh, overcame his reluctance to talk, he told us he got the idea Yates had a fortune hidden on his farm and thought he could stir him so crazy, he could go find it. His partner was at the farm this morning to search for it. That fella made a pass at Ms. Yates and wound up thrown out of the house on his posterior. He wanted payback. Our guy confirmed the two knew about the drainpipe. He's been following Yates around the past few days, showing him a weird light, and whispering out of the dark. Drove the man mad, I'd guess."

Morris and Jackson exchanged a glance, neither man ready to describe what they'd seen.

"I think he realized the truth back there in that house," Morris said. "He knew what he'd done and what had been done to him. Much too late for it to help him."

Jackson supervised bringing the prisoner back to town while Matheson brought the bulk of the search party over to the Yates farm. An hour later they'd caught the second man, who'd hidden in a bloody kitchen cupboard when Morris and Jackson were present. They stuck him in a cell in the town jail with his partner. Betsy broke into tears as Morris explained how the men had tricked Yates and taken advantage of his faith. He spoke of the searing hands that had reached out of the light to pass judgment on the man but made no attempt to explain them. He did not yet know how.

Betsy gripped Morris's arm. "What am I to tell Thomas?"

"The boy's smart, strong," Morris said. "He should know, despite all, that his father was a flawed man who believed too much and questioned too little. He ought to be able to honor his family's memory. I say, tell him the truth."

LET'S MAKE A DEAL

John L. French

A COLLECTIVE MOAN WENT OUT OVER CLANCY'S POUR HOUSE AS THE NEW goalie of the Baltimore Constellations hockey team again failed to stop the York Cavaliers' forward from shooting the puck into the net. That put the Baltimore team down by two goals.

"Where'd they get this guy?" Jake Barker asked.

"Belle's just out of college," Fred Boyd answered. "He was a French major from the Bronx."

"Well he plays like there's no eyeholes in his mask. What the hell happened to Richardson?"

"It was in the papers the other day," Donna Chavez said. "His wife caught him in bed with another woman and put four bullets in him."

Jake snorted a laugh. "Well, he blocked more shots than Belle has tonight."

Just then the buzzer sounded to end the second period. "Clancy," Carly Livingston shouted, "A round for the house."

"Why so generous, Carly?" Fred asked.

"Because she's a Cav's fan." Donna said, not so lightly punching her wife in the arm.

Carly shrugged. "Hey, I grew up in York. Now how about those drinks, Clancy?"

"Right away, who wants what?" My real name is Peggy Rivers, but I was getting used to being called "Clancy." Clancy was the bar's original owner. Whoever owns the Pour House gets called by his name. I was the sixth, or maybe the seventh "Clancy;" nobody was quite sure.

Sipping a Guinness Blonde, I thought back to my first visit to the bar. I was working off a contract, one that ended well for me—enough money to last a few lifetimes, a clean slate, and a fresh start—but not for a guy named Donavan. He had been the target and from what I later heard about him he richly deserved the lengthy prison sentence he was now serving. At least he got to drive both a hot car and a hot woman before he woke up in bed next to my dead body. Well, the body I was using then.

The buzzer sounded and the teams skated out to start the third period.

With his team back on the ice, Fred Boyd shushed everyone, his eyes riveted on the tiny screen over the bar. He had been a hockey fan since age eight when his father took him to a Baltimore Clippers game. He wanted one thing, for the Constellations to bring a hockey championship to Baltimore. It didn't matter that the Federal Hockey Association was the ice-equivalent to AA baseball, Fred wanted a championship. The Ravens, the Orioles, the Blast—all had at one time topped their leagues. Fred believed that if only the Constellations could join them, their attendance might pick up and guarantee their staying in Baltimore for at least a few more seasons.

By the way The Constellations were playing that night, it wasn't likely. They had had losing seasons their first three years and it didn't look good for the fourth.

"What I wouldn't give for the Constellations to be winners."

"The question, Mr. Boyd, is not what you wouldn't give but rather, what will you give?"

A woman emerged from the back of the tavern. There were booths there, for privacy should someone bring a date, or have to have a private chat, or to drink without being bothered. All eyes on her, she walked toward the crowd who had stopped watching the game to watch her.

She was dressed in jeans, boots, and tee-shirt—all in black. Her skin and hair were just a shade less dark than her clothes. Her face and arms bore scars from old battles. The glass in her hand contained something… dark. Her eyes, however, her eyes shone with a light that made you not want to stare into them for fear of discovering what stared back.

Where did she *come from?* I asked myself, not liking the only possible answer. It wasn't through the front door, I would have remembered.

The only back door was behind the bar and there were bars on the bathroom windows.

The woman took a sip of her drink and asked, "Well, Mr. Boyd, what would you give?" and that's when I knew.

She was a deal maker, just like the one who had approached me just after my husband moved out and left me with nothing. The man in black showed me how to get out from under my debts and be financially secure for the rest of my life—no matter what. All it would take was a favor.

I looked around at the patrons of the bar. One or two seemed to be thinking the same thing. I was about to order the woman, if that's what she was, out when Fred spoke up.

"Just what do you mean, ma'am?"

"I think you know." She whistled a few bars of *Whatever Lola Wants*. I knew the tune, and the musical it had come from. So did Fred.

"Well, Miss Lola, Joe Boyd and I might share a name but I'm not about to sell my soul for anything, especially not a hockey team."

After Fred said this I looked at the TV. The game was paused, which was odd. It's not that smart of a TV. I looked at the clock on the back wall. The time hadn't changed since I had last checked it. I looked at my watch. The second hand was frozen.

Lola laughed the laugh of someone who knew a joke no one else did. Then she shared the joke with those in the Pour House.

"We don't need souls, Mr. Boyd. 150,000 people die every day, and a surprising number come to us. What I'm asking, in exchange for what you want..."

Lola turned her attention away from Fred and toward the other bar patrons. Her gaze didn't linger, but her eyes touched theirs just long enough for them to realize what she might be and that her offer was genuine.

"...is a service, a favor. A day of your life, a week, maybe a month. It might be as simple as mailing a letter or dropping off a package. You might have to fly to Houston and bump into the right person at the right time. Or you might be asked to help someone you can't stand, or to take a risk you normally wouldn't take. Do that one thing and we're quits." She turned and looked at me. "Right, Ms. Rivers?"

She knows, I thought as I shrugged and replied, "If you say so."

"How will we know the price?" Jake Barker was a businessman. He made deals every day.

"You won't, not until the time comes. And it will come, you can trust me on that. I don't lie. It's one of the rules. But the bigger the ask, the bigger the price, Mr. Barker. And when the time comes, you will pay. Our deal here will leave you with no choice. Now then, Mr. Boyd, what's it to be?"

I spoke up before Fred could answer. "Take it in the back, those of you who want to. No sense everyone knowing each other's business."

Lola nodded, so did Fred. When they went to a back booth, I joined them.

"Clancy," Fred protested, "what the hel … heck?"

"Well, Ms. Rivers, what about privacy?"

"My bar, my customers, my rules. I'm here to keep you honest."

"As I told you, I don't lie."

"Which could be a lie. And even if it isn't. Someone asks for eternal youth, they end up six years old forever. Someone wants to win a half-billion lottery. They do but lose the ticket. I've danced this dance before and I'm going to make sure the right tunes are played."

To my surprise, Lola agreed. "How about you, Mr. Boyd?"

Fred shrugged. "Like Clancy says, her bar, her rules. And if you can't trust your barkeep, you shouldn't order the beer."

"Very well, Mr. Boyd. As I understand it, you want the Constellations to win a championship, correct?"

Fred was about to agree when I butted in. "The FHA *Baltimore* Constellations to win a championship, with Fred alive and healthy enough to enjoy their victory. Payment to follow."

Lola nodded. "Well done, Ms. Rivers. Sound good to you, Mr. Boyd?"

Fred thought a moment. "Time frame, within the next three years."

"Five years," Lola countered, and held out her hand. Fred took it and they shook.

"Done and done, Mr. Boyd. Oh, and don't get too attached to your Noel Price autographed Clippers' jersey." She smiled as Fred realized that the price of the Constellations victory might be one of his most treasured childhood possessions.

I moved so that Fred could get out of the booth. As I slid over to the wall side I said, "Fred, you've worked behind a bar before, right?"

"Back in college."

"A round for the house on the house and send back whoever's next."

Vincent Cape came strolling back. A young man just out of college. He had majored in history. I remembered that from the graduation party that his parents had given in this very establishment. I also remembered asking myself what good was a B.A. in history. From the look in his father's eyes, he was thinking the same thing even as he told everyone how proud he was of his son.

Vincent slid into the booth. He was clearly nervous, fidgeting in his seat and not making eye contact with either of us. I suspected that if I dared to touch his cheek it would be warm with worry and embarrassment. I was about to take his hand when Lola put hers on his.

"What do you want, Vincent?" she asked in a gentler tone than I expected. When he didn't answer she said, "Let me guess. You have a student loan that falls just short of usury. And you have a degree that you can't use outside of academia but that would require you to pursue a graduate degree which would only add to your debt."

Vincent nodded and spoke for the first time. "The loan debt isn't as bad as some. I got a partial scholarship from Morgan State University and I lived at home so I didn't have any boarding expenses. But yeah, me and my parents do owe a lot of money and there's nobody hiring history majors. If I go back to school..." He left that thought hanging.

"You know the terms?" Lola asked. When Vincent nodded, she turned to me.

"So, Ms. Rivers, what does he want?"

Vincent was about to object, but Lola said, "She's done this before. If you don't like her terms, you can change them."

The young man was smart, smart enough to know when to rely on someone smarter or more expert than he. At his "okay" I said,

"A job in his field that pays enough for a decent living *and* lets him pay the interest and the principal on his loan. A legal job."

Lola smiled. "A legal job. And I suppose a moral one as well?" She shook her head. "That leaves out gunrunning, human trafficking, drugs, and politics. Shame that. I could make you a congressman within ten years, a senator in fifteen. We need more people like you running this country."

"Don't you have enough of that kind of people running things?" Vincent asked.

The woman in black shook her head. "Never enough for what we need. But the price for such power may be a bit high for you. Let's see.

You studied history. Can you just repeat facts, or can you analyze them as well?"

"I like to think I can do both."

"Okay, let's see. There's a world that's completely covered in clouds. Its sun and the stars have never been seen and there is no moon. What kind of religion would its inhabitants develop?"

At first, Vincent was taken aback. Then, after a few minutes of thought, he said, "No sun god, obviously. Maybe a storm god, weather permitting. A Thor instead of an Odin. Or possibly an earth-based religion with the planet itself as God and the Storm as the Evil One. Uh, no offense meant."

Lola smiled. "None taken. Go on."

"With Earth as God, its inhabitants might see their role as taking care of its surface. Planting crops would become a religious rite, while hunting and the hewing of wood might require a sacrifice."

"What kind of sacrifice?"

The young man stared into Lola's eyes and said, "The bigger the ask, the bigger the price."

Another smile and nod. "You'll do." Suddenly, Vincent's text message alert went off. "Go ahead, look at it. It will tell you that next Tuesday you have a phone interview with a New England research firm. They specialize in studying past and current events from a religious viewpoint to predict future events. You'll pass the interview and will be asked to go north for a face-to-face. You have no objections to relocating?"

"To where?"

"Salem, Massachusetts. It's an old firm—a very, old firm. Now, as for your salary."

His text alert went off again. This time he looked at his phone. There was the confirmation of the appointment and below that a possible starting salary.

Vincent stared for a moment then said, "That is a lot of money. That should help pay off the loan."

"What loan?" Lola asked. "As of the minute you agree to the deal, you won't owe anyone anything. Well?"

"What's the price?" Vincent asked.

"From time to time over the next ten years, you'll be asked to 'adjust' your analyses and recommendations in ways we will recommend. If you fail to do this, you'll lose your job, and the forgotten loan will suddenly be discovered."

Vincent probably always thought that his most important decisions in life would be about marriage and his family. He now knew he was wrong. He considered the offer for a long moment. Then he said,

"My father always told me to go with what feels right. And though this seems to be the wrong thing to do, for some reason it feels right."

I had never felt that. When I made my deal, I knew it was the wrong thing to do. The problem was it was the only thing I *could* do.

"So you have a deal," Vincent said, "on one condition."

"And that is?"

"I won't root for the Patriots."

That got a laugh from Lola. "That's okay. None of us do."

When Vincent left, Lola and I decided on a break. I got a Dr. Pepper (without the rye, I had had my drink for the night.) and she taught me how to fix Hotter Chocolate. There was now a line to the back, maybe four or five deep. *How bad must things be,* I wondered, *if this many people are willing to make these kinds of deals?*

I didn't judge, how could I. I'd been there once. Fortunately, my deal worked out. I dared to pray that theirs would too.

Donna and Carly were not in line. Taking my soda, I walked over to their table.

"Not joining the crowd?" I asked, looking at the line.

Like the true couple they were, their heads shook in unison. "We've got everything we need," Donna said. "We're young, in love, and each married to the gal of our dreams. Maybe next year a baby." Not that I was going to ask, but Carly answered my unspoken question.

"My brother with Donna. Then, for them, me and his husband."

"Sound like a good deal," I said. *And it won't cost them anything extra,* I thought as I returned to the back booth where Jake Barker sat waiting for me and Lola to join him.

He came right to the point. "Last Thanksgiving, no, the one before that, there was a car. Good looking gal drove it in. Donavan and her drove it away. Well, Clancy, I guess you heard what happened with him. Damn fool. Who knows why he did it?"

I did. I was that gal but in a different body. As for what happened, let's just say it was part of the deal.

"I want that car, or one just like it," Jake said plainly.

"It" was a Moran '97, a car that only one percent of the one percent could afford.

"I know that case, I know that car," Lola said quickly. "Stolen, but the owner never claimed it. The Pennsylvania police will have it up for auction in two months."

East Bound and Down briefly played on Jake's phone. His text message alert. *Just how does she do that?*

"The information is now on your phone. Bid whatever you have to win the car. Don't worry about the payment. That will be covered. Ms. Rivers?"

What the hell... I thought. *Let's see if she'll go for it.*

"No tickets, no accidents, no damage — ever. It gets the mileage of a hybrid and no questions asked about how he bought it."

"Why not? There's just one thing. There will be a twenty-thousand dollar deposit. Can you help Mr. Baker with that? You'll be repaid, and not by him."

She knew about the box, the one I can never lose, the one only I can open. The one that's always filled with thirty-grand in fifties no matter how I much I take out of it. Yeah, I'll get repaid, the next time I open the box.

"I'll owe you," she said.

Damn straight you will, I thought as I nodded.

She held out her hand. "Deal, Mr. Barker."

"Deal, Miss Lola."

After they shook, she said, "Expect to be making a few cross-country trips in that car, Mr. Barker."

"South bound and down, Miss Lola. I'll even pick you up some Corrs."

"You can buy her a six-pack on your way out, Jake."

"Sure thing, Clancy."

After Jake, there were a few more. One wanted a big lottery win. Lola gave him a drawing date and the winning numbers. I made sure they would be the only winning numbers. Another wanted true love. Lola suggested a dating site and gave her a name to look for.

"Text her his photo, and may they live together healthy and happily to a ripe old age."

Lola smiled. "Of course."

Two different people asked for the deaths of two separate elected officials who lived and worked down in DC. She told them, "Can't do it. We need them just where they are and doing what they're doing. Besides, you couldn't afford the price."

Both left extremely upset, one saying mostly to himself, "I'll just do the job myself."

"Excuse me," she said when the last one was gone. She took out her cell phone, dialed a number. "McPhail, yeah, it's me. Two more tonight. I'll text you their names and addresses."

And then it was over. No more line, no more deals. When Lola and I walked to the front the clocks were all working and the hockey game was back on. The Constellations had just scored.

I looked over my customers. They seemed different—quiet, more sedate. Why not? They'd just traded a part of themselves for something they thought they needed or wanted. Maybe it would work out for them, maybe it wouldn't.

The Constellations won by a goal. "Your doing?" I asked the woman in black sitting at the end of the bar working on her second Hotter Chocolate. She just smiled and shrugged.

With the game over, my customers soon left. They were mostly working people who had to work the next day. The late nights, the ones who would stay until closing, would be in soon.

"Staying for round two?" I asked the deal maker.

"No, I got who I needed."

"I can't believe that that many people took you up on your offer."

"Maybe they knew a good thing when they saw it."

She said this in a strange way, then laughed quietly, again like she knew a joke I didn't.

"I wonder if they'll come back."

"They will," Lola assured me, "once they realize that nothing bad will happen, to them or anyone else…or at least, not because of the deals they made tonight."

Suddenly, I got the joke, or thought I did.

"You're not…" I pointed down.

Another laugh, this one louder. She looked up, past the ceiling and to the heavens.

"Why should the Pit have all the fun?"

"But why?"

"Recruitment, Peggy. There's a battle coming and the people tonight, and others like them, are going to help us win it."

"But you…"

"Lied? Think back. I never once directly said what I was or who I worked for."

I thought about this. She was right. "The bit about the Patriots should have clued me in. Tell me, what kind of deal did they make?"

"None with us."

"Listen, Lola…"

"My real name is Nika."

"Okay, Nika. You said that you owe me."

"I do. What is it that you want?"

"Donna and Carly. They're planning to have a child."

"I know, a girl. In about eighteen months. Have fun keeping that to yourself."

"Yeah, thanks for that. Anyway, what I want for the child, all of their children, are the fairies' gifts."

Lola… no, Nika smiled. "Beauty, wit, grace, dance, song, and good-ness. But, I imagine, no spindles or anything like that. Agreed. But now I must be off. The back lot is clear. Please, walk me out."

I did and, in the middle of the empty lot, Nika unfurled her wings. They were beautiful, their feathers ash-grey with blackened tips, as if they'd been burned in a fire.

"Farewell, Peggy Rivers. We will meet again."

Her wings moved gracefully, bore her up into the night, and she was gone.

A BLUEBIRD FROM ASPEN

Robert E. Waters

CHIMALIS SCREAMED AND BEAT HER FISTS AGAINST THE STEERING WHEEL OF
her '95 *Corolla*, but that did not keep steam from rolling out its overheated engine, or keep the car from sputtering, choking, then dying.
Crying, she steered it off the road and brought it to a quiet halt in a patch
of mangled weeds and torn guardrail. She hit the brakes. The car skid
an extra foot before it came to a stop. The engine hissed, popped,
banged, while steam engulfed the car like fog. Chimalis screamed again.

And kept screaming until all the worries of her life bled away: her
children, her cheating husband, her stressful work, her stupid, fucking
car that she had intended to replace over and over but had never gotten
around to doing. Now here she was, stranded somewhere off Route 24,
in the cool dead of night, on her way to Aspen, with only a smattering
of traffic. She was stuck. She was alone.

My phone!

She fished it out of her pocket, opened her car door, and climbed
out. She tapped numbers on her cell as she moved carefully through the
engine steam and around to the passenger side, a safer place to be with
18-wheelers blaring past with no regard or desire to stop and offer help.
She tapped numbers as she leaned against the car. She put the phone to
her ear. She waited, waited. Nothing. She checked the number again.
The number was fine… but no bars. No reception whatsoever. Dead…
just like her car.

Chimalis slid down the passenger door, crying all the way.

Why hadn't she just stuck to routine? Take I-70 to Glenwood
Springs, and then take 82 all the way home? That was her preferred

route back to Aspen from Denver, since it offered more opportunity to stop and get help if something like this happened. But not tonight. Tonight, she'd decided to take 24 to 82. Why? Tired. Exhausted. Not thinking clearly. Wanting to get home faster. Wanting to get home to her kids and her husband, despite all their personal problems. *Stupid, stupid, stupid!*

Chimalis calmed and tried the phone again. For a moment, it seemed to work. Her spirits rose, then the bars blinked out. She whimpered, wiped a tear from her face, and said, "Damn! What am I going to do now?"

A car pulled up behind her. A compact with high-beams close. An American model of some kind with a low profile. It stopped, bathing Chimalis in bright white light. She stood, wiped her face again, turned toward the light, smiled, waved, and shouted, "Hello! Can you help me?"

There was no indication that the person behind the wheel heard her. Chimalis waited a long minute, wondering what was going on. Then the lights dimmed, and an old lady stumbled out.

She was short, squat. It was difficult to see what she looked like in the blinding beams. She was more dark silhouette than a real person. Then she moved to the front of the car and stepped into the light.

"Do you need help, honey?"

Her voice was high, sweet. Her hair was long and mostly grey. She wore a dress, though Chimalis could not tell whether it was polka-dot or covered in small red flowers. She wore white tennis shoes. Her skin was dark. Not black. Hispanic, perhaps? Native American? Slightly overweight. Her face was pleasant with puffy bags below the eyes. Her cheeks were round. Her smile was soft.

Chimalis walked forward. "Yes. My engine's overheated, looks like." She waved her phone. "Can't get a signal on my phone. Do you have a phone?"

The old lady shook her head and smiled. "No, that's devil stuff. I don't touch it. All that new technology burns the humanity right out of you."

Chimalis nodded. "Yes, well, I need one that works, so I can call Triple-A for a tow." She hugged herself for warmth. "I don't suppose you know anything about car engines?"

The old lady laughed. "Even less. But my home isn't far away. Just a few miles. I'm going there now." She motioned to her car. "I'd be happy to take you. Your phone would probably work there. And if not, I have a phone on the wall. One with a cord, but it still works... I think."

Get in the car with a stranger? Chimalis balked. "I don't know... I..."

"I promise, you are safe with me, honey." Her eyes were dark, almost charcoal black, but endearing, soulful. Her smile was perfect. "All I have is a contrary cat named Benny. After Benny Goodman? I loved that man's playing. Anywho, he might hiss at you, but otherwise, he's harmless. You can make your call, and I'll bring you back here. Shoot... you could walk back if you prefer. I'm that close."

What choice did she have? Either that or stay here on the side of the road until someone else drove by, a smelly old trucker or some leering teenage boy trying to make an opportune score on a MILF? The little old lady looked like the better deal.

"Okay," Chimalis said. "Let me get my purse."

She returned to her car, fished her purse out of the back seat, turned the hazard lights on, and locked her doors.

The old lady opened the passenger door and waited for Chimalis to climb in. When the door was shut, she returned to the driver's side, climbed in slowly herself, buckled in, and started the engine.

A relatively quiet, smooth engine on an old *Pinto*. Chimalis was surprised that the damned thing was still running. When was the last time she had seen a *Pinto*? Her father had had one long ago but had promptly taken it back to the used-car dealership after the transmission blew out on a hill. His was a stick; this old junker was an automatic, and the old lady steered them slowly out into the sparse traffic.

Chimalis tucked her hand into her purse and gripped her mace.

"Where were you headed, sweetie?" The old lady asked.

Chimalis sighed deeply, breathing in the warm, slightly stagnant air blowing through the car's ventilation. "Aspen. I live there."

"What do you do?"

"I'm a traveling nurse. I go where I'm needed. Denver, mostly. Sometimes Boulder, Glenwood Springs, sometimes Carbondale." She reached out her hand, and then remembered she was riding in a car and the driver was holding the steering wheel with both hands. She pulled it back promptly. "Sorry... my name is Chimalis, by the way. Chimalis Burton."

The old woman tilted her head to the right, like a dog, as if she were thinking it out. Her breathing was steady. Her eyes blinked rapidly, but

in the faint dashboard light, Chimalis couldn't determine how many
times. "You're Indian... I mean, Native American?"

Chimalis nodded. "Partially. My mother was Zuni."

"Your name means Bluebird, yes?"

Chimalis nodded. "Yes. How did you know?"

The old woman chuckled. "I'm native as well, couldn't you tell?"

Chimalis stared at the old woman's exposed arm. In the faint
light, it was difficult to see it clearly, but indeed, as she had surmised in the headlights, the woman was not white. Her skin was
dark, crepey. She had to be eighty at least, if not older. "My name is
Saya, by the way."

"That's pretty. What does it mean?"

Saya paused, then said, "Nobody knows."

Chimalis cleared her throat, said, "Well, Saya, I'm glad to meet you
and I'm thankful for your rescue."

"Think nothing of it, honey. I save them all. All souls who break
down out here on this devil highway. Men, women, truckers, teenagers,
nurses... anyone who needs a hand, I'm willing to give. It's my way to
pay it forward, isn't that what they say? The Jews say, 'Save one life,
you save the world entire.' I've been saving the world forever, it
seems." Saya paused, then offered her hand to Chimalis. "Will you
do me a favor, honey? Will you rub my hand? My fingers, they get
numb sometimes, gripping the steering wheel for so long. You being
a nurse, a bluebird and all, I'm sure you have the soothing touch of
an angel."

Saya's hand was larger than Chimalis would have guessed. A man's
hand. Rough, but not brittle. Crepey like her arm, but with thick
workman-like calluses on the palm and big knuckles, knuckles that
seemed inflamed by arthritis. Chimalis could see the red markings on
the palm where the tight grip had occurred. A very tight grip by the
looks of it, for such an old woman.

"Are you sure you should be driving at your age?"

The question stunned Saya. She looked at Chimalis, surprised, then
smiled.

"I'm sorry. I don't mean to be rude. It's an occupational hazard,"
Chimalis said. "I've seen a lot of people your age get badly injured in
accidents driving for longer than they should."

Saya nodded. "It's okay, honey. But I'm just fine. I've been driving
forever, it seems. And it gets me out of the house, onto this highway

where I can save people like you. Don't you fret none, sweetie. We'll be just fine."

Saya wiggled her sore fingers. Chimalis reached for them, then pulled back quickly. She checked her phone. "Look, I have three bars now. I should be able to call someone. If you like, you can just pull over here, and I'll make the call. We don't have to go all the way to your place."

Saya chirped like a bird. "You make your call if you like, honey, but I doubt you'll get anything. It's near impossible out here in the mountains, but you keep trying. My exit is right there."

And so it was. Saya took the exit, and Chimalis tried making a call. It would connect, ring a time or two, and then die. She tried again. Still the same. After a third time, she threw the phone in her purse and cursed, again on the verge of tears.

"Sweetheart," Saya said, her voice rising. "You're too young for such frustrations. What ails you?"

"Everything! My car, my job, my life..."

"Your life?" Saya shook her head and turned off the exit and onto a small, pitch-black road. "Such a beautiful, young thing like you? You must have a family and a man."

Chimalis nodded. "Two boys and a husband, yes."

"The center of your world, I'm sure."

Chimalis huffed. "Yeah, if I ever got to see them. I'm gone all the time. They barely notice me when I'm home."

"Pish-posh! As lovely as you are, I can't believe it." Saya chirped. "Your man must eat you alive when you come through the door."

"Eating someone else alive, probably." Chimalis rubbed her face and forced herself not to cry again. "I'm sorry, I don't mean to bore you with my problems."

"It's all right, honey. You can tell me anything. That's what I'm here for. To soothe your pain."

"I have no proof, but he's just not the same guy I married. We hardly ever... do it... when I'm home, and when we do, it's over in like a minute or two. He stays on his laptop nearly all the time, texting at night when he thinks I'm sleeping. Typical kind of things that someone with pussy on the side might do. I'm sick of it, but I don't know what I'm going to do about it." She paused, then, "Nothing, I guess. What can I do?"

"Well, sweetie, there are all kinds of ways to end a bad relationship. I know. I've been married a few times myself. All bad people in the end, showed their true colors. Well, I took care of it, you can goddamn rest assured I did. And now I live on my own, free from their shackles. All I need is a quiet place to lay my head, a car that can get me places, a good cooking pot, and a mangy old cat. That's all I need." Saya turned her head slightly to the right and winked. "Oh, and a bluebird from Aspen, I guess." She pressed the brakes and turned the wheel to the left. "We're here."

Saya's driveway was short. She pulled in and brought the car to a halt in front of a garage. She did not open the garage door. She just parked the car in front of it and turned off the engine. She sighed, deeply, then opened her door. Saya tried to get out, then stopped. She turned to Chimalis.

"Can you get my seatbelt, hon—"

Chimalis unfastened it with one quick move before the old lady could bring her hand down to the buckle. "I'll make that call quickly, ma'am, and then get out of your way." She climbed out, closed the door on the *Pinto*, and walked to the front of the car. She waited for Saya to join her.

"Forgive the mess," Saya said, moving to unlock her front door. "I'm a bit of a packrat. I save everything."

Her house was small, plain. A single-story ranch with two windows in the front. Nothing fancy. Brick bottom. Wooden top.

Saya cursed while opening her front door. She flicked on her light, stepped in, and Chimalis followed.

A wall of cat stench struck her like a bat. The kids did not have a cat or a dog. Chimalis's nose was not used to it. Unlike Saya, who tossed her purse onto her old, worn couch and walked through the living room to the kitchen as if she were walking through roses. "Make yourself at home, honey," she said. "I'll brew some tea."

Chimalis put the strap of her purse around her neck and hugged it tightly against her body. "Thank you, Saya, but I don't need anything. I'll just make my call, and that's it."

Saya laughed. Her voice carried through a maze of junk: piles upon piles of newspapers and boxes, dusty books and old empty shelves lining the walls of the living room. The couch that Saya had thrown her purse onto was bare, save for an embroidered throw of green. It was old and the pattern on it was Native American. A hawk flew above a field of flowers, red and golden. It was a pleasant tableau, but something about it, the way the light from the dusty overhang picked up the red stitching… it seemed like blood trickling from the bird's talons. And the face of the "thing" gazing up at the sky was human—in shape anyway—but big, very big. Broad and muscular in the shoulders, but hairy like a beast, a giant. Chimalis shivered, turned, and dared take a few steps into the cluttered living room. "Where is your phone?"

A cabinet was opened, a rustle of pots and pans. Water was turned on and began filling a teapot. "In the hallway, sweetie. Right above Benny's litter box."

Oh, great! That's all she needed, to stand above a cat toilet and dial a number. She'd have to hold her breath. *As if I don't have enough to worry about.* Chimalis shook her head and went to find the phone.

It was easy to find. The house was small. The light from the kitchen fell into the short hallway that led to the back of the house. Chimalis found the phone in the shadow of that light, and as Saya said, there sat the litter box. And there sat Benny. Chimalis found the light switch on the wall and flicked it.

Benny was a beautiful cat, and not so old and mangy as Saya had said. A standard orange tabby, sitting there, trying to take a shit, she supposed, in the box. Chimalis paused, waiting to see if the cat would finish. She smiled, made kissing sounds to try to soothe the cat. Benny was having none of it. He arched his back and hissed.

She waited, then whispered, "Don't fuck with me, cat. You don't know who you are dealing with."

"Whadya say?" Saya asked from the kitchen.

"Oh, nothing, nothing. Gonna make my call now."

She mouthed the word *Move!* to get Benny to scoot. He hissed again and bolted into one of the back rooms with a spray of cat litter like car wheels spinning in dirt.

Chimalis stepped over the litter box and picked up the phone. She pressed it to her ear. A dial tone. *Thank God!* She reached into her purse to get her wallet. Her Triple-A card was in there somewhere. That was the first number to dial, and then her husband, and then…

She glanced up at the wall above the phone. There, covered in newspaper clippings, was a corkboard. Some of the clippings were yellow with thumbtacks showing rust around their edges. Some clippings were so old that they had faded beyond legibility. Chimalis winced and tried to read the ones that were newer.

Molly Pierce was a student from the University of Colorado that had disappeared three years ago. Her abandoned car was found on Route 24. No signs of struggle.

A trucker named Jamal Gruber disappeared five years ago. His abandoned truck was found not that far from where Chimalis was standing now. No sign of struggle.

The Harris family was en route to Denver when their Ford *Taurus* skidded off an icy Route 24 and struck a tree. Police and EMT were dispatched to the scene, but by the time they got there, everyone was gone, including little Jennifer Harris who had left her plushy white unicorn behind, presumably thinking she'd come back. Again, no signs of struggle.

And just three weeks ago, Milo Mathers, a retired coal miner from Colorado Springs apparently blew a tire while heading to Denver to visit family. His car was found, abandoned, battery nearly dead from the hazard lights.

Esther Rosewood... Jerimiah Childes... Conner Colwith...

On and on and on, decades of names and mishaps. Decades of missing persons and abandoned vehicles. All, Chimalis surmised, within five miles from where she stood.

Her stomach churned, her heart raced. Saya was still in the kitchen, humming a tune, fiddling with something that Chimalis could only surmise from shadows dancing across beige cupboards. Chimalis hung up the phone. She placed her hand in her purse and gripped her mace. She looked down to ensure that she did not step in the smelly box. Her foot nudged the edge of it and shook loose some of the greenish-blue litter.

A finger bone appeared, nice, white, and shiny, with only a speck of dried sinew attached.

Chimalis squealed, dropped her purse, and made for the front door.

Saya appeared in her path, holding a teacup. The old lady smiled, ear to ear, and said, "There you are, honey. Your tea?"

Chimalis did not answer, did not reach for the tea. She stood there, staring at Saya's face, wondering when it would change, when it would reveal. *How fucking long does this have to go on?*

"Tea? But how can that be, miss? I didn't hear the pot boil."

Saya's smile grew broader. She shook her head just enough to be noticed. "You're a smart one, sweetheart. Perhaps the smartest soul to come through that door in a long while. You're right. There is no tea."

She let the empty cup drop to the floor. She then looked past Chimalis to the corkboard. Her smile, its pleasantness, bled away. Her eyes grew larger, redder, and they did not blink. "What does Shakespeare say about it, dear?" she asked. "What did you see in those papers, that you lose so much complexion? I'll tell you what's really there, what's beyond the facts…"

"Esther Rosewood had an opiate problem. She'd tried kicking the habit for years but didn't have the courage to commit. She begged for death.

"Jerimiah Childes was going home to tell his parents that he was gay, but he hated himself so badly that he'd rather die than see the face of his disappointed father.

"Conner Colwith had just beaten his wife so badly that he was afraid he'd killed her. He was driving Route 24 with a pistol on the passenger seat, trying to drum up the courage to put it in his mouth at 65 MPH."

"And what about little Jenny Harris?" Chimalis asked, her hand shaking, her knuckles turning white gripping the mace. "What was her weakness? Her *fatal* flaw?"

Saya smiled, huffed, wiggled her nose. "Well… some innocents always get trapped in the net. It's inevitable."

"I'm innocent," Chimalis said, on the verge of tears.

"Really? You think your husband's cheating on you. You want to kill him. I can see it in your eyes. You'd like nothing but to go home, put a bullet in his head, and watch him die. He's the innocent one I'll be saving… from you."

"But you can't read my mind, can you?"

Saya shook her head. "No, I can't. You're a strange one. Who are you, really?"

Saya waited for an answer. Chimalis did not give her one.

"It hardly matters now, honey. You're here, and I'm hungry."

Chimalis looked up at the ceiling. No sound. Nothing. *Where are you?*

Time had run out. Chimalis could wait no longer.

She lunged forward with her mace and sprayed it into Saya's eyes, screaming, even louder than her fake screaming over her broken car, and emptied the entire container into the old woman's face. Saya stood there, smiling, letting the burning liquid coat her skin. Her eyes steamed.

"That will not work, honey. Nothing you have will stop me."

Saya grew two feet, snarled, and smacked Chimalis across the hall.

Chimalis struck the wall, hard, and fell to the floor, disrupting the litter box and casting tiny granules of litter and clumps of waste across the hall. The wall where she struck caved, and Chimalis fought to keep from passing out. Her ribs hurt where Saya had struck, but it didn't feel as if bones had been broken. The back of her head and her spine ached as well, and she could feel a warm trickle of blood running through her hair. She struck the floor with a scream and tried crawling away from the beast that reared up before her.

Saya was gone. In her place, a hulking brute of seven or eight feet rose, so tall that it could barely fit within the hallway. It had large, bulging eyes with no lids, which accentuated its blood-red glare. Saya's large-man hands had grown even larger, with the tough skin of her knuckles being replaced by a ridge of tiny horns that squirted a green ooze. Large yellow teeth and tusks replaced Saya's diminutive mouth. The beast slammed its jaws together as if it were chomping bone. Saliva poured from its maw and pooled on the hallway floor.

Chimalis screamed again. She kept crawling toward her purse, toward the back of the house where the cat had gone. The beast followed, slowly, savoring its prey, for that was certainly what Chimalis was now: a meal to this demon that pursued her.

She grabbed her purse, but kept sliding back as the beast, its shoulders now growing thick black hair like a wolf, barked something in Zuni. Chimalis could understand some of it, but it had been so long. Arcane words, deadly, threatening words, and with each word, a gallon of spit erupted from the beast's mouth and ran down its chest like a cataract of white foam.

Don't come any closer! Chimalis mouthed the words, hoping the beast would see and enrage it even further. She reached into her purse. She grabbed a pen. *No.* Her hairbrush. *No.*

The demon grabbed her foot and pulled Chimalis close, close enough for her to feel its hot, sickly breath on her face. Its eyes were larger than her head, its face as broad as a tree stump. She'd never seen anything like it in all her life, and the utter horror of it was almost too much to bear. She could feel herself float away, feel heartbeats in her ears. She tried fighting the sensation that crawled up her legs and arms, a tender prickling of hair that told her it was time to sleep. She closed her eyes. The beast leaned in and opened its mouth wide for a bite.

Whirling helicopter blades high above the house burst through her lethargy.

Chimalis perked, gripped the blade of the knife in her purse, drew it out quickly, and plunged it into the beast's throat.

The demon staggered back, tried gripping the handle of the knife that now pulsed a clear light. White striations leached out from where the blade had struck and began running the length of the demon's body, like cracks in a window. It roared. It lurched left and right. It tried to grab Chimalis' ankle, as if in its rage and fear it was going to finish the job. But there was no strength left in its movements. The blade held firm in its neck and began drawing the beast's last breath from its terrible mouth.

A moment later, the beast collapsed in a shower of black-and-red ash, and in the center of the pile lay the blade, unburnt and pristine, with luminous white light sparking off its tough blade. A ritual blade. A Zuni blade of sharp bear bone and turquoise. A family heirloom. Chimalis never left home without it.

She lay back and breathed deeply, the pain in her body taking control. She smiled. She closed her eyes as the front door of the house was blown open, and men with guns and flashlights swarmed in.

Chimalis awoke to a mass of FBI agents rummaging through everything in the house and carrying mountains of boxed evidence to a white van parked outside. Her head hurt. She had a nagging headache and bruises on her side where the demon had struck. She felt nauseous. But she would live, and this certainly wasn't the worst beating she'd experienced in her long career.

"Lucky you got here JIT," she said to Agent Halsey kneeling beside her. He had a much more pleasant face than the one that had just tried to bite her. "Five more minutes and I would have been dead."

Everything had been planned. The car breaking down, her screaming, the tears, the anguish. The kids, the cheating husband. All a ruse to get the demon to *feel* her helplessness, to sense her fear and sorrow, and to come and lend a hand like a good, model citizen. Just like it had done with all those many victims whose final stories now covered its wall. Yep… it was all a ruse. Save for the lousy cell connection.

"We didn't get your signal until the exit ramp."

"Yeah," Chimalis said, rubbing her sore neck, "tell the local authorities to boost the cell service out here. It'll save a lot of lives."

She stood, with help, and watched as agents began their forensic sweep. "You should find everything you need in this demon's graveyard."

Agent Halsey nodded. "Yep, a treasure trove of goodies already. What kind of demon was it, anyway?"

"An Atasaya, or an *Átahsaia* depending upon your bent. A Zuni demon. A cannibal. It set up shop here along Route 24, with a veritable smorgasbord of tasty snacks just whizzing by. So arrogant it used part of its real name as an alias, thinking no one would know. Foolish demon! I've been tracking it for years." Chimalis sighed, shook her head in sorrow. "I wish I'd have found it faster. We'd have saved a lot of lives if I had."

"True," Agent Halsey said, "but at least we can now bring closure to the families of its victims."

A rookie agent stepped up. "Agent Bluebird? The helicopter is ready for you."

Chimalis nodded. "Let me get my blade."

Placing her hand on the wall for balance, she walked back into the room where the demon's ash pile and the knife lay. She bent slowly and picked up the blade. She wiped it clean of black soot and ran her fingers across the turquoise handle. A new symbol was now etched into the stone. One representing the *Átahsaia*. It took its place among the other dozen symbols already there, each one representing a demon or malevolent spirit that it had vanquished over the years. What a marvelous, dangerous blade it was. Perhaps the most dangerous in the world. If it ever fell into the wrong hands…

"What do you want me to do with that?" Agent Halsey asked behind her.

Chimalis turned and saw orange Benny in the hall. The cat was quiet, calm. It stared up at her through a forest of neat whiskers. Its eyes were coal black. It purred, but something wasn't quite right about it. Something ancient, something sinister looked at her through those eyes.

"Leave it alone," Chimalis said as she walked carefully to the blasted doorway. "That's a demon for another day."

Chimalis, Agent Bluebird of the FBI, stepped out of the house and boarded the helicopter.

WORLD-WIDE WINGS

Jenifer Purcell Rosenberg

IF YOU'RE GOING TO BUILD A STARTUP, DO IT WITH AUTHENTICITY. THAT IS what Aethel kept trying to convince herself, at least. Every morning, before heading into the office, she would give herself the old pep talk. *Sometimes humans must seem confused. They must have insecurities. They must exhibit their individual imperfections while trying to cloak them. Showing too much confidence tended to make others lose trust. Too little, and they would lose confidence in you. Most importantly: remember to blink and occasionally sneeze or yawn in their presence. Even if they weren't aware of it while awake, their minds picked up on little oddities. It was important to come across confident enough to run things, and human enough to not cause any alarm.*

Aethel had been tasked by Heaven with making Earth a better place. The plan was to live among humans and find a way to bring more peace to the world. Too many had been lost in recent decades, and the poor buggers needed help saving themselves. Since searing light did not mix well with the mortals, Aethel selected an identity, a gender, and a new visage. She chose a woman of average height with deep brown eyes, curly dark auburn hair, and golden brown skin. She had freckles and dimples and a dainty gap between her two front teeth. While she had created a human image and backstory that worked, she had unfortunately gotten naming conventions all wrong. Everyone blinked when she introduced herself as Elf Magnitude. But that's what was on all of the paperwork, and she didn't want to have to re-do all of that! People always asked if her parents were hippies, so she began to use the excuse when someone questioned her human name.

Once she had an identity, housing, and the very important credit (with a little divine help on that one), Aethel set to work starting an Internet company. Shiny Meme was intended to bring happy, uplifting content to the Internet, to try and counteract the negativity that often saturated the online world. Since she possessed the inherent charisma of most angels, Aethel had been able to get the company featured in several articles and news features. Between offering something good for the public, and paying her employees a real living wage, she had become somewhat of a media darling overnight.

Of course, the thing that made Shiny Meme such a great company is that Aethel was not only putting uplifting content online, but showing the right memes to the right people precisely when they were needed. The world thought that Elf Magnitude was an eccentric who spent hours locked in her office doing who knows what. Yoga? Gaming? Dorking around with the stock market instead of working like many a CEO? Macramé? But regardless, the cheerful demeanor and general aura of love and kindness she exuded when she wasn't locked in her office made up for the rumors of a quirky woman, and she became a celebrity sensation, with brands and shows seeking her out in the hopes that she would agree to have her face plastered on everything in exchange for some cash. Many an angel had fallen while on this kind of assignment because of the lure of fame. But Elf Magnitude would not sign with any brand but her own, and meme consumers were thrilled. They would likely have been less thrilled if they knew what Elf Magnitude did.

All those hours locked in the office were devoted to entering the Internet. Not going online, but going IN online. While Elf Magnitude was sitting at a modern desk with a top-of-the-line machine, Aethel was plugging in, stretching out through the Internet like streams branching across a landscape. Had anyone walked into the office, they would have been completely unable to rouse her, because her consciousness was a brilliant light swirling through the data connection in search of ways to make people happy. It was easy to follow feelings back to the source because emotions traveled out into the ether with the data that was being sent. The thoughts and feelings pinged past, it was a rush, diving through millions of swirling ideas, all glowing in a vast array of brilliant colors. It was like jumping into a swimming pool full of multicolored nonpareils, something Elf Magnitude had experienced at a party thrown by an eccentric billionaire who claimed to want to invest in Shiny Meme but had actually been hoping to purchase it and turn it into conservative political memes. Just as living things have auras, so did the thoughts of those people. Some talented humans, and most angels, could tell the mindset of an author by the color surrounding the words on a page. It was part of what made humans so fascinating to Aethel. So many emotions!

One afternoon, after bestowing cute puppies and kittens upon several thousand people in need of a hug and a smile, Aethel became aware of a particularly strong emotional thread. The pull of the negative emotions felt like the pull of the tide on the sand beneath one's feet. Rushing, tugging, drawing one deeper into the sand. Instead of resisting the pull, Aethel allowed her light to glide toward the point of origin. Following words took you back to the source, showed you who was there, offered a literal window, via phone or computer screen, into the world of the person behind the message.

The room was dark, hung with gauzy black material over bluish lights. A young woman sat, her features illuminated only by the glow of her laptop screen. Tears had blended with heavy eyeliner and mascara, forming inky rivulets down pale cheeks, dripping from a pointed chin onto the keyboard.

The sense of despair was so intense, Aethel pulled some threads of angelic light from other tasks to help focus more energy on this unhappy human. Pushing outward, into the room, Aethel began to read the thoughts of the saddened woman. This was always an available option, but it was important to save such invasive procedures for special cases. This was one of those instances.

Rora Hill was at the end of her wits. Her heart was broken, and she no longer wanted to exist. Her best friend, Rhys Lucas, had died in a fatal auto accident half an hour after they had argued. Rora blamed herself for the fact that they were gone. If only she hadn't voiced her concern about their new partner, maybe Rhys would still be here. She believed they had passed while still angry with her, and she wanted more than anything to trade her life to bring them back. She was looking for someone who could help her try to make this trade.

While casting around everything connected to Rora on the internet, Aethel discovered a chat message stuck in the queue from the day of the fight. "Hey BB. Sorry we fought. I know Dove can be an ass. I don't wan 2 be mad at U xxx, Rhys." Making certain that it would show a time stamp that would put it on the proper day (having messages from the deceased show up late was already unsettling, but especially if they seemed to have been sent post-mortem), Aethel pushed the message through. Once it went, another message, along with a photo bubbled up. Rhys had sent a photo from the back of a rideshare, along with a reassurance that they were not driving because they had consumed too many drinks. Aethel pushed those through as well and waited. While she was waiting, Aethel noticed strange traces of unctuous energy seemed to be closing in, stifling some of the residual positive glow she was shining. It was important that Rora see the messages from her bestie and then walk away from the computer quickly. Breaking protocol for the greater Good, Aethel constructed a new message from Rhys: "I hope U don't spend all night staring at the computer. Go paint your feelings. Love U." Now the woman just needed to realize she had messages, before this dark energy, clearly also following the forlorn signature, caught up to her.

Just as Aethel was a being of light, so were there beings of darkness. Some were minor, some were major, just like the angels. They were opposite sides of a coin, in essence. The exalted and the fallen. The demons, as the fallen called themselves, had become attached to humans. So much potential for greed and malice that could be exploited. So much opportunity to infect world leaders, feed agitations, and wage war. Different factions would represent different regions on the planet and would battle it out using humans as pawns. They fed on the fear and anger they inspired in the poor unsuspecting people. This was why angels had been attempting to intervene. They wanted to nurture loving kindness, happiness, and creativity. The problem was, with angels doing good work all over the universe, and the majority of demons preferring to stay on this one small planet, angels were often outnumbered.

Sensing the dark energy approaching, Aethel tried to push positive energy and light out from Rora's location, to cover the source of despair. As Rora finally clicked to see her messages, Aethel could feel the mix of complicated emotions pouring forth: surprise, fear, relief, sadness, and love all mixed together. When she read the message about painting feelings, she nodded, said "Thanks, bruh," and shut the laptop to gather painting supplies. Good. It would help her work through her grief and get her offline while Aethel investigated the presence that had been seeking out despair.

Pushing through with haste, Aethel followed the void left in the wake of the traces of darkness. Like whispers in back alleys, the evil echoed after it was gone. Each thread led to another terminal, connected to another site, another blog. Aethel realized that a magnetic pull was occurring, and darkness was leaving a mark on spaces online, as it congealed at the crossroads of hate and fear. The cracks in the veneer of these sights were easy to penetrate, and operated as back passageways into darker things still. The deepest evils of humankind were hidden there in plain sight. Conspiracies, assassination plans, human trafficking, thievery, and countless debasing acts that Aethel could barely comprehend, much less imagine. The fervent cruelty burned like fire, and Aethel was concerned that this psychic damage might translate into damage on her physical avatar. Backtracking, and noting a few of the less incendiary sites that still contained threads in common with the darkest ones, she withdrew to check on Elf Magnitude. The Good Work couldn't continue without its front person.

No sooner had Aethel re-entered her body than she realized she had missed a summons. Periodic reports on how the Earth people were faring were required to track progress. When she found a single, arctic-white feather on her desk in front of her, she knew it was time to pay a visit to the oversight division. Since Aethel was working through the Internet, her direct supervisor was St. Isidore of Seville, the Patron Saint of the Internet. Isidore was a stickler for detail and protocol, as might be expected from someone who wasn't declared a saint for over 1300 years after passing. Always making sure none of his actions could be called into question, especially since so many humans thought he was a false saint. However, given the look on Isidore's face, this was no routine check-in.

"Ah, Aethel. Good of you to join me so soon," he said in Latin, "could we perhaps discuss what happened today?"

Aethel glanced away, trying to quickly determine what the Saint might know before she continued. "Oh! Do you mean the young woman who was mourning her friend? I saw some messages from the deceased human were snagged in a server, so I pushed them through." She shrugged as if to say, "Computers. What can you do?" From the tight-lipped expression on Isidore's face, Aethel wondered if he had seen through the lie. Finally, her supervisor nodded. "That is an acceptable action. Thank you."

As she was dismissed, Aethel felt her astral body drop back into the physical body of Elf Magnitude. She had not been caught stretching protocol. Perhaps she was not as closely watched as anticipated. This was a good thing because that negative presence needed to be found, and it would be easier without anything being obscured by the presence of other positive beings. As the CEO of a company, though, Elf Magnitude needed to attend some meetings and put in some time with the staff. A party had been planned so that the employees could have some time to unwind and celebrate their success. She opened her smartphone and read a list of conversational phrases, to make sure that she had the local vocabulary in order, then headed out.

Although Aethel rather adored humans, the amount of subtle cues, subterfuge, and anxiety within them could feel a bit overwhelming at times. As Elf Magnitude, Aethel had to project herself as an outgoing, jovial person who was full of compassion while still being considered cool. Truth be told, it took more energy than stretching out through the never-ending tendrils of the Internet. Although she was genuinely happy for her employees, and cared about them more deeply than they realized, all she could think about while at the party was getting back online and finding the thread of evil that had been stalking Rora. She promised herself to log some extra time afterward.

Seeking to search out the presence she had felt earlier, Aethel took her tablet to a space-age style lounge chair in the corner of her office, propping the tablet on a black acrylic desk arm that was connected with a chrome bar to the black velvet and metal lounge. It would be easier to search with her body in a safe position, since trauma to the vessel could rip her light form from the far reaches of the Internet too quickly, which would make it more difficult to stay in disguise. They still hadn't thought of a great explanation for the few times angels posing as Earth-beings had shone brightly through their human bodies. Normally, it was explained away as spontaneous combustion. It always ended up in the exposed angel being removed from Earth duty—and that meant being removed from some of the most creative of God's creatures.

As her human body relaxed, Aethel flowed again into the Internet, searching for the source of the unctuous energy she had sensed before. She immediately discovered another thread of cruelty oozing around in cyberspace, dripping evil wherever it passed. Aethel paused with each stopping point to make certain those receiving the stain were safe. It seemed an email message filled with racial and religious hatred had been sent to several thousand people. Someone had created a mailing list of people who did not fit a specific profile, and the message being sent to them was baiting, triggering. Aethel pulled the message back from as many recipients as she could, hoping to prevent the emotional pain of receiving such hate in an inbox. She then followed the source back to its origin. To her surprise, she did not find a demon there, but a human who was part of a group advocating for genocide. Definitely influenced by evil, then, but not a genuine demon. Focusing on the middle-aged man sneering in delight at the hate messages he was sending, Aethel tried to gain insight into where this evil had originated. What she found was the biological equivalent of a corrupted hard drive, infected with the malware of hate and xenophobia. *This person is dangerous,* she thought while going through his computer files. She knew she needed to act.

Reaching out to the man's memories, she found a few people who had been the moral compass for this guy when he was a child. He had been fond of his third-grade teacher, Mrs. Anderson, a tall, blonde woman with a smoky voice and a mischievous sparkle about her. He had been happy in her class, and then his family had moved away to a different community where he had been subjected to an abusive teacher. Aethel realized that had been the beginning of corruption in this human. They were resilient creatures, but there was a negative stigma against soothing the soul and healing the mind. It was sad to see someone who had once had the potential of all humans — to be loving and kind — but had been harmed and never given a chance to heal. She had to heal him! Pulling from his memories of his teacher, Aethel bent her light into the shape of Mrs. Anderson and leaned forward through the man's screen.

"Billy Dixon, I am disappointed in you!" she said in a far-away voice that captured the vocal quality Bill remembered his teacher having, but making it sound slightly more otherworldly. Billy had been looking at another roster — he'd bought several from a hate group that peddled hacked lists. When he saw what he believed to be the ghost of his teacher, his eyes grew wide and his jaw dropped. Aethel continued, basing what she said on Bill's memories of the third grade. "We didn't work so hard to include all members of the class only to have members of our team go out and hurt people! Did you know your reading partner Micaela is on your list? What happened to you? What was our class mantra, Billy?"

Bill looked sheepish and mumbled something unintelligible. "What was that, Billy?"

"Bullies are not welcome here," he said, pushing his wrists against his eyes to stop the tears from flowing.

"Why are you bullying people, Billy?"

"Ah. I. I don't know?"

"That's because you know that it is wrong. We do not hurt others. We make peace. Now I want you to sing the peace song."

Bill looked around as if making sure nobody else could see him. He took a deep breath. Before he started singing the peace song, Aethel moved into his mind instead of just reading it. She unraveled the hate, the fear, and the cruelty, and restored a conscience to this broken human. When he was done singing, Aethel appeared in front of him as his old teacher. "That's better, Billy. Perhaps you can make things right now."

Bill nodded and sat there staring, confused, at all of the hate para-phernalia on his wall. Aethel pulled back into Bill's computer and found his contact lists. Not just his targeted victims, who she removed from his possession, but also all of the other people in his hate group. She went to investigate them.

For the rest of the night, Aethel went through every hate group, every underground server, every discussion board, message group, and personal computer of each of Bill's contacts. They were easy to find, because they all left the same kind of pervasive evil wherever they went. Well, at least everyone in a folder labeled "old bills" did, anyway. Bill's sister Meg was a political activist raising money for homeless families, and several of his co-workers gave to charity and shared happy memes on social media without ever causing others any deliberate pain. But the ones leaving the evil in their wake needed to be dealt with.

The method she had used on Bill worked for the majority of the people on her new healing list. She identified someone who had been important to them and impersonated their ghost before briefly pos-sessing the body of the intended target to heal their minds and show them the path of kindness. There were roughly two dozen people for whom that method did not work — people who seem to have simply decided that they enjoyed destruction and pain. People who had aligned themselves with actual demons or were beholden to them. These people were the most dangerous and worked the hardest to try and convince their underlings to treat other people terribly. As she delved into the contact lists of these seemingly higher rank evil hench-men, Aethel made a startling discovery. The higher up the chain of evil you went, the more powerful the evil people were. By the time she started feeling the warning signs that her body needed her to return, Aethel had uncovered proof that many of the world's most powerful CEOs and politicians were, in fact, demons. They were commanding their legions through listservs and cryptocurrency. That was not good.

She returned to her body and, as Elf Magnitude, she left the office building at five in the morning, took a cab home, and left a message on the office discussion board letting everyone know she had a bad cold and couldn't come in that day. She realized they would all think it was a hangover, but that was fine. It made her look human, and she often forgot to feign illness sometimes to keep herself believable. After a hot shower and some sustenance, the body was refreshed, and Aethel could get back to her light form and finish her latest project. This was so much more amazing than puppy memes and dancing cows. Once you started those, most humans would share them, and the happiness and goodwill would spread throughout the world of people connected to the internet. But with what she was about to do, lives would be saved. People who had been unable to afford a computer or an internet connection would be positively affected by this, too.

Aethel found the people who had not been shiftable the night before, and took over their social media, deleting hateful messages (for some, that was everything they had ever posted), posting public confessions of crimes they had committed and, where possible, sending evidence to the authorities with a written confession. She found hidden bank accounts used as tax havens and hate funds, and she re-distributed that wealth to every person the hate groups had targeted. It was a good thing she could focus her light in so many places at once, because she was managing to change lives very quickly. While she was unable to put money in accounts for people who did not have bank accounts, she discovered that she could shift the funds around to pull struggling people out of debt. Suddenly, several Senators made charitable donations for things like children's cancer and public libraries. She had brought so much good to the world, and now she was ready to take on one of the senators whom she had realized was actually a demon.

Taking on a demon is not easy for most beings. Aethel knew it was a risk, but she simply had to try. Demons in places of power could create atrocious conditions for innocent people. As she was approaching the senator's office computer, she felt the summons to go have a chat with St. Isidore of Seville again. Right while she was in the middle of changing the world! Such timing! Hadn't she just been summoned yesterday? Aethel sighed and responded to the summons, appearing in front of her supervisor.

His thick, shaggy eyebrows waggled as she approached. He seemed to be in a jovial mood. Saints tended to keep their original form, but when here, Aethel preferred to be in the form of pure light, as was her nature.

"Great news, Aethel! All of the positive energy you have been spreading seems to be working!" He grinned wildly as he said this. "When they work together, they accomplish so, so much, and when they work against each other, they hurt everyone involved. I am pleased that you are helping them see. We may ask you to train some others in what you are doing, what…erm.. memes are helping the most."

As Aethel returned, she couldn't help feeling a little guilty. After all, she had broken several rules and had bent the truth. That was not supposed to happen! Stretching her human disguise body and making sure to hydrate, Aethel felt a sudden foreboding. There was a demon present.

She turned around quickly and dropped the carafe of coconut water she had been holding. Before her stood a man, but this man was clearly like her, a different being playing at being human. Given how many decades this senator had been in office, this demon had a significant edge over Aethel where experience among humans was concerned. He looked her up and down, snorting.

"You have been a busy little angel!" he said. "I admire your creativity! I look forward to working with you, or at least to having you work for me."

Aethel glared. "I shall never work for you, demon!"

"What do you mean, Miss Magnitude? You've done me an amazing service this day! It seems you are a valuable asset to my team!"

Realizing that she was still standing in front of the open refrigerator, Aethel stepped forward and closed it behind her. "Get out of my house," she said.

The demon senator laughed. "YOUR house? This place has been my home for millennia! You aren't a Dominion. I can feel that you're Seraphim, pure light within that disguise you're wearing. What are you even doing on Earth?"

"I am making a difference," she said.

"Oh, ho! You are indeed!" he crooned, "You have wiped several thousand humans of their free will and personalities! I'm quite sure that's considered a no-no!"

Aethel was taken aback. Had she taken people's identities from them? Did they no longer have free will because she had willed them to not hate? Was it wrong? They had clearly been influenced toward hatred by the Earthbound demons, so how could it be wrong for her to fix that?

"I healed what was sick. I brought happiness and peace to people. That is my directive."

"I betcha your directive never told you to tank their free will!"

"It isn't free will when they are being controlled by a demon!" she countered.

The demon began to square off for a fight. His human form mutated, and twisted, growing, stretching, filling the modern kitchen with a glistening, oily, fierce-looking demon. He was over seven feet in height, with talons and a beak, skin-covered wings tucked in so as not to hit the open glass shelving. A fallen cherubim, most likely, since those most often had animal features to them. His skin looked almost molten, with an orange glow like the logs of a long-burning fire. He wouldn't be able to harm her in her light form, but if she were to exit the body to take on her light form, the vessel would be vulnerable. This was clearly something the demon knew.

"What's your choice, Miss Magnitude?" he asked in a singsong voice, "Do you work with me and mine and keep doing your work here, or do you stand up against me and get pulled back upstairs?"

With a sad resignation, Aethel took a last glance around the glorious home she had been using during her time here on Earth. She had made a difference for many people. She'd paid off medical bills for poor families, helped the sick to heal, and brought joy to millions. She didn't want to let her staff down, but she needed to be sure that this demon was dispatched, even though leaving the body at this time would likely be the end of Elf Magnitude. "I have made my choice," she said.

The demon looked pleased, obviously under the impression that Aethel would join him. His smugness turned to alarm, however, when Aethel surged forth from her vessel, filling the kitchen with a blinding white light. A gigantic taloned claw arced toward her, but it went right through the light. Concentrating herself into a stream of light more precise and intense than a laser, Aethel pushed into the demon's mind through his left nostril. His attempts to block and swat her resulted in injury as the demon flailed at the holy light that was entering his brain. He managed to collide with the glass shelves, resulting in pebbles of broken glass scattering across the marble floor.

The mind of a demon is a catalog of pain, suffering, and malice. The greasy energy Aethel had discovered the day she helped save Rora was clearly originating within the minds of demons, a contagion that created legions. Fighting against the unholy forces of his mind, she managed to figure out how he ticked. She discovered that this was Soneillon, the demon of hate. Aethel pushed her light throughout the entire demon's body, burning off the unctuous ichor of evil, and planting peace within the tormented mind. She could feel her light diminishing as she scoured the cruelty from this beast.

A soft, feeble cloud of light flowed out of the nose and ears of the sleeping old man on the kitchen floor. Glass was scattered everywhere, shining like ice chips in the sun. The day would see the long-time senator as the first of many to resign, citing a need for a new generation of politicians. Aethel struggled with the knowledge that she had gone too far by dismantling free will. Despite the fact that she had defeated Soneillon, she realized that pushing too hard might cause her to fall as well. St. Isidore had been keeping tabs, and praised Aethel for making the right decision. She returned to being Elf Magnitude and focused on sending happiness to humans without tampering with their free will, so that they could share the love with their fellow people, and she could share joy with the humans of Earth.

BRINGER OF DOOM

Christopher J. Burke

WITH A QUICK BURST OF FLAME, A BLACK PALL OF SMOKE, AND A STENCH of sulfur, the demon appeared from thin air through a dimensional rift. He raged, "Who dares awaken Brahk'dahgh, Breaker of Bones, Bringer of Doom, from his slumber?"

This mortal realm had changed greatly since he'd last trod upon it. At that time, humanity dwelled in filth, living in stone caves and mud huts, barely managing fire. These modest trappings of this current abode were abundant splendor by comparison. The inhabitants had mastered tools and forged a nest from a mutilated tree.

The demon stood in the center of a circle of wool. One dozen runic symbols adorned it, but they held no mystic energies that he could feel. He appeared to be neither imprisoned nor bound.

Sensing no snares, he slid his right foot out of the circle. *What foolish human,* he thought, *would invoke my name without even a pretense of precautions? That impudent mortal will feel the brunt of my swift and terrible wrath. The mighty Brahk'dahgh serves No One!*

The small enclosure, with a ceiling scant inches above his horns, was silent and still. This enraged him all the more.

He howled, "Who summons the master of demons?"

Slowly, the head of a little girl poked up from behind the bed. She'd barely provide a mouthful to split between his two gullets.

The child rose to her full height, not much taller than Brahk'dahgh's knee. In his eyes, she glowed with a bright, white aura.

In her eyes, the Breaker of Bones was a walking, talking mountain, at which she stared in silent awe. With some trepidation, she asked, "Mister Demon, sir? Do you want to play tea with me? Please?"

Play... tea? Turning his head, he spied a little table. In the center sat a pot, along with two tiny cups and saucers. There were some small dishes, one of which contained a pile of minuscule biscuits. The demon could not reason the incongruity. This child appeared to live in modest comfort, but without enough to nourish herself. Was this some torment dimension?

"Will you?" she asked again. "Pretty please!"

"And what will you give me if I grant you this request?"

The little girl, no more than four, wiggled out from behind her pathetic fortification of blankets. She ran to the table and picked up a plate. "I have cookies! There's oatmeal and peanut butter."

Brahk'dahgh stood perplexed. Was this child speaking in tongues? "Cookies"? "Peanut butter"?

As quickly as she'd offered it, she pulled the plate back. "You're not 'lergic, are you? Grandma says some people are 'lergic!"

The girl's innocence, her purity, shone like a shield. He couldn't touch her but tricking little children into dropping that shield was a simple matter of the right temptation. But first, he needed to find who'd summoned him. Needing to think, he started to sit down.

"Wait," the child cried. "You won't fit on my chair. But you can sit on my clock rug. Does this mean you'll play with me?"

The infernal creature sat heavily, and the whole room shook.

Mistaking this for a "yes," the little girl put on a pair of white, lace gloves. She picked up the teapot, and said, "My name is Lizzie. Thank you for coming to my tea party."

Her guest growled, "I am–"

"Brock Dag! I know. I heard you. Breaker of Homes." She poured two cups. "That means you're housebroken, right? Would you like to hear a song? I made it up myself!"

Biding his time, the demon listened as Lizzie started singing a nonsense rhyming song. The continuous stream of syllables sounded eerily familiar. Did this child summon me with her made-up play song?

For the first time since an early eon, he let out a loud laugh, an absolute knee-slapping guffaw.

Lizzie smiled. "I knew you'd like it. I can't wait to sing it to Grandma."

Thoughts of corruption fled the demon's mind. He'd content himself with "tea." When they finished, Lizzie taught him how to count using only ten fingers, so they could play Hide-and-Seek. After she hid, he sensed her presence beneath the bed. Still, he chose first to check the narrow gap between the chest of drawers and the wall.

"You're not a shapeshifter, are you?"

He heard giggles behind him.

He wondered if this was joy. He'd never known that emotion.

"Home base!"

He twisted about and saw Lizzie standing by the table with one hand on the teapot. The light about her had flickered and dimmed. Her defenses were waning. "Good game!"

The little girl went to give her huge playmate a big hug. He waved her back and uttered something unthinkable. "I don't want to hurt you."

Both of them were stunned. He no longer wished to harm this child. However, he knew that he would should he remain. Such was his nature.

"This was... fun, my lady." He bowed. "But I must leave now."

The child bawled her eyes out. Tears streamed down her face. This should have delighted Brahk'dahgh, but he was not amused. Her protective shield didn't just drop, it shattered.

"But then I'll be all alone again!"

Was the great bringer of fire and destruction being moved by a child's tears? "Alone? Why are you alone?"

She sobbed. "Mommy's at work, and Grandma laid down on the couch for a nap this morning and hasn't gotten up."

Brahk'dahgh had only experienced horror and dread by inflicting them on others. Could demons even be horrified? Brahk'dahgh learned those feelings in that instant. He ran out the door and saw a pathway down. When he reached the bottom of the steps, he stopped abruptly.

The husk of an old woman lay still on the sofa. Next to it, the woman's soul stood in a pure white dress reaching for an angel's hand.

Brahk'dahgh held up an arm to shield his eyes from the brilliant illumination.

Sensing his arrival, the angel wrapped his wing around the woman's soul. "Begone, demon! You cannot claim her!"

"I didn't come for her! But you must leave her be. Let her live until sundown."

"We shall not fall for your lies and deceits. Get behind me! Clear the way!"

"There's a child alone upstairs!"

An ethereal voice cried out, "Lizzie! My Lizzie!"

The angel steadied her. "Fear not, Elizabeth. The child's innocence protects her. Her soul is safe." They disappeared in a flash of white light so dazzling that Brahk'dahgh dropped to his knees and screamed in pain. When he could see again, he was alone with the body.

From above, he heard, "Grandma? Brock dag?"

Lizzie came down the stairs to find her grandmother by herself, rising from her nap. The grandmother looked at the little girl and smiled.

"Lizzie! Would you like to... bake cookies?"

Brahk'dahgh felt his movements constrained within the old woman's failing body. He saw shadows, echoes, of memories left behind by the departed. Betsy had had a long, fulfilling life of service to family—her parents, husband, children, and grandchildren. With her knowledge and her granddaughter's assistance, the two were able to prepare and enjoy freshly baked treats of proper proportions. Brahk'dahgh rather liked the peanut butter.

Lizzie was all smiles now, but something bothered her. "Grandma, did you see my friend leave? He was really big and round, with horns."

"Oh, sweetie! I'm sure I would've remembered seeing such a thing!"

This saddened the child, and her grandmother wanted to make it better. "What would cheer you up?"

"Can I have some ice cream, too?"

Ice cream? A delicious, frozen treat stored in a freezer. "And what will you give me if I grant you this request?" the demon-turned-grandmother asked out of habit.

Lizzie's eyes and mouth opened wide. She jumped up and threw her arms about her grandmother's neck. The strangling hug sent the heat of a thousand white-hot pokers searing through Betsy's body to the demon within, the purity searing him.

Betsy shuffled to the freezer and grabbed a container of ice cream. She pulled off the lid and dug into it with her hands.

A new voice called out, "Mom! What are you doing?"

Lizzie cried, "Mommy, something's wrong with Grandma!"

The woman pulled her phone from her bag. "Mom, I'm calling an ambulance! Lizzie, help Grandma to the couch."

The girl's touch burned, but he didn't mind. He stumbled to the sofa. The frail, old body he'd borrowed had already given out. He'd only been able to keep it warm for a little while. And now the Bringer of Doom was doomed himself.

His vision faded away as he listened to the mortals' panicked voices.

"Grandma!"

"Mom!"

"Grandma!"

Darkness enveloped the demonic essence trapped within the old woman. *Is this how it ends?* he thought.

"She's over here!"

"Code blue!"

Brought low by a child? A warm, loving child?

"Clear!"

A surge of hellfire coursed through every atom of his being, shredding the darkness, and leaving the demon sprawled in a foul, sulfuric pool down in the deepest reaches of the Abyss. He'd shed the human's skin, and regained his own, true nature, brimming with vitality. Immortal again.

Once more, he was Brock'dag, Breaker of Bones, Bringer of Cookies, who could serve the delightful ice cream treat at the next apocalypse, were it not for one thing.

Brock'dag serves No One.

AS YE SEEK, SO SHALL YE FIND

Michelle D. Sonnier

THE PRAYER REQUESTS HAD BEEN TAPERING OFF FOR A LONG TIME. Chamuel liked to tell himself it was because young people had fallen away from the old ways, rather than a lack of belief. In truth, it was probably some of both. But the Archangel Chamuel still felt the frisson of a prayer for help on a more or less regular basis. Believers called out for assistance in finding lost things, and he was there for them.

Watches used to be common requests, but not so much now that most people used their smartphones to check the time. Finding wallets or keys were still popular petitions. His favorite entreaties, though, were help in finding purpose, love, or self. It was eminently satisfying to see his supplicant suffused with the glow of satisfaction and certainty. Prayers to help find lost faith were rare and nearly always heartbreaking. Sometimes he couldn't get them to see the light no matter how hard he tried. Sometimes they were just too far gone to believe anymore, their faith already exhausted despite the prayers they raised.

Then suddenly, near the end of spring, just as the season trended into summer, the number of believers desperate to find things shot up with the mercury.

It started with keys. Everyone was losing their keys, sometimes several times a day. Then Mr. Morton misplaced his glasses ten times in the space of thirty minutes. Chamuel remembered the fearful gleam in the mortal's eyes the last time he nudged the man's glasses back into view. The anxious man had just lost his father to dementia-related complications earlier that year. Chamuel wanted to stay and help him find his lost peace of mind, but that had not been requested of him, and another prayer request thrilled against his skin. Chamuel had to go. Fulfilling a request always took precedence over using his own initiative to find what was lost.

Mrs. Landry needed her sewing scissors. Mr. Wabash couldn't find his debit card, and he was desperate to order a pizza. Ms. Baker was nearly in tears trying to find a critical presentation on her hard drive. Her promotion was riding on that presentation. That was a tough task for Chamuel. Modern technology and angelic grace didn't always play well together. But he nudged her mouse to hover over the right file, which was somehow in the wrong directory, just in time. He waited in silence, invisible at the back of the conference room, hoping to witness her professional triumph.

Another prayer, full of desperation, quivered in his ear. A true supplication full of such faith he had not felt in many a decade.

"Archangel Chamuel, I seem to have lost the family Bible. I know that nothing is truly lost, since God is everywhere, and can see where everything is. Please guide me to find what I'm looking for. Thank you, Chamuel."

He followed the prayer, stepping into a sick room set up in the parlor of a creaking old home in Louisiana. A young woman hunted around the room, lifting the scattered detritus of the sick room with a frown on her face. The prayer did not come from her. In fact, Chamuel could not read her at all. Not even her name, as he could with all other humans. He took a step toward her to examine her more closely, admiring the rainbow of tattoos that flitted across her arms. The prayer tugged at him again. He turned back to his faithful one, a wizened and elegant lady sitting next to the sick bed, prayer falling from her lips like pearls. Mrs. Roberts frantically called for help in finding the family Bible so that she could read a verse to comfort her sick husband. Chamuel's eyes flicked to the shrunken figure in the hospital bed in the middle of the room. He could tell Mr. Roberts would not be earthside for much longer.

"Mama, I still can't find it," the young woman said as she lifted a tray holding the remains of a picked-over lunch. "Are you sure you brought it in here?"

"It's the only place I've had it, Nina." Mrs. Roberts sighed. "You better get on to work, honey. You know how that man feels about you being late." Her nose wrinkled as if she'd smelled something rotten.

"Are you sure? I could call in sick..." Nina offered even as she reached for a small denim satchel on the floor with apron strings trailing out of it.

"No, no, we've got enough sickness in this house without inviting more in with a lie." Mrs. Roberts caressed Nina's trailing hand as she hustled for the door. Chamuel felt a strange electricity in the air as Nina passed him. "You have a good shift, baby. I'm sure it will turn up in time for me to read Daddy his supper verse."

"I love you, Mama!" Nina called out over her shoulder and ran out the front door.

"I love you too, baby," Mrs. Roberts murmured to herself as the car peeled out of their driveway. With a sigh, she began to pray again.

Chamuel spotted the Bible on the floor under the hospital bed, and he nudged it out to bump against Mrs. Roberts' foot.

"Huh, I must be going blind," she grunted as she bent to pick it up. She flicked her eyes skyward. "Dear Archangel Chamuel, thank you for guiding me to find what I'm looking for, which includes this family Bible." She sat back into her chair, opening the pages with a gentle caress to choose a passage to read to her husband. The prayer of true thanksgiving, delivered from a humble heart, fed Chamuel like the mana of ancient days.

Not wanting to leave the woman alone at the time of her need — and more than a little curious about her enigmatic daughter — Chamuel settled in, content to wait until Nina came home. Curiosity trembled through him. Who was this young woman that he couldn't know her as he knew all of God's creatures?

Another prayer pressed against his consciousness. Chamuel sighed and returned to his vocation.

Mr. Hunter was frantic to find his daughter's favorite stuffed bunny. She absolutely would not nap without it. Mrs. Landry misplaced her fabric scissors again. Young Elliot needed to find his dog. Chamuel found the gangly six-month-old puppy under the drooping branches of an old holly tree, fascinated with a chipmunk burrow. It wasn't hard to nudge the distractible young hound out where Elliot could see him.

Chamuel smiled, hoping to enjoy the sweet moment of reunion between the boy and his dog. Yet another prayer request crawled up his spine. Mrs. Landry's fabric scissors again. It wasn't like her to have such troubles.

This time the errant scissors were underneath a small fold of navy crepe she had set aside to sew a new dress for her granddaughter's doll. She murmured her thanks for the answered prayer.

Suspecting something else was at play in this already peculiar day, Chamuel leaned against a wall of Mrs. Landry's sewing room and waited as the woman cut out the front of the bodice for a sundress in pink floral cotton for another granddaughter. She placed the scissors next to her, plainly in view, as she set the cut piece aside. She shifted the pinned fabric and reached for the scissors.

They were gone... again.

"I could have sworn..." she muttered.

Chamuel spotted them now up against her sewing machine on the table next to her cutting table. He nudged them so they clattered to the floor before Mrs. Landry could even say the first words of the prayer. Shaking her head, Mrs. Landry picked them up and cut the back of the bodice.

He continued to watch her precise and methodical steps. *Set the scissors down. Stack the cut fabric with the other cut pieces. Shift the pinned fabric to cut the first piece of the skirt. Reach....*

And the scissors were gone again.

Chamuel frowned and scanned the room. This time they were tucked up on the closet shelf among vintage flour sacks Mrs. Landry had always meant to turn into a quilt but never quite got around to. Chamuel snatched them up. He slid them under the pinned fabric before Mrs. Landry finished her prayer.

Mrs. Landry gasped and took a step back from her cutting table. She stared at the fabric scissors as if they might leap up and bite her. A deep furrow ran between her anxious eyes.

"Maybe I'm just tired," she whispered to herself. "Maybe I should take a break?"

Chamuel saw a flash of red in the corner of his eye. With care, he snatched up the hob by his suspenders and dangled the little wizened creature in front of his face. Mrs. Landry wandered from the room in search of a cup of tea, completely blind to the presence of both angel and fae.

Chamuel quirked up an eyebrow. "Aren't you supposed to be nocturnal?"

"Aren't you lot not supposed to touch us?"

The hob lashed out a foot and connected with Chamuel's wrist. An electric shock shot up his wrist. Time and space shivered for a moment. Chamuel dropped the hob. The hob, however, did not immediately scurry off as expected. He regarded the angel with gimlet eyes and a smirk. Chamuel rubbed his wrist and frowned at him.

"Why are you bothering Mrs. Landry?" Chamuel asked. "Did she offend you in some way?"

The hob shrugged. "This is the first time I've been to this house. She hasn't had time to offend me yet."

Chamuel narrowed his eyes. He thought for a moment. "Have the Fair Folk taken up hiding things for a hobby?"

The hob grinned at him. "I wouldn't call it a hobby."

"What would you call it?"

"A calling, perhaps… A reason for being…" The hob rocked from heel to toe, his grin growing wider.

Chamuel sighed and pinched the bridge of his nose. "Why? Why are you doing this? Just give me a straight answer."

"So you'll notice me, of course!" chirped the hob brightly.

"Why do you want me to be interested in you?" Chamuel sighed.

"It's not me that wants your consideration." The hob wagged his finger at the angel.

"*Who* wants my attention?" Chamuel crossed his arms across his chest.

"His Majesty, both prince and king, the Lord of…" the hob began.

"Oberon?" Chamuel interrupted. "*Oberon* wishes my attention?"

The hob pouted. "You don't have to be rude."

"I apologize if I have offered any offense, good sir," Chamuel said through gritted teeth. "Perhaps you might guide me to good King Oberon so I may make his acquaintance?"

The hob sniffed and lifted his chin. "Only because His Majesty would have my hide if I didn't. Really, you angels are supposed to be so full of grace. One would think that would come with some manners."

After the hob led Chamuel through enough twists and turns to confuse even Odin's ravens, they arrived at the court of Oberon, King of the Faeries. Brambles and vines formed a baroque masterpiece of vaulted architecture. Honeysuckles gilded each curve and lavender carpeted the floor, so each step Chamuel took brought a calming scent. Oberon himself lounged on a chaise of braided ferns. Tiny faerie cousins flitted about his head on watercolor wings, vying to be the next to offer him a morsel of food. A disheveled elf sat at his feet, trussed up like a Christmas goose.

Chamuel gave Oberon a deep bow. "My Lord, thank you for the honor of visiting you in your domain."

"Temporary domain," Oberon mumbled around a grape. "I know better than to invite one of your kind into my true realm."

"We don't know what would really happen," Chamuel said with a smile. "It's never been tried."

"My people are too precious to me to risk their lives on an uncertainty," Oberon growled. He waved his hands, and vines grew up out of the floor to form a chair. "You may have a seat if you wish, or not."

Chamuel inclined his head. "You are too kind," he murmured as he settled himself into the vine chair. He clasped his hands in his lap. "Now, how may the heavenly hosts and the Lord, Our Father, be of service to the King of the Faeries?"

Oberon sighed dramatically. "No pleasantries? Just straight to the point?" He frowned. "Not even the veneer of civilization..." he sniffed.

Chamuel tilted his head to the side. "We know you don't care for contact with us. I was merely thinking of your comfort in keeping this meeting as short as possible." He forced a smile. "How may we help you?"

Oberon waved his hand. "I don't care about any of those other heavenly fools. And that 'father' of yours can keep his distance, thank you very much." Oberon narrowed his eyes, focusing on Chamuel. "My business is with you, and only you."

Chamuel raised his eyebrow. "I see. So, what is it I may do for you?"

Oberon became suddenly fascinated with a fold of his robe. He murmured something under his breath.

Chamuel leaned forward. "I'm sorry, I didn't quite catch that. What?"

The elf at Oberon's feet spat out the wad of leaves stuffed in his mouth. "He needs you to find something for him, ya ninny. Why else would he need to call on the likes of you?"

"Hush." Oberon sent the wad of leaves back into the elf's mouth with a flick of his finger. He turned his attention back to Chamuel. "This is..." he cleared his throat. "A bit of a sensitive subject."

"I should say so," Chamuel murmured. He made a show of examining his fingernails. "I thought your power within your domain was absolute. That it would be impossible for you to lose something...

unless you wanted to lose it." Chamuel paused. "Did you want to lose it?"

Oberon sat bolt upright, his face like thunder. "Absolutely not!" he roared. The tiny faeries scattered and hid behind the leaves of the honeysuckle. The elf at Oberon's feet cowered. Chamuel remained calm.

"You understand that I have to ask?" Chamuel kept his tone calm and even. "If it is something you *meant* to lose, my finding it could be quite disastrous. Isn't that right?"

Oberon took a deep breath, then closed his eyes and counted to ten. "Your assessment is fair, Angel."

"I ask again," Chamuel said, smooth as silk. "Did you mean to lose it, or do you truly want it back?"

"I want it back," Oberon's voice came in a rush. "I do truly want it back, and I'll do anything you ask."

Both of Chamuel's eyebrows jumped for his hairline. "Anything? My, that is quite an offer. Are you sure?"

"Very sure." Oberon's shoulders sagged. He leaned forward with his elbows on his knees.

Chamuel waited for him to speak, but when the Faerie King remained quiet for too long, he said, "If I am to find you something so precious, first you must tell me what I'm looking for."

"My Little Whimsy..." Oberon's voice cracked. "I can't find my Little Whimsy, and it's all his fault!" Oberon kicked the bound elf at his feet. The elf spat out the wad of leaves again.

"It was a game!" he protested.

Chamuel cleared his throat. "Excuse me? But whimsy seems a bit... insubstantial. I don't think there is enough substance to the whim of the Faerie King for me to find it."

The bound elf rolled his eyes. "Not *it, she*. Little Whimsy is his daughter."

"And you lost her!" Oberon roared.

"For the last time, it was a game! She was having fun!"

Chamuel's eyes darted back and forth between Oberon and the gamesman at his feet.

"Can't you just call out her true name?" Chamuel asked. "She'll hear you wherever she is, isn't that how true names work with the Fae?"

Oberon glared at the elf. His eyes narrowed to slits. "This one made her forget her name. No matter how many times I call for her, she doesn't hear."

"Yes, well," the elf brought his shoulders up to his ears. He forced a laugh. "That was part of the game... It was supposed to be like hide-and-seek, but it wouldn't be fair if I could just call out her true name and get her to reveal herself, now would it? But when I cast the spell, I stuttered and both of us forgot her true name."

"You could have just agreed not to call out true names for the duration of the game," Chamuel reasoned.

"Well, yes," the elf sighed. "Hindsight is 20/20..."

"You lost her!" Oberon bellowed.

"She had to hide! That was part of the game!" the elf squeaked.

"How long has she been lost?" Chamuel asked.

"Feh." Oberon waved off the question. "I am not concerned with human time." The bound elf flopped over on his side and began to crawl along the floor like an inchworm. He halted at Chamuel's feet.

"Take me with you," he hissed. "If I'm out of his sight for long enough, once he has his Little Whimsy back, he might forget what I did." He gazed up at Chamuel with pleading eyes. "Please. I'll owe you a favor in addition to whatever Oberon promises you."

Chamuel gave a small, almost imperceptible nod. The bound elf sagged into the lavender with a relieved sigh.

"Knowing what size child to look for will make my search faster," he said. "I know you wish to have her home as soon as possible."

One of the tiny faeries zipped down from her hiding place in the honeysuckle. She whispered in Oberon's ear. He nodded.

"She's only been gone a decade or so," Oberon said. "She may appear to be grown to humans, but I assure you she is still very much a child by Faerie standards."

Chamuel nodded. "She is lost somewhere in the human realm, I gather?" When Oberon nodded, Chamuel looked down at the elf at his feet. The elf grinned up at him. "May I take this one with me? Having him as a guide would shorten my search."

Oberon waved away the thought of the elf. "Take him." A feral grin stretched across his face. "Perhaps you can lose him in the human realms for a while. I would consider it a great kindness."

Chamuel stood and dusted his hands together. "Now, that would place you further in my debt. Is he worth it?"

Oberon sniffed. "No. No, he isn't."

"Then it's agreed, Oberon, King of the Faeries, will owe the Kingdom of Heaven one favor in return for finding your Little Whimsy?" Chamuel extended his hand.

Oberon coughed. "Not quite. I, King Oberon, will owe *you*, Chamuel the Archangel, one favor when you find and return my Little Whimsy to me."

Oberon grunted. "Agreed?" He extended his hand.

"There is one more small matter," Chamuel said with a smile. "I do need to know her one true name, not just what you call her."

Oberon jerked back his hand. "That would give you power over my daughter."

"I cannot find her without it," Chamuel reasoned. "Do you not trust an archangel to have honor?"

Oberon narrowed his eyes. "I trust you as far as I can see on a foggy day."

"It's a good thing then that your eyesight is so keen," Chamuel teased.

Oberon grunted and thrust out his hand again. "Deal."

As their palms met, the world around the archangel and the Faerie King shuddered and twisted. Reality groaned. The floor bucked beneath them, and the walls warped to and fro. Oberon leaned forward and whispered into Chamuel's ear. When they released their grip, the world settled back into its more or less natural order.

"OW!" the bound elf shouted. "Can we never do that again?"

Chamuel bowed to Oberon. "I will have your child safely returned as soon as I can, your Majesty."

Oberon nodded regally. "I don't suppose I can trust you to keep this matter under your halo?"

Chamuel placed his hand on his chest and gave Oberon a mock wounded look. "I am the very soul of discretion."

"Angels don't have souls," Oberon grumbled.

Chamuel grinned and winked. "Who would I tell?" He turned to leave the temporary court of brambles and vines. The bound elf inched along the floor after him.

"Don't forget me!" he cried.

Oberon rolled his eyes and shook his head. He snapped his fingers, and the bonds fell away. The elf scrambled to his feet. He stumbled along in Chamuel's wake, working the blood back into his legs.

"You do have a very long stride, don't you?" The elf puffed.

Chamuel glanced back at him. "I'm going to need something to call you."

"You may call me Bedlam," the elf said.

Chamuel shrugged. "Seems a bit obvious, but fitting."

"This is the last place you saw her?" Chamuel's voice dripped with disbelief. He took in the wide-open parking lot and bustling stores of a strip mall in southern Louisiana. "You thought *this* was the perfect place to play hide-and-seek with King Oberon's daughter?"

"In my defense, ten years ago there were a lot more trees and much less asphalt," Bedlam muttered, his eyes wide with shock. "How do humans change things so quickly?"

"It's not quick for them," Chamuel murmured. He closed his eyes, reaching out with his senses to find the lost princess.

"I mean, why would you ruin a forest with all this... this..." Bedlam gestured. "Retail?"

Chamuel sighed. He looked down at Bedlam. "I need to focus. Finding a faerie princess who has been lost for a decade is not as easy as finding recently misplaced keys. Please, be quiet."

Bedlam pouted but said nothing. Chamuel closed his eyes again, just catching a glimpse as Bedlam stuck his tongue out at him. Ignoring the elf, Chamuel spun in a slow circle, palms held out and up. He stopped almost immediately, his eyes snapping open. "Huh."

He looked down at Bedlam again. "You must not have looked very hard." He pointed across the divided four-lane highway at a run-down 24-hour diner. "She's right over there."

Bedlam frowned. "Well, I did hide in Canada for a few years. I kind of forgot who was looking for whom. Then Oberon found me... And well, it's a little hard to think when you're hanging from your toes," Bedlam said with a shrug. "I'm going to have to get all new shoes. None of my old ones fit right anymore."

Chamuel shook his head and crossed the street. Oil spots in the diner's parking lot shimmered with iridescence in the humid Louisiana heat. Chamuel sent a shiver through his form to hide his divine nature and adjust his visage to appear more human. Then he stepped fully into the mortal realm. He turned to Bedlam and held out his arms. "How do I look?"

Bedlam grimaced. "So... Human."

"Good." Chamuel grinned.

"Don't smile like that," Bedlam said. "Your teeth are too bright."

Chamuel put his hand over his mouth for a moment. He smiled again. "How about now?"

Bedlam nodded. "Much more human."

Chamuel headed for the diner, Bedlam invisible on his heels. A tinny bell rang as he opened the door and stepped in, causing his shoulders to twitch. The poor excuse for air conditioning made the diner marginally cooler but still clammy. Chamuel spotted Little Whimsy right away. She was the only harried waitress in the place. Her back was to them as she loaded her tray with plates from the service window.

"Sit wherever you like. I'll be with you in a sec," she called over her shoulder, her pigtails seemingly plain brown, until he looked deeper and caught a rainbow shimmer to them. Something familiar teased at the back of his mind. His brow furrowed as he noted at least three different rainbows tattooed on her bare arms.

Following her direction, Chamuel slid into the booth offering the most privacy from the other diners and pretended to peruse the menu shellacked right into the tabletop.

"Can we get onion rings?" Bedlam begged. "That's the one thing humans got right. Mmmm… Onion rings."

"We're not ordering food," Chamuel murmured under his breath. "We're only here to remind her of who she is, then give her a push on home."

"I'm hungry," Bedlam whined.

"I don't have time to feed you," Chamuel said. "I have prayer requests backing up while I tend to this. And besides, you're the one who owes me a favor."

"Spoilsport," Bedlam grumbled.

"Maybe she'll get you some onion rings after she remembers who she is," Chamuel said. "Did she like you before you made her forget her name?"

Bedlam looked thoughtful for a moment. "I'm not sure. She was kind to everyone, so you couldn't tell who she really liked and who she was just being polite to."

Chamuel jumped when Little Whimsy arrived at the table and chirped, "So, what can I get for you?" Her name tag read "Nina Faye." She was the young woman Mrs. Roberts had called daughter.

"What do you recommend?" Chamuel asked, buying himself a moment.

Nina Faye's eyes flicked to the kitchen over her shoulder, then back to Chamuel. She leaned in with a conspiratorial whisper, "Jacob's on the grill today, so better stick with something fried."

"What was that? My hearing isn't too good," Chamuel said, motioning her closer.

Nina Faye leaned in, drawing in her breath to repeat herself. Before she could speak, Chamuel put his mouth next to her ear, his lips nearly brushing her earlobe. He breathed out the name Oberon whispered in his ear.

Little Whimsy gasped. She leaned forward and gripped the edge of the table as she swayed on her feet. The blood drained from her face and her chin sank to her chest. For a long moment, she held that position, her head swaying and her breath sawing in and out. Then, suddenly, she dropped the crumpled order pad she'd balled in her fist and jerked upright. Her eyes grew round as the realization of whom and what she was sank through her skin. Her gaze slid to the seat next to Chamuel, which had appeared empty only the moment before. Bedlam grinned and waggled his fingers at her.

She put her fists on her hips, her eyes blazing. "How could you leave me here for *ten* years, Bedlam?"

"We were playing hide-and-seek!"

"And you cheated! This does not count, the angel found me, not you," she said with a pout.

"You are without a doubt the champ of all champs at this game." Bedlam thrust both fists in the air, grinning.

Little Whimsy pursed her lips. She crossed her arms across her chest, her foot tapping on the worn linoleum.

Bedlam dropped his arms. "I suppose now would be a bad time to ask for a basket of onion rings?"

"Now would be a good time to disappear until I forget how mad I am at you," Little Whimsy growled through gritted teeth.

"Hey! Space Cadet!" Jacob shouted from the order window. "Stop flirting with the customer and come pick up this food!" Little Whimsy started to turn, but then jerked to a stop, confusion on her face. She shook her head to clear it.

"Sorry, game's over!" she called out as she whipped off her apron and dropped it on the floor. Change and half-used pens scattered everywhere. "It's time to go home, Papa misses me." She turned to Chamuel and Bedlam, concern puckering her brow. "He does miss me, doesn't he?"

"I can assure you, Your Royal Highness, your father does miss you," Chamuel said. "He promised me an open-ended favor to find you and send you home."

Little Whimsy's eyes widened and her mouth rounded into an O. "Really? I must get home then…" She took a step toward the door, then paused. Another cloud passed over her face. "But what about Mama?" she murmured under her breath. "I can't leave her all alone…" She turned back to Chamuel, her gaze tormented. "What do I do?"

"The choice is yours, Princess." Chamuel favored her with a gentle smile. "But nothing says you can't come back again after you reassured your father that you're alright."

"Right." She nodded emphatically. "Say goodbye to Mama, go home and let Papa know I'm alright, then come back home… eerrr… back here and help Mama." She nodded again.

Then, Little Whimsy waved goodbye to the startled customers and skipped out of the diner. As Jacob and the other diners watched her go in puzzlement, Chamuel and Bedlam slid a bit sideways out of the range of human perception. By the time the humans turned their gaze to the booth where she'd been about to take the order, it appeared empty.

"I'm not getting my onion rings, am I?" Bedlam asked with a sigh.

"I don't think so," Chamuel said. He looked down at Bedlam with something bordering on fondness. "You probably shouldn't go back to the Faerie Realm for a little while."

Bedlam nodded. "Norway is nice this time of year."

Chamuel slid out of the booth. The humans around him took no notice as they chattered away about the waitress's shocking exit. "I must get back to my rounds."

It didn't take long for Chamuel to clear out the backlog of prayer requests, now that the faeries were no longer actively hiding things to get his attention. All the keys, purses, scissors, and pets were back where they belonged and stayed there as much as they ever did.

Out of curiosity, he returned to the old house in southern Louisiana. Little Whimsy stood at the edge of the forest that bordered the back yard. The golden light from the kitchen windows highlighted the tears on her cheeks.

"I thought I might find you here," Chamuel murmured. "Do you need any help finding your way home? I can show you the path even if I can't follow you all the way."

Little Whimsy shook her head vigorously and sniffed, dragging the back of her hand across her nose. The archangel waited with her quietly in the dark until she was ready to speak.

"Daddy's gone. He went before I could get here." She lifted her mournful face to Chamuel. "How can I leave her alone?"

"She's not alone," Chamuel comforted. "She's never alone."

Nina nodded, but her eyes dimmed with worry. "What if I forget about her once I cross into my homeland and I don't come back to her like I promised?" her voice quivered.

"Then you wouldn't remember her enough to be hurt yourself, I suppose," Chamuel said thoughtfully.

"But *she* would remember and hurt." Little Whimsy dashed more tears from her eyes. "Mama never asked to play games with the Fae. She just found a little girl crying in the woods and raised her and l-loved her as her own because that was what needed doing."

Chamuel nodded. "She is a good woman."

"She could never have children of her own," Little Whimsy choked. "If I forget her, she won't have anyone else."

Chamuel looked down at Little Whimsy. "Then don't forget her. Don't forget the you who is Nina Faye, or how much you love your human mother."

"Is it that easy?"

"It is if you decide it is."

Little Whimsy nodded and turned to walk deeper into the woods. She paused and looked back over her shoulder. "Thank you. I will not forget." She bit her lip. "Or at least I'll try…"

Chamuel smiled tenderly "I have faith in you."

After Little Whimsy was well gone, Chamuel walked out of the woods and into the house to stand in front of Mrs. Roberts. She sat in the dark of what was now no more than a parlor, grief pooled around her like murky shadows. The empty hospital bed still crouched in the middle of the gloomy room. Tears slid down the tracks of the wrinkles in her cheeks. Her body rounded in as yet another sob tore through her. Clutching her own shoulders, she tried to pray. The words caught in her throat and she choked. She tried again and only a keening wail slipped past her clenched teeth. She threw her head back and howled.

"WHY??" She sucked in a deep breath and cried out again. "Why? Was it too much? Did I ask for too much?" Mrs. Roberts crumpled forward again, weeping.

Chamuel waited until she lifted her head again and opened her eyes, then slipped back into human reality. With a roll of his shoulders, he purposely let his divine nature shine. He reached out to brush the tears from her cheek. Chamuel suddenly knew exactly how he would use his promise from the Faerie King.

"I can't bring Herman back to you, Beulah. Father called him home. But I can promise your Nina won't stay lost for long. I will guide her home to you as soon as she has completed her task."

Beulah Roberts gasped. "Chamuel?" Her voice quavered. She brushed her fingertips against his hand on her cheek.

Chamuel nodded, giving her a beatific smile as he began to rise. Beulah clutched his hand, holding on as long as she could, rising from her chair with her eyes fixed on the angel. As he ascended back to his station in Heaven, he held her gaze, watching the glow of faith rekindle in her eyes.

ON THE SIDE OF THE ANGELS

Danielle Ackley-McPhail

Stately lilies pure and white
Flooding darkness with their light.
-Louise Lewin Matthews

THE WORLD IS NOT WHAT IT HAD ONCE BEEN. NOT BY A LONG SHOT. AND it never was that great, to begin with. But now…? If I hadn't already had it on good authority that I was on the side of the angels, I would have wondered if all of us weren't already in Hell.

My given name is Lys, but that isn't the name I was born with.

The name my mother chose for me is Charlotte Evangeline Scalia. Don't bother asking if any part of that came from my father. The paper pinned to my blanket didn't say. I wouldn't know myself, having been all of hours old.

My best friend, Maria Anna Martucci, she used to call me Char. She still would, if she could find me. But I'm good at hiding. Well, from her, anyway. To me, she'll always be Maria. Only, her name's Shousan now.

For sixteen years, the Sisters raised us by our birth names, exercising them in their entirety way too frequently, until the day they died.

Yeah, the day they died. The Sisters *and* the names.

That was the day Maria and I both took the Order of the Lily.

Don't worry, I never heard of it either.

That's how it is with secret orders.

Now, do you want to hear our story or not?

On the day our world ended, I finally embraced my faith. Kind of hard not to when demons are chasing you. Even harder when a Saint calls you out. Not that I knew about either of those things then.

It wasn't difficult. I've always believed in God just fine. It's religion I don't trust. Not the Sisters, not the individuals, but the greater institution—the collective clique. Have to figure I'm not alone in that.

Organized religion has always drawn more sinners than saints. The problem is that too many of the former actually, wholeheartedly believe they're the latter. Those are the ones that give the rest of us a bad name.

That, after all, is his plan.

No, not *His* plan, *his* plan. You know... the other guy.

The forces of Evil exist, and I am sure it will not surprise you that they fight dirty.

Anyway... back to the story.

By the time we fought our way out of the catacombs beneath the cloister where we'd been raised, I knew what we must do. I only hoped I had enough holy water for the job.

Not. Even. Close.

I did, however, discover I didn't need it. That in itself was both a blessing and a curse.

How? Well, be quiet, and I'll tell you.

I didn't just walk out of those catacombs with a new name and a solemn vow. I had been entrusted with a sacred object. A reliquary.

And before you even start, if you don't know, don't ask. It skeeves me, and I owe the thing my life.

Where does the curse come in? You try carrying out a sacred charge with a big fat target hanging around your neck.

No... not literally! I have more sense than that.

I would have been just fine as a foot soldier in this divine war, but no... The damned thing had to make me a bodyguard.

It makes sense, though. Maria wouldn't have stood a chance. I guess that's why they gave her the book. She's more of a thinker than a fighter. No, that's not right, not anymore, but she still would have had a harder time than me. I'm used to being a target. I've fought my entire life— whether I needed to or not if I'm honest.

Now I have no choice.

For a long time, I went out on my own. Keeping in touch with Maria, but also keeping my distance. It was safer for her. She worked the book—the field guide, as it were, that Lilja gave to us—and I worked the street, hunting for the evil others couldn't see.

Yeah... you didn't know about that, did you? Didn't think so.

More than my name changed that day.

The revenants were only the first wave, the toehold in our world, corrupt flesh serving as a vessel for corrupt spirits. A fleeting threat. Obvious, easy to avoid, easy to banish, if you knew how.

Heck, even if you didn't. Dust to dust and all that, right?

Yeah. That's where we got cocky.

Don't look so shocked. I never claimed to be a saint.

Besides, there is no other way to put it. We thought we had super-powers or some shit like that. Like, with the divine on our side, we were untouchable. Yeah, you can guess how long that lasted. We learned better real quick. I have the scars to prove it, but I'll be damned if I will. I have more important things to do than play show-and-tell.

Come on. We've been here too long.

Excuse me?

What are the revenants?

Where have you been, living in a convent?

Oh… wait, no. That's me.

Yeah… so I'm a wise ass, too. And you're just figuring this out now? How are you even still alive? The Christ isn't the only one capable of raising the dead. He just does a nicer job of it. The other guy…well, he's more of a puppet master. See, the infernal aren't native to this plane. They need an anchor, something to hold on to.

Better hope that's not you.

Oh, relax! I'm just giving you a hard time. It doesn't really work that way. Right? Not yet.

See, demons need a vessel, but there isn't exactly enough room inside us to make that practical. They'd spend too much time fighting for the wheel, if you get what I mean. Those guys aren't too fond of extra effort. There's a reason Sloth is one of the Deadly Sins, after all. And the jolt they get from tormenting a lone soul? It isn't worth the energy it takes to hold on.

They are testing the limits, though. Revenants aren't very effective. Fire or water—holy, of course—takes them right out, even the fresh ones. Believe me, I know! Sure, there are a lot of bodies around, but what shape are they in? Rotting or crumbling, take your pick. Either way, they're hardly going to go unnoticed. Ashes to ashes and dust to dust aren't just metaphors. Convenient if you want a quick disposable army, though. Just saying.

Not that I endorse demonic overlords.

They got pretty far on that shock-value alone, though. Too far. And all of us were too stupid to realize what the hell they were up to. A means to an end, that's all it was.

Huh? You sure do like to interrupt.

Why do I wear leather?

It sure as heck isn't because it looks sexy. Or bad-ass. I'll tell you what is a metaphor… the armor of God! Not that I've turned my nose up at *that* protection, but give me good thick leather, besides. Any day I have to face down the hellspawn, I'm damned well going in protected, body and soul!

What? Do you seriously think I care what I look like when I'm fighting a demon dead set against getting sent back to the netherworld? Sorry to shatter your preconceived notions. Proper leather is a lot tougher than denim and doesn't show blood near as much.

I'd say stop watching so much TV, but how many of us get to do that anymore? Too busy trying to survive with our souls intact.

Of course, *you* don't seem too worried. I'd say that's pretty stupid, but the Sisters taught me better manners than that.

Sorry… was that out loud?

What can I say? I may have learned the manners, but that doesn't mean I have to use them.

Anyway, they're looking for a permanent place on this plane.

The demons! Who'd you think I was talking about? Stay on point here. See, we might have been slow to get there, but we figured out what they are after. Well, Kenn figured it out first. He's not a Lily, but he has fought beside us, a soldier on the side of light. On the side of the angels. Just like me, if you can believe it.

Hell, even if you can't.

Sorry… back to the demons… This is what they're looking for…

A step up. A way out. That anchor I was telling you about. The planes are about balance. Darkness descends. Light rises. Shadow exists between the two, constantly in flux. The demons are reaching for a bit of light, or as close as they can get on the mortal plane, to balance out their darkness, to keep them afloat. It's hard to find, but it's out there. We aren't called to be perfect. That would be setting us up for failure. But some of us have hit just a bit closer to the mark than the rest.

Oh! Not me. I struggle just like everyone else. Being called out by a Saint doesn't make me one, but it did open my eyes.

No, seriously. That wasn't a metaphor.

A Saint's soul glimmers with the light of Heaven, and so does the vessel that held it, even after the spirit ascends. *That* is what the demons are after. The reliquaries. The *true* reliquaries.

Go ahead and laugh. I've seen it. So has Kenn. All too often.

With a holy relic in their possession—no pun intended, but shit happens—demons attain balance, of a sort, enough to raise them out of their deep, dark shithole into this one. Free to walk around with no one the wiser. Mostly.

Until they run across someone with open eyes.

By the way... Your horns are showing.

Hmm... did I say blood? I meant scorch marks. Leather doesn't show scorch marks near so much as denim does.

UNGUARDED

Keith R.A. DeCandido

"*MAMÍ*, I THINK I MAY HAVE A CLIENT FOR YOU AT SCHOOL."

Yolanda Rodriguez blinked in surprise at her fifteen-year-old daughter Kamilah. They had just sat down to dinner. Kamilah's older sister, Analia, had made pork chops and Yolanda had been about to compliment one daughter on her cooking when the other one hit her with that particular bombshell.

"You haven't been telling anyone at school about what I—" Yolanda started.

But that just got Kamilah to look at her with annoyance from over the top of her plastic-framed glasses. "*Mamí*, come *on*. Do I look stupid?"

Her youngest, Eduardo, who was eight, looked up and said, "Can I answer that?"

"Don't even think about it," Kamilah said to Eduardo, then looked back at her mother. "My friend Haroun—I think he's been cursed."

Yolanda chewed her pork chop thoughtfully. If anyone else had said this, she wouldn't have taken it seriously, but Kamilah knew more about the supernatural and the weird and the magical than most of Yolanda's fellow Coursers.

"What signs have you seen?" Yolanda asked.

Before she could answer, Yolanda's husband Carlos asked, "Wait, isn't that the boy who beat you out for best GPA last year?"

Quietly, Kamilah said, "Yeah."

"So this isn't just you wanting revenge?" Carlos asked with a big smile.

"No, Haroun's a good guy! Really!" Kamilah shook her head. "He's smart and funny and he's on the basketball team — he even made varsity, even though he's only a sophomore!"

"So what happened?" Yolanda asked.

"Everything's going wrong! He made six fouls in two minutes in last night's basketball game, and he missed every shot he tried to make. Then today he tripped over his own two feet and banged his head on his locker — so he can't play anyhow 'cause he also sprained his ankle. And then in math class, he got all the answers wrong — he *never* gets the answers wrong in math."

"Maybe he just got all stressed out 'cause'a the ankle," Analia said.

Kamilah almost pouted. "It's not just that! He doesn't *get* stressed out! Last year, his grandmother died and he still played basketball, still got everything right in class, and he didn't ever fall down! I really think he's got a curse on him."

"How long's this been going on?" Yolanda asked.

"Couple days."

Yolanda sighed. "Tell you what, Kamilah, give it another couple days, just to be sure."

"But —" Kamilah started, but Yolanda cut her off.

"Kamilah. We don't know for sure that this *is* a curse. You find any hex bags or symbols in his locker or his bags?"

"Not — not yet."

Torn between pride and concern over Kamilah's use of the word "yet" there, Yolanda then asked, "And do we have a client?"

Kamilah looked down at her food. "No."

"Right. This is a *job*, remember? Unless someone's payin' for a Courser, ain't nothin' we can do. All right?"

"Yes, *Mami*."

But Kamilah did *not* sound happy about it.

Later that night, Yolanda and Carlos were getting ready for bed. Carlos had taken off his prosthetic leg and was lying down while Yolanda was changing into her nightshirt and making sure their pet dragon, Magellan, had enough water in his dish.

"You sure you weren't too hard on Kamilah, Lala?"

Yolanda sighed. She knew it was true love with Carlos because she let him call her that without punching him repeatedly in the throat.

"You think I was?"

"If it was Analia or Eduardo saying it, I'd be right there with you, but Kamilah knows from curses."

Nodding, Yolanda pet Magellan once on the head. The dragon said, "Croooo," breathed out a tiny bit of smoke, and then settled down to sleep.

Then she moved toward her side of the bed. "Yeah, she does, but we still ain't got a client. Besides, it could be a curse, but it could also just be a kid havin' a bad couple days. And it's not like I can go wanderin' around the school without cause."

"Why not? You used to teach there," Carlos said with a cheeky grin.

"Yeah, and they just *love* it when former volleyball coaches go around pokin' into students' lives for no good reason."

Carlos chuckled, then his face grew serious. "Oh, yeah, speaking of clients, Jake finally called me back. Accounting screwed up *again*, so I won't get the payment until next week."

Yolanda sighed as she crawled under the covers. "Dammit. And the full moon ain't for two weeks."

The night of the full moon was almost always a busy one for Coursers, because there was always *some* manner of phenomenon that needed a supernatural hunter-for-hire like her to deal with.

Ever since a Wendigo chewed off Carlos's leg — the incident that led to Yolanda taking on the job of Courser — he'd been working as a freelance comic book artist. Unfortunately, the publisher's accounting department had never been reliable. When he first started working for them, they couldn't cut checks right; now, they couldn't get a simple wire transfer to go smoothly.

At least Yolanda still had her job at the cross-fit place which, along with Carlos's disability, brought in some regular income. But with three kids, that was never enough.

She drifted off to sleep, her dreams filled with images of zeroed-out bank accounts and empty plates on their dinner table.

The next day, Yolanda put in a full shift at Pinehurst Cross-Fit. She spent all morning and afternoon helping people get into shape in the storefront workout joint on 181st Street a couple of blocks from their apartment, in the Washington Heights neighborhood of upper Manhattan.

By three p.m., she had finished with a pair of clients and headed to the small office she had been given. As she went, Shaniqua, half of the couple who owned the place, said, "Yo, you got somebody waitin' for you!"

"Thanks." That was probably a Courser client. Ever since she'd gotten rid of a leprechaun infestation at Pinehurst, Shaniqua and her wife DeAnna had allowed Yolanda not only to continue working for them but to use her office as an unofficial home base for her Courser work.

Sitting in the guest chair of her tiny office was a tall, skinny man wearing a turban and a long linen tunic over loose linen pants, all of which were light brown. After a moment, she recognized him.

He rose to his feet as she entered. "You are Ms. Rodriguez?"

"Yeah, I'm Yolanda Rodriguez."

"I am Thara Uddin, and I am hoping you might be able to assist me."

As Yolanda sat in her chair, the springs squeaked a bit. Uddin retook his seat more silently.

"You're the imam at the mosque over on St. Nicholas, right?"

Uddin nodded. "Indeed. I have been tasked with a very important mission, but I am afraid that the means to complete the task are beyond my abilities. I understand, Ms. Rodriguez, that you are a Courser, yes?"

"Who, ah, who tasked you with this mission, if you don't mind me askin'?"

"The *hafazhah*. They are the guards of Allah's people, and all who are dedicated to Islam have four such assigned to them to protect them until they have reached their appointed time." Uddin shook his head. "My apologies, as a Courser, I'm sure you know all this."

In fact, Yolanda didn't — she had a great deal of trouble keeping track of all the different magical beings in the world. Kamilah usually backstopped her on that stuff. But there was no need for Uddin to know that, so she just nodded and said, "It's okay, go on."

"The issue is with the four *hafazhah* who are assigned to a young man named Haroun Ayad."

Unable to help herself, Yolanda smiled.

"Something amuses you?" Uddin asked tightly. He sat up straighter in the guest chair, his entire body tensing. He obviously thought this was no laughing matter.

"It depends — is Haroun Ayad a sophomore at Cardinal Marini High School?"

"Yes. How did you know that?"

"I used to teach at Marini, and both my daughters go there. Haroun's friends with my younger daughter, Kamilah."

"Ah, I see."

"What's the problem with Haroun's *hafazhah*?"

"They have been blocked from performing their duties."

Suddenly, Yolanda felt really bad about how dismissive she had been of Kamilah at dinner the night before. If Haroun had four guardians protecting him and they were suddenly yanked away, that could make it look like he was cursed.

Although the fact that Haroun was obviously a devout Muslim raised another question. "If you don't mind my askin', Mr. Uddin — why is Haroun attending a Catholic school?"

Uddin gave a small smile. "I don't mind at all, Ms. Rodriguez. Haroun's father is Muslim, but his mother is Catholic."

"That musta been a *fun* wedding."

"I could not say, as the nuptials occurred before I came to New York, but nonetheless, both Haroun and his father are regular attendees at our mosque. However, his mother is an alumna of Cardinal Marini."

Yolanda nodded in understanding. Children of alumni and present and past faculty got tuition discounts at Marini, which was part of why Yolanda and Carlos sent their daughters there, and likely also true of the Ayad family.

"Okay — what else have the *hafazhah* told you?"

At that, Uddin hesitated. "Very little, I am afraid. The guards do not commune directly. I was told by a colleague that Coursers had means of doing so?"

"We do, yeah." It was going to mean a trip up to Kawtha's shop on Vermilyea and 207th Street, though the cost of the amulet she'd need could be added to the imam's bill. "I need to assemble some materials — can we meet at your mosque tomorrow?"

"Absolutely. You may come by *after salah* — say two-thirty?"

"Great. Now we gotta talk about my fee."

After discussing remuneration with the imam, Yolanda finished her day at Pinehurst. Around six, she picked up Eduardo from his afterschool facility and walked him home, then told everyone of their new client over dinner.

"So he *was* cursed!" Kamilah said triumphantly.

Yolanda pointed a finger at her daughter. "Maybe. I'm gonna talk directly to the *hafazhah* tomorrow. Gotta head uptown first and get me a Perrone Amulet."

Analia said, "Say hi to Kawtha for me!" at the same time that Kamilah said, "You can't use a Perrone!"

Making a mental note to give Kawtha Patel regards from her older daughter, Yolanda replied to her younger one: "Why can't I use a Perrone? It's for summoning angels, right? And the *hafazhah* are basically guardian angels."

But Kamilah was shaking her head. "Perrones are *just* for summoning *Christian* angels. It won't work for *hafazhah*, or for a Zoroastrian angel or a Sikh angel, either. You need a Knudtson Stone—that's for summoning *any* kind of godly messenger or servant."

Yolanda sighed. She seemed to recall that a Knudtson Stone cost about twice as much as a Perrone Amulet. She hoped she had enough in the account to cover it—while the imam would reimburse her once the job was over, she still needed to front the cash for the thing.

"All right, thanks, Kamilah. See what else you can dig up about *hafazhah* tonight after you get your homework done."

"I'll do it right after dinner," Kamilah said with a smile.

Yolanda shook her head. Of course, Kamilah already had her homework done before dinner…

After bringing her checking account dangerously low to purchase the Knudtson Stone, as well as a new silver stick—the last one had fallen down a sewer drain—Yolanda headed to the mosque on St. Nicholas Avenue and 175th Street.

As she entered the surprisingly small space—it was on the ground floor of an apartment building, across the street from a much more ostentatious Roman Catholic Church—she saw several men standing on the brightly colored and intricately patterned red-and-gold carpet. Uddin stood at the center of the group, today wearing darker brown. Most of the other men were also dressed in long tunics and loose pants, though they all wore simple white caps instead of turbans.

Uddin approached her and gave a small bow. *"As-salamu alaykum. Welcome, Ms. Rodriguez."*

Although she wasn't Muslim, Yolanda thought it only polite to give the appropriate response: *"Wa alaykumu s-salam.* I'm ready to summon the *hafazhah,* but—uh, why the audience?"

"Forgive the indulgence, but many of the brothers wished to witness this great event."

"Yeah, okay." She bit back a retort asking if any sisters were invited, reminding herself that the client was always right.

Yolanda reached into her purse and rummaged around to try to find the small bag containing the Knudtson and its accessories, which she finally located underneath her cell phone and a vial of holy water.

First, she placed the small handkerchief on the floor of the mosque, then put the Knudtson Stone atop it.

One of the men standing with Uddin asked, "What is the cloth for?"

Yolanda grinned as she unscrewed the bottle of planetary oil. "To keep your carpet clean." Then she poured the oil onto the stone and said, *"Jag kallar* Haroun Ayad *vaktmästare. Jag kallar Allah tjänare."* The stone started to sparkle with a mild blue glow.

A bright light seemed to come from nowhere, bathing the room in incandescence. Yolanda held her arm up over her face and blinked spots out of her eyes even as the light dimmed as fast as it had brightened.

Standing in a circle around the stone were four forms. Two were dark red and shimmering with what seemed to be fire—Yolanda saw smoke wisp off them. The other two were a pale white—and she saw condensation wisp just like the smoke off the first two.

All four faced in the same direction, not looking directly at Yolanda—or at anyone else in the room.

One of the fiery ones spoke first, with a harsh voice, like a truck driving over broken glass. *"You who summoned us, are you who was promised by the scholar of this structure?"*

"Assuming you mean Mr. Uddin, then yeah. I'm Yolanda Rodriguez. I understand that—"

One of the two icy ones spoke in a quiet tone like snow falling. *"We are the guardians of one who is dedicated to Allah."*

The other icy one added in a louder, more intense manner that sounded like wood cracking, *"We have been denied our task."*

"You will fix this," the second fiery one said, and that one's voice was whispery and faded.

Belatedly, Yolanda realized that all four angels faced southeast: the direction of Mecca.

"I'll do my best, but I gotta know *how* you're bein' stopped from protecting Haroun."

"*Your question is meaningless,*" the second icy one said.

The second fiery one repeated: "*You will fix this.*"

"I don't know what 'this' is yet!" Yolanda sighed. "What happens when you try to protect Haroun?"

"*We are unable to.*" The second fiery one was starting to sound angry.

The first fiery one said, "*She is not a child of Allah — she must be instructed.*"

"*Our task,*" the first icy one — who had the nicest voice, so Yolanda was grateful that she got to give the lecture — said, "*is to guard the child of Allah. In time of day, my sister and I guard him, I in the front, she behind. At night, our brothers take over. But three days ago, all attempts were stymied. We could not guard him, could not approach his personage, could not do anything. In anguish, we came to the scholar of this structure, and he came to you.*"

"You will fix this!" the second fiery one cried, and Yolanda felt the mosque shake.

Uddin exchanged nervous glances with his comrades. All of them were openly gaping at the presence of the *hafazhah* in their midst.

"Like I said, I'll do my best. One more question — you said this started three days ago?"

The first fiery one said, "*When my brother and I were to take our turns three days past, we were denied, and all attempts to fulfill our function have failed.*"

"*We* must *serve our purpose,*" the second icy one said. "*The child of Allah may visit a fate not his own if we cannot act!*"

Now that she had a specific timeframe, it gave Yolanda something to work with. "If it's okay, I'll look into this, and summon you again tomorrow."

"*There is no need for further summonings,*" the first fiery one said.

The second icy one added, "*It wastes effort and serves no further function. And we find it cumbersome.*"

"You will fix this!" the second fiery one bellowed.

"For the third time, I'll do my best. *Jag släpper dig.*"

With those last three words, the four guardians faded and the Knudtson Stone's sparkly glow did likewise.

The gathered men were still gaping and now were talking amongst themselves in what Yolanda thought was Arabic.

Uddin, however, didn't join the gabfest, and instead came over to her. "Do you now have a course of action, Ms. Rodriguez?"

"I think so, yeah, but I need to talk to the Ayads. Can you take me to their home?"

"Now?" Uddin asked hesitantly.

Recalling that Haroun was in school with Kamilah right now, and his parents probably both worked, Yolanda said, "No, tonight, once everyone's home."

Uddin removed a smartphone from one of the pockets of his tunic and then recited an address on 184th Street. "I will meet you there this evening at seven-thirty."

Yolanda wasn't thrilled at the imam inviting himself along, but he *was* the client, and besides, his presence might put the family at ease.

That night, Yolanda gathered up Kamilah and Magellan and headed to 184th Street.

Analia had also wanted to go with them, but she had to help teach a karate class. "I can get out of it," she'd said—having recently achieved her junior black belt, Analia often accompanied Yolanda on her jobs for extra muscle.

"It's fine," Yolanda had replied, "this *probably* won't be dangerous. And if it is, I got Magellan."

Kamilah did *not* usually accompany Yolanda on her jobs, as her specialty was lore and research, but Haroun was her friend, and Yolanda thought having her around would make them both happy.

As for Magellan, the small green dragon had followed Yolanda home from a job years ago, and Analia and Kamilah had insisted she keep him. (Eduardo was still a baby at the time, though as he got older, he was very confused as to why none of his friends had pet dragons.) Yolanda had named him after the dragon in *Eureeka's Castle*, one of her favorite shows from when she was a girl. He'd proven handy on more than one job. Right now, he was curled up inside Yolanda's purse, fast asleep, away from prying eyes.

They were buzzed into the large apartment building on 184th and then took the rickety old elevator up to the seventh floor and the Ayad apartment.

Uddin was standing in the doorway when they exited the elevator. "Welcome, Ms. Rodriguez."

"Thanks, Mr. Uddin."

He led them into a very cluttered hallway, filled with short bookcases stuffed with books and magazines. To Yolanda's right was the kitchen, and on the left were three closed doors. The far end of the hallway opened into a large living room, which had an entryway to a dining room that also had its own door to the kitchen. Yolanda suspected that Haroun had spent a lot of time running around in circles in this place, especially when he was Eduardo's age.

The living room walls were also covered in bookcases, aside from one wall that had exposed brick, and they had hung pretty works of art on it. Seated on the couch that was against the brick were a dark-skinned man in a polo shirt and slacks, a pale redheaded woman in a flower-print sundress, and a very tall young teenaged boy with coffee-colored skin wearing a Spider-Man T-shirt and jeans. He was barefoot and had an Ace bandage wrapped around one foot. Yolanda assumed that was the ankle he had sprained. There was also a square-shaped bandage on his forehead.

As soon as they walked into the living room, the boy brightened. "Hey, Kamilah!"

"Hi, Haroun! My *mamí*'s here, and she's gonna fix everything!"

Yolanda winced. "Well, I'm gonna try anyhow."

The two parents stood up. "You're the Courser?" the man asked.

Nodding, she held out a hand. "Yolanda Rodriguez, and that's my daughter Kamilah."

"I'm Zaki Ayad," the man said, returning the handshake. "This is my wife, Siobhan."

The redhead also shook her hand. "A pleasure. I have to ask — what *is* a Courser, exactly?"

Yolanda chuckled. She got this a lot. "We've been called a lotta things, but we're basically supernatural hunters-for-hire. I don't really get the name, myself, I just do the job, y'know?"

Kamilah said, "It's actually an old hunting term from the 17th century — it originally referred to hunters who worked by sight instead of by scent."

Haroun laughed. "Don't get her started, Mom. Kamilah's like a walking Wikipedia."

That got Kamilah to peer at Haroun over her glasses, and Yolanda was amused to see that she wasn't the only one who received that doleful look. "I'm *better* than Wikipedia, thank you *very* much."

Siobhan, however, looked dubious, to say the least. So did Zaki, and they both shot a glance at the imam.

He nodded, and they both nodded back and sat down.

Yolanda blew out a breath. The biggest impediment in her job was dealing with people who didn't believe that what she did was real. Hell, until the Wendigo chomped off her husband's leg, *she* hadn't believed that what she now did was real.

The living room also had a loveseat, an easy chair, and a rocker. Haroun joined Kamilah on the loveseat, while Yolanda sat on the rocker, gently setting down her purse so as not to disturb Magellan. Uddin remained standing.

"I got to talk to your *hafazhah*," Yolanda said to Haroun. "They said they —"

"You *spoke* to them?" Siobhan was rolling her eyes now. "Oh, come *on*."

Zaki put a hand on her thigh. "Sweetie, *please!*"

"He's just had a couple of bad days! It happens!"

"Please, Ms. Ayad," Uddin said, "trust in Allah."

"I respect that you — that all three of you — trust in him," Siobhan said, "but I don't."

"Just hear Ms. Rodriguez out?" Zaki asked. "Please?" He was now staring at his wife with wide brown eyes.

Siobhan let out a very long breath. "Fine."

Yolanda had been tempted to let Magellan out of the purse just to see her reaction, but it was best to keep the dragon in reserve. Instead, she looked back at Haroun.

"Your *hafazhah* said that they stopped being able to protect you last Sunday around sunset."

Haroun said, "That was dinner time. Aunt Maureen came over."

Siobhan added, "Maureen's my sister. She found a few things in my mother's house when she was cleaning it out, and brought them by, and stayed for dinner."

Yolanda recalled Kamilah mentioning that Haroun's grandmother had died. "I'm sorry for your loss."

"Thank you."

"Did any of the things Maureen found go to Haroun?"

Haroun said, "I took that pretty coin." Reaching into the pocket of his jeans, he took out a dark coin, which looked like it was made of copper, with a bright shape engraved on it in what looked like gold.

Kamilah stared at it. "Can I see that?"

Shrugging, Haroun said, "Sure. I just took it 'cause it reminds me of Grandma. She always carried that coin around. Said it kept her safe."

After turning the coin over in her hands, Kamilah looked over at Yolanda. "That's a Jerusalem Cross." She held it up and Yolanda saw that the engraving was a Greek cross—which meant it was even on all sides, instead of looking like a lower-case letter T the way a lot of crosses did—and there were four more crosses, one in each corner of the big cross.

Siobhan added, "Ma always said that coin was for her guardian angel."

Suddenly, Yolanda got a very queasy feeling.

She reached into her purse and pulled out the Knudtson Stone. That disturbed Magellan, and he flew out into the living room.

"What is *that*?"

"That's *Magellan*," Kamilah said in her best teenager *duh!* voice.

"He's our dragon," Yolanda said, "and don't worry, he ain't gonna hurt you."

Magellan flew lazily around the living room. Haroun was staring wide-eyed at him, while Siobhan and Zaki looked like they were trying to crawl *into* the couch.

Uddin, though, was apparently more interested in the Knudtson. "The *hafazhah* said they were blocked from even being near Haroun. You will not be able to summon them here."

Yolanda smiled. "They're not who I'm summoning."

She placed the cloth on the hardwood floor of the living room, then put the stone on top of it. As she poured more of the planetary oil onto the stone, she said, "*Jag kallar* Haroun Ayad *vaktmästare. Jag kallar Yahweh tjänare.*" As the stone started to gain a sparkly blue glow, she said, "Everyone cover your eyes for a minute."

Another bright light, which dimmed, and then a glowing figure appeared in the center of the room. It had no discernible features and only a basic human form but made up entirely of light. Yolanda had to admit to being disappointed at the lack of wings.

The form seemed to turn and face Yolanda. *"Why have you brought me here?"*

"You're the guardian angel attached to that coin, right?" Yolanda pointed at the coin in Kamilah's hand.

"The bearer of that talisman is entitled to my protection only if that bearer is of the faith."

"And there's the problem. Haroun ain't of the faith — he's Muslim."

"Then he is not entitled to my protection."

"Yeah, but you're blocking him from the protection he gets from *his* guardian angels."

"Your words are meaningless to me. The talisman must be given to one of the faith. Now release me, mortal, that I may return to my duties."

The angel started moving toward Yolanda, but Magellan interpolated himself between them. Smoke issued from his nostrils as he said, "Mneh!"

It started getting very hot in the apartment, and the angel's glow intensified.

"I've no wish to harm you, but if you do not release me — "

Yolanda had everything she needed anyhow. *"Jag släpper dig."*

The angel disappeared and the stone's glow faded.

"What — the *hell* — was *that*?" Siobhan was almost hyperventilating.

"Your mother's guardian angel, looks like," Yolanda said. "You said she carried that coin everywhere, right?"

"Yeah, she said it gave her luck, but — " Siobhan shook her head and got up from the couch, pacing across the front of it. "This is crazy! She didn't have a guardian angel!"

"I know you don't believe in this stuff, but I just *called* it — "

Waving her arms back and forth, Siobhan interrupted Yolanda. "No, forget that, I'm talking about Ma. Her life *sucked*. How could she have a guardian angel?"

Uddin stepped forward. "I can only speak to how the *hafazhah* behave, Ms. Ayad, but I suspect the Christian guardians are similar: they do not protect from all harm, but rather keep them from harm that is not part of their fate as preordained by Allah." He smiled and bowed his head. "Or, in your case, by Yahweh."

Yolanda said, "But what's happening here is that the coin is keepin' Haroun's *hafazhah* from doing their jobs of protecting him *and* the angel attached to the coin *also* ain't protecting him, which is why he's been such a mess. It's like getting the opposite of being protected, and twice as much."

Zaki asked, "So what do we do?"

"Duh, Dad," Haroun said, "I don't keep the stupid coin! You can have it, Kamilah."

"Actually," Yolanda said, "I think Siobhan should have it."

"I haven't set foot inside a church in twenty years, Ms. Rodriguez," Siobhan said, "and I'm not about to start now." She smiled. "But my sister has. I'll give it to Maureen."

"That should solve the problem," Yolanda said.

Magellan, meanwhile, had landed on Kamilah's lap, and Haroun was now petting him. "He's *great*!"

Uddin walked up to Yolanda and offered a hand. "Thank you, Ms. Rodriguez. I believe that you have brought peace to this family."

"I don't know if I'd go that far," Siobhan said. "You just turned my entire world upside down with a stone and some oil, and it's gonna take me a while to be okay with that."

Zaki stood up and put a hand on his wife's shoulder. "Haroun should be safe now. That's what matters."

Siobhan smiled and put one of her hands on his. "That's definitely true."

Yolanda said to Uddin, "I'll e-mail you an invoice."

Before the imam could respond, Zaki said, "No, e-mail it to us. You helped *us* out, we should pay for your services."

"The mosque is happy to—" Uddin started.

"No, Zaki's right," Siobhan said. "He's our son, our responsibility. Thank you both for your help."

"My pleasure." Yolanda and Siobhan exchanged e-mail addresses, then she turned to her daughter. "Okay, Kamilah, we should—"

But then she saw that Haroun and Kamilah and Magellan were all goofing off on the loveseat.

Turning back to Zaki and Siobhan, Yolanda said, "Maybe Kamilah and Magellan can stay for a while?"

"I think Haroun would love that," Siobhan said. "We were gonna order pizza for dinner. You can all stay if you want."

"I must return to the mosque," Uddin said.

Yolanda smiled. "I should get home, too—Kamilah, you can get yourself and Magellan home on your own, right?"

Kamilah just peered at her from over her glasses. "*Mamí.*"

"That's what I thought."

THE DOG LISTENER
Christopher J. Burke

SOMETIMES, I WISH I COULD TELL DAD HOW MUCH I NOW APPRECIATE some of the things he used to say. Other times, I realize that if he were still here, I probably wouldn't give him the satisfaction of hearing me say that he was right. But I've come to see the reasoning behind some of his general complaints.

In particular, he used to say, "Virgil, getting older stinks, but it beats the alternative." The click-bait version of the Stuff-That-Dad-Said-Stunk-the-Most would start: *1. Everything hurts. 2. Everything changes.*

I haven't written that one yet, but I'm starting to understand where he was coming from. Except for his time in the service, Dad lived his entire life in this town. He liked it here, but he used to like it more "the way it was."

In the middle 1800s, Newfield was just a bunch of farmland, notable solely for being a mile marker on the road from Oakfield to Churchville Junction. I can only imagine that some farmer, likely named Cotter or Gersh, stood in his field, and thought to himself, "This is good just the way it is." Do you think he railed against new home construction? Might he have stood in the way of western expansion until someone said, "Hey, what if we named a street after you? Or a park?"

A century later, Newfield had grown into a typical small town, complete with a couple of square miles of wood-framed houses, a few schools, a church, and a town square, with a scattering of parks and playgrounds strategically placed for family excursions. The place had a lively downtown most weekends, with dance halls, bijous, and a bowling alley.

In the 'good ol' days,' Dad worked as a shoemaker in his father's shop, before taking over the family business. He also did carpentry on his days off for a little extra income. When he met Mom, she started mending garments at a table by the front window. It was a simple life, but the two of them were happy to spend their days together in that little store, nestled between the florist and the barber. The customers would come in to have the soles of their shoes repaired and the buttons on the jackets replaced while they got their hair cut. Dad loaned them a pair of slippers to wear while they waited. When they picked up their goods, he'd remind them to buy a bouquet for the missus from next door on the way home. Small towns were like that then.

Newfield seemed frozen in time for a couple of decades. Life was good. Not many complaints. But then, everything changes.

Times change. People change. Shopping habits change.

When folks stopped bringing in shoes, Dad tried selling them instead. And then he sold the entire shop. I think he was glad I didn't go into the family business. Not that he ever said that out loud. I wish he'd had more time to enjoy his retirement.

Newfield has grown quite a bit since then. Dad would have liked it to stay the way it was twenty-five or thirty years ago. I would have settled for maybe five or ten years, before Oakfield expanded and gentrified. Once their excess population made its way down the pike, my neighborhood felt the effect.

From my apartment on Gerst Street, on the east side of town, I've watched most of the older stores close. Boutiques and cafes replaced them along the main avenues. It's great if you need pet grooming or artisanal spices...

Overall, I'd say that it's been a net positive because I like craft brews. But there wasn't anything wrong with how Newfield was just a couple of years ago. Plus, I miss Schmitty, the old guy at the newspaper shop. But when rents get higher, people retire. At least, it gives me something to write about.

Maybe you've read something of mine... under the byline Virgil Schuster? You probably haven't seen my blog, but I have a regular gig supplying columns for a couple of online tech magazines. Aside from that, I supplement my income with other opportunities around the Internet.

I'll admit that I've dashed a few of those promoted lists you see on social media. What can I say? "Seven Things You Missed the Last Time You Clipped Coupons" paid for a month's groceries. But I've also penned work for publications that pay a month's rent.

California Audubon? Whatever you want to know about the Mourning Dove and the Yellow-rumped Warbler! Ecclesiastical youth ministries? Let me tell you how we can serve our elderly and our world. Canadian road trips? I am so there! Well, not literally, but satellite images paint really awesome pictures, if you know what I mean. I can research anything online. It's relatively simple, and the fun usually outweighs the frustration. And I get to meet a lot of interesting people who have contacts in a lot of areas. I just have to be careful because some of them can be a little shady, and the areas of the web they haunt can get pretty dark.

I prefer to keep the Sun on my face, thank you, which I do every day.

Since my apartment is my office, there isn't any reason to leave it in the morning. However, staring at the same computer screen all day, or at my signed posters of *Cat Girls From the Stratosphere* and *The Panther Woman's Nine Lives*, would drive me mad. Thankfully, setting my own hours allows me the flexibility to go out whenever I want. Take a walk, get some fresh air. Moreover, since a nasty car accident last year, desire has yielded to necessity. If I sit in one spot for too long, everything hurts. *Yes, Dad, you heard me.*

Getting outside and moving around helps me work out angles for new pieces I've outlined. It's difficult concentrating when you're in pain. Plus, people-watching and trend-spotting are my bread and butter. If something sparks an idea, I jot down a note and research it when I get home. It gets my mind off my back.

Around 10:30 am, I left the apartment, and walked up to the avenue. The fusion takeout place wasn't ready for business yet, but the little shop where you can get a hundred kinds of hot sauce had its front door open. I can't complain about that place. Not only did it spice up my Buffalo chicken salad, but I made $400 on an article I hammered out after perusing the shelves.

Two blocks west brought me to Cotter Park, a little downtown oasis filling a full city block. It's surrounded by storefronts, three-story office buildings, and the occasional food truck. It's where you'll find my favorite bench, overlooking my favorite patch of grass, between the fountain and the playground. It has long been the "Number 4 is my favorite" on my list of "Top Six Places to Go and Things to Do in Newfield."

And yet I have mixed feelings about it.

For one thing, coming here is like returning to the scene of the crime. The crime was jaywalking, but it ended with a flipped wreck.

A year ago, I met Dan Underwood in real life for the first time. DanU238 had a lot of contacts and was usually one of the first I'd ping when networking for a lead on an article. It turned out we had common interests. To be honest, a chiller movie pinup convention in Brickton wasn't one of those, but Dan convinced me to give it a try. He promised to introduce me around and said he knew many of the models from previous cons. I can't say that I didn't have fun. I bought two movie posters, had them autographed, and even posed for a photo with one of the actresses.

The fun ended when Dan drove us home. He kept hinting at some of the crazier schemes he'd been involved in. He might've been sussing out my interest level, to see if I'd want to take part in some future wacky operation. I said little, but smiled a lot, feeling stress levels build toward a dam burst. Then, it happened.

A late-night walker came out of the park, crossing in the middle of the block with a leash stretched out in front of her. Dan swerved to avoid her and plowed into a parked car, going fast enough that we flipped over. Despite the seatbelt, I was tossed around, banging my head. First, I saw stars, then things went all red, then all black, and finally bright white lights blinded me. Everything hurt.

My next memory was the woman screaming. As I crawled away, I heard her shoes clacking against the pavement. She stood over me, asking, "Are you okay?"

A dumb question, to be sure, but one I heard repeated over and over as I drifted in and out of consciousness. It sounded like a higher pitch, and more excited, to the point of panting. "Are you okay? Are you okay? Are you okay?"

I assumed it was the concussion. When I told one of the doctors that I'd heard a floppy-eared dachshund talking to me, she ordered a whole battery of tests. The MRI tech checked for neurological issues, but couldn't find any medical rationale for hearing voices. I mused that maybe it was a sign that someone from above was watching over me. He laughed, fairly certain that messages from beyond probably weren't transmitted through wiener dogs. He thought it was a sign that I had a vivid imagination.

It wasn't my imagination. It *isn't* my imagination.

As I walked up the steps at the park entrance, an eager Lhasa Apso nearly tripped me as it romped by. It yipped, "Oh, boy! The park!! Oh, boy! The park!!" Keep something in mind here. I'm not interpreting what some yapping might mean. I'm saying exactly what I hear.

A young blonde woman wearing an "Ask me if I care..." T-shirt followed the pooch, at the other end of the chain, mindlessly chatting on the phone. She tilted her head toward me and contorted her face for a moment. I don't know if that was explanation or apology, but she continued on her way, neither breaking her stride nor interrupting her call with "Phyllis."

I pulled out my writing pad and started a note. Ms. I Don't Care was definitely going on a list.

The evolution of Cotter Park is the biggest change in my life in Newfield. Physically, the park itself is the same, with its trees, grass, and playground. The people ambulating within its stone walls and iron fences? They're a different story.

Sure, some of the old-timers still show up. They need their daily allotment of exercise and sunshine as much as I do. Old Mrs. Bluecoat sat in her usual spot, hushing her basset hound. She concentrated on her knitting, but snuck glimpses at the guy working out in a tank top.

I can't fault the folks working in those office buildings from strolling out with their bagged lunches on sunny days. Sometimes I stop to chat with Paige from Accounting, second floor, above the panini place. She's quite pleasant to talk to, even though she's dating Lenny from Sales. But they aren't who the park oasis was meant for.

The children are missing. There are no kids running around, climbing all over the slides and seesaws. These days, I could sit on a swing for an hour, lost in my thoughts, and it wouldn't bother anyone. There's no one to bother.

Where'd they go? Grown and moved on is my guess. Families have left the cramped apartments of these old wood-framed houses. No one wants to be like my grandfather, who swore he slept in a bed with his six brothers. I was lucky to only share a tiny bedroom with my sister until Dad put up a partition.

More fully-detached homes have sprung up along the county roads heading up into the hills, and down toward the interstate. They were a great attraction for parents with growing families. And when you have a backyard and open land, you don't need to bring the kids into town for the playground in Cotter Park.

The younger crowd that's moved in isn't interested in begetting progeny just yet. They're happy with their little dogs.

Why not? They're man's best friend, right? Even mine, until I turned thirteen. That's when I found out I was allergic to Prince, my family's Doberman Shepherd mutt.

Now the allergies alone aren't enough for me to alter my daily constitutionals. Yes, maybe it's becoming a dog park, but there's still plenty of fresh air. I can distance myself from most of the fur and dander. And, to be fair, most of the owners clean up after their companions better than some parents ever did with their kids.

No, it's not the air, but the noise pollution that bothers me. The sounds of children's laughter and their shrieks of joy have been replaced with a constant barrage of "Fetch!" and "Who's a good boy?" Not the guy in the oversized college football jersey, fake-throwing the tennis ball for the fifth time! He's not a good boy.

As inane as the human chatter can be, it's nothing compared to their canine pals. You can think that I'm lying or just plain nuttier than a pound of organic trail mix. Despite what the MRI guy thinks, I can hear dogs' thoughts. I *understand* what they're thinking. Ever since the accident, I can literally tell what's going on inside their heads. And let me tell you, it isn't deep. Definitely not anything I could quote in an article or use for insight or background.

It's all, "Fetch the ball. Where's the ball? He still has the ball. He threw the ball. There's the ball. Bring it back. Bring back the ball. He threw the ball. Fetch ..."

"Rub my belly. Rub my belly. Rub my belly..."

"I'm a good dog! I'm a good dog! I'm a good dog!"

"Oooh! A tail!! Catch the tail!! Ouch! Something bit my tail! Oooh! A tail!"

Mind-numbing to the point of my wishing just one of them would go all "Cujo" or something.

Their conversational choices are limited. I can't even speak to them. Believe me, I tried. They don't understand me. They just tilt their heads and stare, like I'm the odd one. Maybe I am.

Some days, the cacophony of voices is hard to take.

This morning, I saw a Labradoodle greet a Yorkie by the fountain. "Hello, friend. You smell like George! Hello, George!"

On a patch of grass behind me, a German shepherd was chatting with an Irish terrier and talking Shih Tzu.

Under the shade of a maple tree, a pug was... *getting to know* that Lhasa Apso, with the owner, still on her phone, blissfully unaware.

I've heard more stimulating conversations on entertainment news shows, except those hosts don't start singing along whenever a fire truck rolls by. Have you ever been serenaded by a mastiff karaoke version of *O Solo Mio*? You probably have, you just don't know it.

I sat back, looked down, and pondered my feet, trying to relax and refocus my mind.

Then it happened. All at once, there was a lull in the incessant chatter. I closed my pad and scanned the assembled canines. Their ears had perked up, their snouts all pointing toward the back of the park.

"He's coming." Every purebred and rescue dog chanted as one in a low, hushed whisper, as outwardly they fidgeted and whined. "He's coming."

The owners and walkers could only see their pets were agitated. I was the sole human who knew why. As it turned out, forewarned was not forearmed.

But it was four-legged.

A huge, black breed of wolfhound, wearing a thick, spiked collar, bounded into the center of the park. Frowning, I looked around, searching for a frantic owner but spying no such thing. Seriously, it couldn't be here alone. Would anyone think it was a good idea to let a creature that size roam free? Where would you even keep an animal that big in the middle of Newfield? I wasn't getting near it to check its tags.

Thank God, there weren't any children about to frighten. That thing creeped the bejeezus out of *me*. But only me. No one else seemed to notice anything, except that their animals crouched low to the ground.

My allergies kicked in just looking in that thing's direction. If it decided to pad my way, I'd need more than a box of Kleenex—I'd need a new pair of boxers!

It plodded over to the old milestone marker, a four-foot-tall obelisk, and stood on its hind legs. Then it rested its front paws on it as if it were a podium and surveyed the crowd.

I sat immobile, staring at it with my head tilted sideways and my brow furrowed as I tried to figure the beast out. I hadn't heard it utter a sound. Was it too far away, or had fear overtaken my brain?

Then, in the back of my head, I heard a low, gravelly... *demonic* voice sounded in my head. "FETCH THE SOUL! WHERE'S THE SOUL? FETCH THE SOUL! BRING IT BACK!!"

It turned and gazed right at me... right through me. "HAVE YOU SEEN THE SOUL... VIRRRR-GIL?"

I selected "flight" from the psychological checklist, but this devil dog closed the gap to my bench with only three strides. Before I could move, the cursed canine rested a paw on either side of me. Brimstone exuded from its nostrils as acidic drool dripped onto my lap, burning holes in my jeans.

With its face inches from mine, the beast's fiery-red eyes stared through the windows of my own soul.

"I HAVE TO FETCH THE SOUL. HAVE YOU SEEN THE SOUL?"

I heard its thoughts, just like any other dog, only this time I knew it could also hear mine. I felt it inside my head, calling up a wave of images from my memory. Snippets of everyone I'd seen today. One lingered a second longer than the rest, tank-top workout guy. Muscle-bound with a crew cut, he took in the Vitamin D, unconcerned about the possibility of melanomas.

The Beast pivoted its enormous snout nearly a full 180 degrees. Behind it, on the far side of the park, I spotted his quarry. As if he felt our combined stares, he turned toward us. His face reddened as he *saw* the Beast, and me with it.

Dan? What the Hell? Was that *Dan?*

He broke into an all-out sprint for the wall and scrambled over.

The hound took off like a bat out of...well, you know. Galloping at a speed that would shame a Derby champion, it hurdled the high stone wall like it was a little red wagon. Maybe it was just an afterimage burned into my tearing eyes, but I would swear that ungodly creature left a trail of black smoke as it disappeared from view. I shut my eyes, tried to catch my breath, and anxiously listened to the chorus of mundane puppy commentary that accompanied the thumping heartbeat pounding in my chest.

Oddly, no one else in the park seemed to have noticed any of what had just taken place. Just me, the dogs, and...well, Dan. Of course, a few of the closer park patrons were now staring at me, clearly wondering if I was going to clean up after myself, and the mess I'd just made.

At that moment, I could swear I heard my Dad's voice. *"Virgil, every-thing changes, and we have to accept that. Sometimes, change is a good thing."*

It got me thinking that I did need to change some things. Maybe I could change where I go to meditate on my life. The library could be nice. The chairs might be uncomfortable, but at least it's quiet.

But first and foremost, what I really needed to change was my pants.

IRRADIA'S GAUNTLET

Russ Colchamiro

"Death aaaaaaaand," Irradia said as the seven ball dropped into the corner pocket, "destruction. That's game. Rack 'em, bitch."

Clad in blue jeans, black boots, and a form-fitting black t-shirt, she slugged down the last of her double whiskey.

Nodding her head to Neil Young's "Rockin' in a Free World," Irradia knew Darius was an equally good pool player, maybe better. But like most girls like her, she just wanted to have fun.

"I thought angels were supposed to be better sports," said Darius, an exotically handsome Athenian with a square jaw and a penetrating gaze. He was casually dressed in beige cotton pants and an azure silk shirt with the sleeves rolled up past his biceps. "What's with the sass?"

"Don't complain to me because your pool skills are for shit. I suggest you spend less time whimpering like a little imp and more time on your aim."

A top lieutenant in the Devil's army, Darius was used to her taunts. They turned him on.

Though down three grains of soul—one for each pool ball by which she'd bested him, plus another for each game he'd lost—his mouth pursed into a half-smile. It was all foreplay. "I'm ready for another," he said. "You?"

A beguiling, red-headed creature with a reputation for luring out the sinner masquerading as saint, Irradia turned over her glass to indicate it was bone dry. Her arctic blue eyes were as sharp as an arrow dipped in liquid nitrogen. "What do you think?"

Darius gestured to the waitress—a blonde, tattooed nymph who gave him the finger, her way of acknowledging that she'd bring another round whenever she felt like it.

Smelling of booze, smoke, sex, and unbridled terror, *Mila's* was the last stop before their fates were decided—neutral territory between Heaven and Hell.

Though time was ambiguous in that illusive netherworld, Darius had studied Irradia long enough. He was about to suggest they move to a corner booth—he had plans of his own to set in motion—but then she winked at a bronze-skinned demon two tables over, eyeing his taut frame. Darius knew Irradia was just playing games, trying to make him jealous, tempting him to abandon his truest self. And yet he fell for it anyway.

"I think you're a naughty girl who wants a little punishment," he said as the blistering guitar riffs of ZZ Top's "Legs" thrummed through the speakers. "But I'm not so sure you could handle my game. Up the stakes?"

"Look at you," Irradia purred, her attention back where he wanted it—on him. "Growing some stones. What do you have in mind? Or was that just another tease?"

Irradia had been to *Mila's* before, eons ago. A lousy, undisciplined angel who'd damned more souls than she'd saved, Irradia knew her days in Heaven were numbered.

But God saw potential in her, gave her a choice. Weed out the hypocrites. Thin the herd. Either that or go straight to Hell.

Irradia took to the role immediately. Washing out sinners who'd snuck into Heaven was a lot more fun than babysitting saints.

"Five grains of soul per ball," Darius said. "And another five per game."

Chatter at the nearby tables stopped, all eyes on Irradia. Five grains weren't enough to chisel away at her soul. But ten? Angel, demon, goblin, nymph… any creature would feel it. There's only so many grains of soul one can lose before there's no way to get them back.

Which is exactly what Irradia was counting on.

"That's a little more than I usually play for… but sure," she said as the waitress delivered another whiskey. Irradia took the amber liquor down in one gulp, ordered another, then took her pool cue, bumping Darius in the shoulder, part flirt, part warning.

"Now step aside, fire dick. Let me show you what a real break looks like."

The first hundred souls Darius tormented were loads of fun. He'd blown it with his first one, an accountant from Lisbon who'd embezzled millions of Euros from a cancer center to finance his mistress's extravagant lifestyle. Darius had wanted to take his time, carve the accountant into tiny pieces and feed them back to him sautéed in his own bile. But Darius got overeager and ground his victim's soul into mulch in the first hour.

Oh, well. Live and learn.

After that, Darius had developed patience, to savor each moment in Hell. He hunted with vampires, ravaged with werewolves, dumped child-molesting priests into tanks full of piranha.

But torture, for all of its cruel and infernal delights, had lost its luster. Darius, it turned out, was a demon seeking redemption. Underneath the sinner in his soul, a saint was praying to get free.

"You'll never make the combination," he said to Irradia, who was lining up the cue ball at the far end of the table, to strike the twelve, into the two and, on a thirty-four degree angle, slice the six ball into the side pocket. "You're getting too cute."

Irradia leaned over the table, twitched her hips so her thong was showing, and looked back at him. "You can stare at my ass all night. But there's no getting around that your soul" — she thrust the cue, setting the sequence in motion, "belongs... to me."

She circled around to the other side of the table, analyzing the few balls still left to sink. Despite her early lead, Irradia knew victory was far from a sure thing. Maybe it was her night. Or Darius was letting her win. Classic lure. But that seemed too obvious.

As much as she liked to flirt, tease, and taunt, Irradia was well aware that Darius was, in fact, a demon, and a powerful one at that. She was damn good at her job. So was he.

"There's no chance you're here by mistake," she said, taking it right to him. "How'd you end up at *Mila's*? You can serve in Heaven or vanquish in Hell."

"Kick me when I'm down. Isn't that a demon's M.O.? I thought angels were supposed to be a bit more gentile."

Irradia chortled as she sipped on a beer. "Me? Gentile? Oh, honey. You've got the wrong angel."

Darrius's tormented eyes drew into red glowing slits. If he was ever to escape the clutches of Hell he needed to be worthy of Heaven. But she wasn't making it easy. "And you've got the wrong demon."

He took a beating on that game too, down twenty-six grains of soul. He lost some acuity in his left eye, images of the creatures he'd tortured leaking into his sightline like long-forgotten shadows. But he had more than enough concentration to move the night along.

With Irradia sufficiently cocky, even by her standards, she missed her next shot, allowing Darius to seize the momentum. He went on a half-hour run until he caught up. Dead even.

"Got your groove back," Irradia said as Metallica's "Enter Sandman" blasted through the speakers. "You must be feeling good by now."

There it was. Darrius had been waiting for Irradia to slip, an acknowledgment that she couldn't flirt her way into his psyche. But he understood the impulse. He sipped his White Russian. "That's funny."

Irradia leaned back against a wooden support beam, the mounted clock above her head set at perpetual midnight. *"What's* funny?"

Darius smiled, not to convey joy, humor, or satisfaction... but intent. "That you think I was ever worried. I'm not after the grains of your soul." He strode close enough to Irradia that he could smell the uncertainty oozing from her tainted heart. He grazed his hand across her cheek, tapped one of his gnarly black fingernails on her shoulder, then patted the arch of her wings. "I came for the whole damn thing."

The shotgun blast tore away chunks of ceiling. Drywall crashed on the floor. The music cut short. No one spoke a word.

"There ain't too many rules at *Mila's,*" said Didi, black as the void in Satan's heart. Filled with buckshot ground from Jesus's cross and soaked in holy water for a thousand years, her pump-action shotgun was primed to inflict ontological damage. "You can bet up to a thousand grains of soul and do whatever the hell you want with 'em. But you wanna bet the whole soul"—Didi pumped the forestock again, pointing the consecrated weapon at them both—"you gotta clear it with me first."

"I don't gotta clear shit," Irradia said, her wings expanding majestically. "What I do with my soul is none of your damn business."

There was a collective hush, every creature in the bar hungrily waiting for whatever was coming next.

Didi shifted her arms, revealing the slogan on her T-shirt: *On the Stairway to Heaven is a Highway to Hell.*

"*Everything's* my damn business, you petulant skank. My place, my rules. I know who you are and why you're here."

"Oh," Irradia said, her mouth curled into a smirk. Nothing got her angelic blood pumping like a lethal threat. "I seriously doubt that."

"You're here the same reason as everyone else. You got unfinished business, either above or below. You got sent here until your fate's decided. Until then, you're just killin' time, waitin' to get word."

"Didi," Darius said. "My apologies. Hell may traffic in sin, but I find myself tempted by the saint. If we promise to behave, do we have your permission to consecrate the wager? Soul for soul? You would, of course, get your ten percent, off the top."

Didi lowered her weapon just enough to signal she was willing to negotiate. "Fifteen," she said. "Bitch tax, for stepping outta line. We all answer to the same places, with the same damn consequences. I ain't riskin' what's left of my own soul so you can wager yours."

"Fifteen, then. Thank you."

"Fifteen?" Irradia protested and crushed the shot glass in her hand. Blood spooled down her arm. "I'm not giving that wench fifteen percent of your soul because you couldn't keep it in your pants."

"It's fifteen to him because he broke protocol," Didi said. "It's fifteen to you because you called me a wench. And you got no class. But mostly the wench thing."

With outstretched wings, Irradia rose above the floor. Her eyes glowed a blistering white and blue. Cold as ice. Hot as Hell. The entirety of *Mila's* shook.

Darius shot Irradia a quick glance to keep her in check, then focused back on Didi. "We accept. And if you would be so kind, bring another round of drinks. For the house. We're just here to play."

The lead went back and forth, Irradia now down five grains. Nothing she'd miss. If she turned it around, as she knew she would, returning to Heaven with Darius's soul would go a long way. But if the unthinkable happened and she lost her own before she got what she came for, ending up in Hell would be the least of her problems.

So as the crowd grew around their table, she led Darius where she wanted him to go.

"Hospital," she said while staring down the length of the table. Gripped in her fingers, the cue stick was a surgical instrument, like the one that ended her life.

Darius arched a black eyebrow. "Hospital what?"

"Where it happened. Where I died." With an abrupt stroke, she hammered the four ball into the corner, leaving the ten open for the side. "I was coming out of a supermarket in Phoenix. Some spoiled little brat chased a cellophane bag like it was a giant butterfly. An SUV whipped through the parking lot, going way too fast. I saw the driver, could tell he didn't see the kid."

"I love that moment," Darius said.

Irradia studied her next shot. She knew she could make the ten, but if she wasn't careful, the follow-through would leave her right behind the eight ball. But really she was studying him.

"You know that calculation," she said. "In a split second you decide if you can reach the kid in time, and if the little shit's worth the risk. Cuz let's face it, there are way too many assholes walking around Earth as it is. It's why you're in business."

Darius had long felt the same way, until he accepted that the path to salvation would never come by rejecting sin, but by making his peace with it. He raised his drink. "Amen to that."

"It happened in a split second, but I did the math. I let myself feel the rush. That spike of adrenaline, the fear kicking in, leaning even an inch in the kid's direction, like I *might* go for it. The rush, the danger of it all. The thrill of what could be. Then before I knew it… I knocked him on the asphalt. I saved his life. The car missed him completely."

"But it hit you."

Irradia nodded. "Popped my head like a cantaloupe. They rushed me to the ER. That's when I saw it. Saw Her."

"Did She wear the robes? It's so obnoxious."

"No, actually. She was dressed to the nines, in a Brazilian steakhouse. She handed me a glass of sangria and told me to go on a skewer run—all the meat I could eat. And when I was done, when I'd satisfied my self-indulgence, we would discuss my future. There was work to be done."

The match wore on with no word from Heaven or Hell.

Having knocked back several cocktails—and shaky from the grains he'd lost—Darius' shots, like the grip on his cue, were off the mark. It was time to lay it out.

"My wife slept with the guy next door," he said finally. "Hakan. A Turk. I found them in my gazebo, pawing at each other. The shock overwhelmed me. I saw red. So I grabbed a branch from the garden, bashed Sophia's head in, then went after him. I jabbed Hakan in the sternum. He heaved, bent over. A lacerated liver. But when he went down, he took me with him. My neck hit the stone table. That's all she wrote."

"He die? Hakan?"

"Worse. He was deprived of oxygen for too long. Permanent brain damage. He can't talk or even wipe himself. Which makes us even, in the end. He said to me once, 'the devil takes a hand in what is done in haste.' I didn't understand it then. But I do now."

"He ended up in one kind of Hell. You in another."

"Indeed."

Irradia savored the pathetic nature of Darius's fall. The match wasn't over, yet she felt like she'd already won. And then her instincts kicked in, picking up the signal he'd put out there, whether he realized it or not. "You're lying," she said. "There's more."

The spectators leaned in closer, sensing his weakness. An opening for Irradia to rip him apart for good.

"If you're gonna tell your tale, then do it for real."

Darius had a decision to make it.

He let his head dip, letting it be known that she'd gotten to him. And then he rose, to take his medicine. Or dish it out.

Easy choice.

"I ignored my wife for years. Sophia was never the love of my life, and I was never hers. Or maybe I was. Who remembers? I got... bored with her. Bored with life. But rather than make the most of my time on Earth, savoring every moment while the moments were even mine... I sulked. I vanished in plain sight. Because I knew, as deep down, all mortals know... that no matter what we do, where we go, or what we believe... it all ends the same. In death. So what was the point? And still Sophia tried to snap me out of it, to get me to engage."

"She knew what button to push. And she pushed it. Hard."

"They'd been at it for months, not flaunting it exactly, but not *not* flaunting it either."

"She wanted you to know. And do something about it." Irradia smirked at the spectators. "And then you did."

Darius sighed, swallowing his pride. "Yes. Just… not the way she wanted." Then, as Irradia gloated, his focus returned, knocking down three balls in a row. "Only… in that baby's breath between her life and death—what I know now is an eternity of possibility and hope—I saw the true face of God. I could have relented before anyone got hurt, but looking into the eyes of the Lord, I collapsed, engulfed by Her beauty, grace, and love. I knew I wasn't worthy of it, even though She was telling me through Her heavenly glow… that I was. She revealed to me a place in Heaven, but instead I became an agent of Hell."

"Got you playing for the right team."

"It was then I learned the most valuable lesson of all."

Darius snapped the beige cue stick into the white cue ball, slamming the black eight into the corner pocket.

Irradia felt the shift. She didn't like it. "And what's that?"

Darius grinned, pulling the spectators back to his side. "The kingdom of Heaven may be populated with saints, but most of them grapple with the sinner in their soul."

Irradia took that dig for exactly what it was. And exactly what she wanted. Her wings itched. It was time. "You've got a lot of opinions about who belongs in Heaven."

"And you… about who belongs in Hell."

"That's true," Irradia said as she sauntered around the table so that she was face to face with her adversary. "But it seems only right, as I speak for the Lord." She expanded her glorious white wings, not to their full plume, but wide enough to demonstrate the time had come to raise the stakes once more. "My opinions are Hers. Her opinions are mine. And," Irradia continued, drawing her blistering white eyes onto him, "so are you."

Basking in the provocation, Darrius levitated above the table, his dark, powerful wings arched, his eyes as red as the crimson skies of Hell. The walls shook. The floor rumbled.

Every creature at *Mila's* grabbed onto support beams, wall hooks, and the bar itself to keep from plummeting through cracks in the paradoxical realm. Piercing through the consecrated membrane, a shard of light—a pulsing fusion of good and evil—sliced the head off a succubus, incinerated a goblin.

Fighting against his own selfish prayers, Darius's voice reverberated with the power of the Devil himself, rancid steam emanating through the walls. He spoke the words he was sent to deliver regardless of how he felt about them. *"Do you make the challenge? Do you have the deed?"*

"Enough!" Didi pumped her shotgun. "You're not sanctioned for this! You cannot—"

Streams of energy—Darius red, Irradia white—beamed from their eyes, concentrated onto Didi's slight frame. The saloon keeper liquified into a foul-smelling puddle of flesh and bone, her meatless skull falling into the ooze that had just been her torso. What little remained of her soul rose from the slop in a sizzling mist.

Mila's creatures huddled together, some frozen in fear, others drooling in delight.

"I make the challenge!" Irradia proclaimed. *"And I have the deed."*

In her hands appeared a holy parchment, marked with the Lord's seal. She unspooled the hallowed document forged in Heaven, aimed at Hell.

"In the beginning, God created the Heaven and the earth. And God divided the light from the darkness. And the Lord God said, 'behold, the man is become as one of us, to know good and evil.' Only it is time, now, my children, to make my kingdom whole. It is thus decreed that I, Lord God, will remain in Heaven, taking dominion over Hell."

Gasps abounded in the wake of Irradia's gauntlet. She continued:

"As agent of Lucifer, the first Fallen Angel, master of the lower realm, do you accede your claim to Hell. Or do you rebut?"

Darius had fought against this moment since the demons of purgatory burned his corrupted soul into molten sin. *"It is not Hell that will come into Heaven,"* he proclaimed against his deepest desires, *"but Heaven that will come into Hell."*

"A duel, then," Irradia said.

"A duel. There will be no Heaven, there will be no such place as Hell. The first Fallen Angel will reclaim his throne—Lord of the Afterlife, all and one."

Darius folded down his wings, set his feet back upon the floor. Irradia did the same. The walls no longer shook, cracks in the membrane sealed themselves up.

"First to five," Darius said as he chalked his cue. "Winner takes all. Do you accept?"

The barmaid brought them another round. Darius raised his glass. Irradia did the same. "It is decreed."

"It is decreed," Darius said.

Demon and angel sipped their drinks, each convinced they had advantage over the other, aware the stakes were beyond further ascension. Even the smallest mistake could determine the fate of every soul that had, did, or would ever exist.

Because what they also knew, in the embers of their very souls, was that the Lord and the Devil were ultimately not so different, if they were different at all.

The nerves got to her. Irradia struggled with the break shot, the cue ball glancing off the pack. The nine ball drifted toward the corner pocket, the remaining balls clustered mid-table, setting Darius up for an easy game.

He did not disappoint, making a run on the table. But if Irradia had learned nothing else as an agent of the Lord, it was to never concede defeat when victory was within reach and, as Jim Morrison sang, the end was always near.

In her mind, she slapped the stupid off her face and reminded herself who she was. And who she was really up against.

"You took it down hard," she said. "That's a tough act to follow."

Darius chuckled at her obvious attempts at mind games, the desperate ploy of a desperate adversary. "It's easy to stay focused when you know what you're playing for."

"And I don't?"

"Knowledge is a devious concept. There's no way you can beat me now unless you can answer one question: Are you willing to risk a war in Heaven by granting peace in Hell?"

Panic shot through Irradia's heart. Maybe she was in a little over her head, yet so was he. She'd prepared for his anarchy, expected his deceit. But why had he rattled her? And why now?

She racked the balls for another game. Darius unleashed a thunderbolt with his cue stick, sinking the eight ball on the break.

"Is it getting hot in here?" he taunted. "Or is it just me?"

Irradia was losing herself, down two games to none, the grains of her soul depleting with more depth than she could handle. Three more games and Heaven would lose dominion to Hell.

She knew the spectators were spies from above and below. The pressure was suddenly so great she nearly burst into pure soul energy.

The great purge. The final release.

Instead she collected the scattered balls and set them back inside the rack, focused only on their smooth edges, her face reflected back in the gleam of the red seven. It was there she met her own eyes, taking her back to her last day as a mortal.

The child scampered across the parking lot, his feet trundling on the asphalt.

Can I reach him in time? Should I?

And then she heard Darius's voice again. *What are you playing for?*

Her chest tightened, her face went flush. With humiliation. Rage.

Not because she'd hesitated to save the boy, but why. In her mind's eye, in the parking lot, she stood beside herself.

"Grab him," her angel-self instructed.

"I can't," Irradia's mortal-self replied.

"Why?"

"I'm not ready."

"Ready?" her angel-self said. "Ready for what?"

Irradia's mortal-self looked at her angel-self, who, after eons of immersion in the spirit world, finally made a proper confession. She hadn't toyed with the thrill of *almost* and *what if?* She'd pretended to be a cynic trapped inside a saint. Only her hesitation in the parking lot had been all too human, an instinctual selfishness, a sane consideration in an insane moment, an impulse of self-preservation.

"The car's coming fast, and it's either me or the kid. I hate him for making me choose and I'm ashamed to let him go." Irradia's mortal-self stared at the child who's fate was in her hands. "But I don't want to die."

With that admission, she gasped like a drowning woman who'd finally found her breath.

Staring at the red seven she looked at her reflection once more, only the eyes staring back were not the ones she'd learned to loathe. She'd spent the entirety of her immortal life punishing herself over a moment of reasonable doubt, diminishing the stark reality that she'd sacrificed herself for a stranger. A child.

She turned to Darius, and with that glance, reclaimed herself. She felt it deflate him. And empower her.

Though he made a solid break, he missed an easy shot into the side pocket, giving control back to Irradia, who won four straight games, fully in command.

"So what's it like down there?" she said as she sank the two ball and, with perfect draw, set herself up for the twelve in the corner. "I know it's all fire and brimstone, but committing to sin? To the pain of others? Making them pay? It doesn't sound half bad."

Irradia made her next shot, too, only three balls left until she could sink the eight.

On the verge of eternal defeat, Darius thought then of his long nights in the underworld, Heaven out of reach, overlooking a crimson river of death and into the farthest reaches of Hell.

"You have your entire mortal life to feed the soul," he said, "to bring more peace than pain, to love more than to hate. You might not succeed. But it's virtuous to try."

Fueled by the duality of existential adrenaline and fear, Irradia went in hard. "*Try* sounds like another word for *fail*."

Yet as that insidious word—fail—left the perch of her lips, the self-inflicted implication immediately took effect, unleashing a virus into the striations of her soul. Irradia missed her next shot, giving it back to Darius.

"Your time on Earth is but a blink in the eternal eye," he said, feeling his strength return. His precision. "You don't have to reconcile sinner from saint, good from evil, or even right from wrong." With that declaration Darius sank the nine ball, the three and, off the bumper, the fifteen. "You just have to care about something, or someone… somewhere, sometime… more than you care about yourself."

In short order, Darius won that game and the next, tying them up at four apiece.

"You know why I really ended up in Hell?" he said, taking command of the final game. He felt Irradia's distress, the incompatibility of her role in God's army, her very nature, and the task at hand.

Defiant to the end, she stood tall. "Enlighten me."

Darius ran the table until only the eight ball remained. "Because as much I hated my wife and she hated me, I still held the capacity to love. The only question was… would I allow the light into the chasm of my soul or would I forsake my redemption? It should have been an easy choice. I just waited too long to make it."

Though his eyes were crimson fire, Darius knew this was his best chance to make the wager he'd come for all along.

"The depths of Hell may be lined with sinners, but some of us, despite our wicked and evil ways, long to be a saint. You don't belong in Heaven, just as I don't belong in Hell. Take my place, Irradia. And let me… take yours."

The eight ball rolled toward the corner pocket, each revolution of that sacred orb building kinetic energy aimed at Heaven, delivered from Hell. As it did, the cue ball drifted toward the opposite corner. It would either just miss the pocket… or scratch.

Too close to call.

Mila's rumbled again. The walls shook, the floor rattled, light blistering from cracks in the realm.

The spectators scrambled, leaving only Irradia and Darius, ready to attack, wings spread, arms pulled back. Their palms were open.

To give. And receive.

"You violated terms!" Irradia accused, her eyes glowing white. *"You forfeit your claim!"*

Fear and contempt enveloped Irradia like the inferno of damnation's flame. Heaven's secret temptress detested him for exposing what she coveted most of all. "You are pathetic and weak. Unworthy 'til the last."

"I was weakest at the moment I most needed to be strong," Darius conceded. "I have burned in Hell for it since. But I pledge my eternal soul to rectify my misdeeds in this life and the last. Let the Shepherd of Heaven take me into her grace, and the let the Master of Darkness… take you."

"How dare you corrupt me, you damn, demonic fool!"

"I'd rather be a fool of the righteous than a mongrel of the wicked."

Only then did Irradia understand why she'd been pitted against Darius, lonely desperate tears thick in her throat. They hadn't been sent to wager Heaven or Hell. The choice had never been theirs' to make.

"The Lord was testing my loyalty," she revealed to Darius—and to herself. "Just as the Devil… was testing yours."

Darius smiled. "For once I'm happy to fail that test."

"Maybe you are," Irradia said, rueful of his plan, envious of his of peace. "But I'm not!"

With no other moves left for them to make, supernatural energy erupted from their winged bodies until, finally, with apocalyptic thrust, there was a great collision of power.

The Rapture. Creation.

The end. The beginning.

Spread across the world was eternal darkness.

And then, after a time, there was light.

"A shot and a beer," Thaddeus said to Didi, *Mila's* saloon keeper. The blistering guitar riff from Rainbow's "Since You've Been Gone" roared through the sound system. "And make it fast."

"Holster your halo, there, pal. I'll get to you in a minute."

"Just hurry it up," the sinewy angel said. "I got a live one."

Didi raised an eyebrow. "Oh, yeah? Who's that?"

The angel gestured past the throng of creatures, eager to fornicate, fulminate, or fight. A sign above the cash register, quoting C.G. Jung, was mounted on the wall: "*No tree, it is said, can grow to Heaven unless its roots reach down to Hell.*"

"See that demon over by the pool table?" Thaddeus said. "Near the jukebox?"

Didi wiped down the bar. "What about 'er?"

The angel licked salt off his fist, slugged down his tequila shot, then chewed a lime wedge. "Says she's up for a game. And if I play my cards right, we'll have all night."

SEVEN RAVENS

Michael A. Black

IT WAS ONE HELL OF A HOLE. I STEPPED OVER TO WHAT WAS LEFT OF THE rear wall of the trailer to survey the crime scene. The smell of blood and death was pervasive. Broken plywood and torn aluminum littered the concrete slab upon which the trailer rested. I turned and looked for any discernible tire tracks in the dirt leading up to the slab and saw none. But on the cement itself there was something: a bloody stain that resembled the shape of a massive footprint. My first reaction was that the killer was also a graffiti artist. The footprint was much too large to have been real.

Inside, the bodies of three men lay in a twisted pile. Each man had been decapitated and their heads strewn about the room, which was a mess. Or rather, an explosion of murderous rage. Papers were scattered over the floor, a computer monitor was smashed, a desk was overturned, and the walls, once painted a light beige, were now splattered with blood. The rest of the furniture, six chairs and a couple of metal filing cabinets, had been smashed. The center of each cabinet was crushed. It looked as if the killer had jumped up and down on it.

"To do this kind of damage," I said pointing toward the demolished wall, "he must've had some heavy equipment. It looks like it was pulled outward." I turned and looked back at the bodies. "And this looks like it was done with an axe."

Warren, one of the FBI agents on the scene, looked at me, smirked, and spoke with a condescending lilt to his voice: "Three tribal council members all decapitated and pretty much dismembered...What else could it have been, sheriff?"

Howard Redpath, the Tribal Police Chief, glanced at me with wary, dark brown eyes. He said nothing. I knew he didn't like the idea of the feds being here anymore than I did. But we both knew they were going to take over handling things. They were the FBI.

"You got the State ET's coming in?" I asked. "Or do you want me to call my people?"

"Either or," Agent Warren said. "We've already got a strong suspect."

"Care to enlighten me?"

The FBI man rolled his eyes, like I was a moocher asking to borrow twenty bucks and pulled a small tablet from his shirt pocket. Flipping up the fine leather cover, he said, "Charlie Whitefeather."

"You're saying that Charlie Whitefeather did all this?"

"He was seen lingering around the area of the lodge earlier," Special Agent Warren said.

"And he's also on record as having made threats against members of the council," Agent Vickers, Warren's partner, added. "Allegedly, for their failure to allocate any casino money to buy out some mining company, which he also threatened."

I was familiar with Charlie's comments, but put it off to the rantings of a drunk. "Ward Ellis's company," I said.

"Right." Warren raised an eyebrow. "I take it you've heard of him?"

I looked at Redpath, whose face remained as stoic as ever.

"Everybody around here has," I said.

Ward Ellis was a big, boisterous man in his mid-fifties, and his appearance was often compared to John Wayne back in his hey-day. His company had moved in quietly about four months ago, buying an old, abandoned missionary school near the northern edge of the Rez. The school had once housed and educated Native American children but had been closed for over twenty-five years. Ironically, one of those children who'd been forced to attend the "mainstream cultural assimilation education" at the school was Charlie Whitefeather.

Nobody paid much attention to the situation until Ellis started moving in a lot of heavy equipment in the last few weeks. Then he announced his plan to start excavating the land adjacent to the Reservation. The Deer River was the dividing boundary line, and when the Tribe protested that his plans would pollute the river and devastate the land, Ward Ellis responded with his middle finger. He'd purchased the mineral rights to the area, he told them, and intended to start work in a few weeks.

The news media immediately seized upon the story and its environmental impact, but the boorish owner responded in kind: "What are you all complaining about? It'll bring jobs to the area, for Christ's sake, and give those Indians more money to spend at their casino."

The Tribe and a lot of the local sportsmen didn't see it that way. They took Ellis to court but found out there was little they could do. As a last-ditch effort, the tribal council was approached to make a buy-out offer to Ellis, to purchase the land and thus stop the excavation. This seemed to be a feasible plan and had been used in the past, but when it came to a vote, three of the five members voted not to allocate the funds.

Naturally, the disenchantment was palpable, and rumors of Ellis making under-the-table payoffs ran rampant, spread most notably by Charlie Whitefeather.

"Whatever," Warren said, taking in a deep breath. "We don't normally get involved in local disputes, but since these murders happened on the Reservation, it became a Bureau case. This one seems pretty open and closed, though."

"If we can go pick up the Whitehorse fellow," Agent Vickers said. "Maybe we can get back to Madison by nightfall."

They were both dressed according to standard FBI protocol: immaculate medium blue suits, white shirts with ties, and black Oxfords so shiny that you would have thought they were patent leather. And maybe they were, but I wasn't about to kneel down and check.

"Making threats is a far cry from doing something like this," I said. "And it's White*feather*."

"All the more appropriate," Warren said. "The white feather's a traditional sign of a coward."

"Charlie Whitefeather's no coward," Redpath said.

Warren waved his hand dismissively. "Whatever. He's disappeared from the area, right, Chief?"

There was a condescending lilt to the way he said "Chief." The trace of a smirk remained on the Fed's face as he turned to address Redpath. If the Chief caught it, he didn't show any emotion, but that was typical of him.

I remembered thinking these two FBI guys had a lot to learn about Fulton County, the indigenous personnel, and homicide investigations as well.

Redpath turned to me. "Jim, I have no jurisdiction outside of the Rez. I'd like for you to handle things on this one."

"Just a minute, Chief," Warren said. "This crime occurred on federal land. It's a serious felony, and therefore falls under the Bureau's purview. We know how to handle these things."

Redpath turned toward the FBI agent, his somber face still showing no more emotion than if was watching a horse fly landing on a pile of dung.

"Yeah, Mr. FBI," he said. "You know how to handle *things*, but do you know how to handle *Indians*?" He turned back to me. If he saw the smile on my face, he again didn't show it.

"Any idea where Charlie's at?" I asked.

Redpath shook his head. "I sent my deputy over to his house."

"At my direction," Warren said.

"His truck's gone," Redpath said.

"We figure he's headed up to get Ellis," Warren said. "The Chief here was telling me that Ellis lives in some kind of facility up there?"

"He does," I said. "It used to be one of those old cultural assimilation schools. It's pretty large."

"This is all fitting together like the pieces of a puzzle," Warren said. "I take it this Whitefeather guy's a militant Native American environmentalist?"

"No," Redpath said. "He's an Indian."

The FBI man's face tightened into a frown, and I figured, despite my glee at Redpath's retort, it was time for me to step in.

"So you think that's where he might be headed next?" I asked. "After Ellis?"

Redpath nodded. "Be my guess."

"Well, it's safe to operate under that assumption," Agent Warren said. "You know where it's at, I assume?"

"I do," I said. "We'll need to alert the state police, too," I said. "Put out a BOLO. They've got a pretty good air patrol."

"Better tell them to hurry," Redpath said. "Fog's moving in."

"Fog?" Warren said. "My weather app says it's going to be as clear as a bell."

"That another one of those glass balls you can see through?" Redpath asked.

Warren frowned.

"In any case," Vickers said. "You need to start assembling some of your deputies."

"If he's headed north toward Ellis," I said, "we'll need a guide. That area's pretty dense."

"I have none of my people to lend you," Redpath said, "with Dave Wolf being off sick, but I can give Tom Blackbear a call."

Agent Warren's brow furrowed. "Who's that? Another reservation cop?"

"No," I said, smiling. "He's sort of an unofficial game warden."

"Huh?" Warren said. "I'm not too keen on having some non-law enforcement, civilian slowing us down."

"He won't," I said. "But if it'll make you feel better, I'll deputize him."

I called Ward Ellis at his facility to warn him about the possible threat.

He didn't seem to take my warning very seriously.

"Charlie Whitefeather," he said, drawing out the pronunciation of the three syllables. "That drunken idiot's been spouting off nonsense and threats toward me and this project for weeks."

"He has," I said. "But there's a possibility now that he may be backing them up."

I told him about the murders, and he was silent for a moment.

"Are you saying he did it?" he finally asked.

"At this point, he's a person of interest in a homicide investigation."

Ellis laughed. "Spoken like a typical, evasive politician. Sheriff, you let me down. I expected more honesty and integrity from the likes of you."

I wanted to respond with, *I likes me just fine*, but instead I said, "Mr. Ellis, you could be in danger. I'd advise you and your staff to come into town until we get this matter cleared up."

"And when's that going to be?" Without waiting for me to answer, he added, "Let the red-skinned son of a bitch come. I've got a first-rate security force here, and my personal Glock's ready and waiting."

I somehow had the feeling that he wasn't going to have to wait long.

Three hours later, my hunch proved right. Tom Blackbear and I stood on the sloping shoulder of the roadway at the intersection of the highway and the mile-long, winding gravel road that led to the old abandoned missionary school that was now Ward Ellis's headquarters. The two FBI agents were busily examining the red pickup that had been pulled under a canopy of trees in the forested area. A state police fly-over had spotted what looked like Whitefeather's truck parked just off the highway. We'd piled into two squad cars and high-tailed it up there. It turned out to be Charlie's, all right. The inside of the cab and the seat showed distinct traces of what appeared to be blood. Warren took one look at the rope and grappling hook in the bed and surmised that was what Charlie'd used to dislodge the rear wall of the trailer. I wasn't so sure. There were no tire tracks at the scene to corroborate that theory. But what else could it have been?

"Sheriff," Warren said. "I suggest that you lock and impound this vehicle until such time that a qualified CSI unit can examine it."

I'd already called in that order, but I let his comment slide. I had other things to worry about, namely an empty bottle of vodka on the floorboards down by the gas pedal, and a torn-open box of .45 caliber cartridges on the seat. Half of them were missing.

"Looks like the suspect's armed and dangerous," Agent Vickers said.

I recalled Ellis's arrogance from our earlier conversation, and it added a new urgency to our quest. We had to find Charlie Whitefeather in a hurry, or one thing was certain: there'd be at least one more body littering the landscape. I sent a mobile unit down to the school to stand guard.

"What are we waiting for?" Agent Warren asked me. "Let's go find him."

"It's going to be dark soon," I said. "The State has a helicopter equipped with good thermal imaging capacity."

"Come on," Warren said. "We're talking about an inebriated Native American here, aren't we? I doubt he'll be that hard to locate."

"Native American?" Blackbear laughed. "We call ourselves Indians around here, Mr. FBI."

"The Bureau mandates we use the more culturally sensitive term," Warren said.

Blackbear smirked. "Too bad the government didn't have all this concern when you federal guys were taking our land."

"That's a debate best left for another time," Vickers said. "Now, can we get on with it? I think quadrant search would be the best, given the terrain."

I glanced down at the FBI man's suit, cuffed pants, and oxfords, and was looking forward to seeing how many brambles would be stuck to those fancy pants once we got into the woods.

"Like I told you, we're waiting on the state police," I said. "And their thermal imaging."

"And as I said," Vickers said. "It sounds a bit excessive, for one inebriated Native American."

"Sounds a bit smart, too," Blackbear said. "To this Indian."

Agent Warren glanced at his watch. "So how long is that going take?"

"As long as it does," I said.

My cell phone rang, and I answered it.

"Bad news on that state police copter," the dispatcher told me. "It's been grounded due to the weather. Encroaching fog. They're asking if you need more people."

"See if they can spare some units to assist in setting up a wide perimeter." I turned to look at the two feds. "Looks like we'll have to do this the old-fashioned way after all."

"It's about damn time," Warren said. He was the younger of the two and appeared to be in top physical shape.

"Be careful what you wish for," Blackbear said, motioning toward the thick forest along the fence-line. "We go in there, you might find more than you bargained for."

The FBI man glared at him for several seconds before he and his partner walked over to their car. They opened the trunk and pulled out two Benelli automatic shotguns. I didn't know if they were loaded with double-ought buck or rifled deer slugs, but either way, it was a lot of firepower. My deputies and I all had our standard rifles and sidearms, an AR-15 and a Glock 19. Blackbear had an old Colt 1911 on his belt. He went behind the seat of his pickup and pulled out a rifle-case. As he unzipped it I saw the wooden stock and knew it was his old M-1 Carbine.

"Brought your father's gun, I see."

He pulled it out of the scabbard. "Yeah, if Geronimo would've had a couple hundred of these…"

"Geronimo? He was an Apache, wasn't he?"

"No matter," Blackbear said. "On his death bed, he regretted that he had not fought to the death."

"I'm hoping we won't have to," I said.

"That makes two of us." Blackbear glanced over at Warren and Vickers. "That younger FBI guy's pretty gung-ho, ain't he? For a fed."

"Maybe he was in the marines, or something," I said.

Blackbear grinned. "No, *I* was in the marines. So was my father. And contrary to what people say, us jarheads ain't as stupid as people think. This ain't gonna end well."

I said nothing, but silently agreed with him.

I had one of my regular deputies and two other special deputy volunteers. It was a far cry from the way I would have preferred to handle it, but beggars couldn't be choosers. After news of the crime got out, and the nature of its gruesomeness, I felt lucky that anybody wanted to go along.

My deputy, Ernie Feldon, hadn't been my first choice, either. He was big and sometimes rather truculent. I kept him on midnights mostly because of his abrasiveness with the general public. Plus, his sheer size, six-six and close to three hundred pounds, not much of it fat, made his closing down a bar fight a *fait accompli*. The other two men who'd volunteered were Vince Clemons and Terry McCarthy, both good-sized and capable. Blackbear did a preliminary check of the area and picked up a trail. I told everybody to pair up and spread out at twenty-foot intervals and follow our lead as we worked our way toward the school. We were odd-numbered, I told Feldon to hang back as a rearguard since he didn't have a partner.

"Above all," I said, glancing toward the FBI men, "Don't forget that Whitefeather's most likely armed with at least a handgun. It's possible he has an axe as well. Don't take unnecessary chances, and don't get jumpy. There are a lot of animals in the woods that could get you spooked. There could be hunters in the area, too, although we didn't spot any other vehicles. So if you have to shoot, be damn sure of your target." I paused to look each man in the face, then added, "We've got radios, so stay in contact."

The wind had kicked up and a grayish mist of fog began to surround us with a foreboding persistence. Redpath had been right after all.

Blackbear and I led off. The forest itself had transformed into a sea of reds, yellows, and a few scatterings of stubborn greens that were holding on. After about twenty-five yards or so it all disappeared into the hovering mists of the fog. Wildflowers colored the grass at our feet, and it almost felt like a group of forest nymphs had thrown rose petals along the away welcoming us to some bucolic gladiatorial arena.

"You know, I saw seven ravens yesterday," Blackbear said to me as we made our way down a narrow pathway through the ungainly foliage. "It was a sign."

"A sign of what?" I said.

"The raven is a harbinger of change," Blackbear said. "It can be good, or it can be bad. Seeing so many can only mean something bad is coming."

"Well, maybe they were crows instead."

He shook his head. "No. They were ravens. I know the difference. And it was no coincidence that the next day you came to me and asked my help in tracking down Charlie Whitefeather. An Indian tracking another Indian for the white man. Much sorrow will come of this."

I didn't reply.

"Seven ravens," Blackbear repeated. "Do you see the significance?"

"Not really," I said. "But I'm sure you're going to tell me."

Blackbear smiled. "Seven ravens, seven of us. Somebody's gonna die. Maybe all of us. Death's in the air."

I glanced back and saw we were way ahead of the others, none of whom had Blackbear or my outdoorsman's acumen. I told him to hold up and radioed a break. I didn't want us to get too far apart.

Between the rapidly darkening sky, the overhead canopy of tree branches, and the escalating fog, our visibility was down to only a few yards. I realized we were placing ourselves in a very precarious situation and decided to pull back. We apparently had him contained in the designated area. If we could maintain a perimeter until the fog dissipated, maybe we could get that chopper with the thermal imaging back to locate him without playing GI Joe in the woods. I radioed for everyone to proceed back to the vehicles and asked for a sequenced acknowledgment.

"Special agents, here," Warren said. "Why are we retreating?"

Retreat was such a negative word.

"We have practically zero visibility farther in here," I said. "Too much risk of friendly fire."

After a few seconds of silence, Warren came back on the radio: "Roger that."

"Ten-four," Feldon said.

I waited for the last reply.

Clemons and McCarthy didn't respond.

After a good thirty-second wait, I was about to tell Feldon to go look for them when I heard the shots.

It sounded like three shots from a rifle, but it was hard to tell.

"Who's firing?" I said into the radio as Blackbear, and I moved at as quick of a pace as we could.

No one answered.

I requested another sequenced acknowledgment.

"FBI, roger that."

"Ten-four." Feldon.

No other response.

That meant that Clemons and McCarthy must have fired the rounds. I ordered the other units to use caution in locating them.

We pushed through more cloying plants and shrubs with Blackbear leading the way. It seemed we'd gone double the distance that I remembered since leaving the cars. The fog had grown so thick that visibility was limited to only a few yards. Wispy gossamer tendrils embraced every tree and bush. Finally, Blackbear stopped and held up his clenched left fist.

I stopped beside him.

"There." His voice was a whisper.

I looked around his shoulder and saw them, Clemons and McCarthy, or what was left of them. Their mutilated corpses lay in pieces over the yellowing grass, their blood matching with some of the decaying deciduous leaves.

"Oh, Lord," I said.

Some thrashing came from our left. I whirled and leveled my rifle but the two FBI men stumbled through the bushes, oblivious. Warren came to an abrupt halt and his head jerked back as he saw us.

"Oh, it's you," he started to say, then stopped. "Oh, my God."

He'd seen them too.

Vickers, the second fed glanced our way, then turned and heaved.

If the scene hadn't been so traumatic and shocking, I would have laughed. Both of them were covered with brambles and burrs, their highly polished shoes now caked with mud and dirt.

"Are they dead?" Warren asked.

"What do you think?" Blackbear said, making no effort to keep the disdain out of his voice.

"What are we—?"

The staccato rhythm of rapid-fire from an AR-15 ripped through the stillness. I grabbed my radio and yelled into it.

"Feldon, is that you firing?"

No reply. And the gunfire suddenly ceased, replaced by a wail of distress, then silence.

Blackbear and I exchanged glances and he hurried toward the sound of the gunfire.

I followed, vaguely cognizant of the danger of approaching the unknown through a haze of uncertainty and fog. I slipped my radio back into its holder and gripped my rifle with both hands, slipping the selector lever off SAFE. Behind me, I heard the sounds of panting and muffled conversation. The FBI boys were on my six.

Feldon's big body was brutalized almost beyond recognition. He'd been twisted in half, with his legs facing downward and his torso face-up. Long, jagged scratches began on the right side of his face and continued in a downward slash over his chest. His right arm lay several feet from the rest of him, the hand still gripping the pistol-grip of the AR-15.

I felt enraged and nauseated at the same time. What kind of monster could wreak such devastation?

"Look there," Blackbear said, pointing to the rips on Feldon's chest. "The angle."

The blow had apparently been delivered with a downward slashing motion, from right to left, which meant the attacker had been holding the cutting instrument in what was most likely his left hand.

"Charlie's left-handed," Blackbear said.

Before I could reply, Warren and Vickers arrived. Vickers looked like he'd thrown up again and traces of vomit clung to the lower edge of his jacket and speckled his pant legs. Both of them were breathing hard.

"Is that your deputy?" Warren asked.

He seemed to be handling the carnage better than his partner.

I nodded.

"There." Blackbear pointed to a section of matted grass, swathed in blood and crushed down by what appeared to be huge, oversized feet.

We approached it cautiously. A few droplets of red spotted some of the larger leaves.

"Blood trail," Blackbear said. "Feldon must have winged him."

My gaze traced the intrusive pathway until it disappeared in a gray swirl of mist.

Blackbear and I exchanged glances and began following it, both of us holding our rifles at the ready.

"Wait," Warren said. "I thought we were going to pull back. Wait for reinforcements."

"We got a wounded killer out there," I said. "And he's heading for Ellis now. You coming?"

The two FBI men exchanged glances, then began walking after us.

"Ain't so gung ho now," Blackbear whispered. "Is he?"

I said nothing, trying to focus on what was happening. I was having a hard time justifying that one man, no matter how determined and how capable, could have dealt out such massive carnage. A marauding army, maybe, but not one man. Blackbear must have been thinking the same thing.

"This ain't just Charlie no more," he said.

"What, you think he's got somebody with him?"

He didn't speak for several seconds, then said, "No. I'm thinking *P'Cate Wendigo*."

"What?"

"A *Wendigo*," he said. "The black devil that devours. A spirit creature."

My rational mind was telling me that this was absurd, but after what I'd just seen, I wasn't so sure he was wrong.

I kept my mouth shut and kept scanning the forest for any signs.

"I know you don't believe in the legends of my people," Blackbear said. "But the ravens, the seven ravens, that's what they were telling me. The *Wendigo* is here to exact vengeance on those who would defile the land."

"You're talking crazy, Tom."

His face remained grim. "I wish that was so. But death is coming."

We continued in silence, and the fog lifted a bit as we approached a section devoid of the high grass. I caught a glimpse of a twelve-foot high cyclone fence with three strands of barbed wire along the top. I reached out for Blackbear's arm as more shots rang out. Single reports, heavy sounding.

A shotgun, I thought.

I glance back over my shoulder, trying to see if the FBI men were close, but two more shots came from somewhere in front of us, beyond the fence line.

"Come on," Blackbear said. "It's coming from up there."

We increased our pace, hoping to catch a glimpse of our adversary. I had a full magazine of fifteen rounds in my rifle, and another mag fitted in a holder on the stock. Suddenly, I wished I'd brought more, but you never brought enough.

Every combat soldier's lament.

When we got to the cyclone fence a large flap had been torn away from the posts. It lay on the ground, blades of grass peeping up through the diagonally angled metal rows of squared spaces. More blood droplets dappled the ground.

Blackbear stepped across the metal fencing. It clinked and groaned as I did the same.

There were no more gunshots ahead of us, only silence. Dusk had settled, but there were several big sodium vapor lights positioned in the surrounding area. It was solid asphalt and the blood trail became more visible. We followed it to an overturned security vehicle. Two guards were in recumbent positions nearby, their motionless bodies indicating serious, if not fatal injuries. We stopped to check them, but both were dead.

How many did that make? Six?

I got on my radio and called to the man I'd sent here earlier.

No response.

I blew out a long breath and looked at Blackbear, who shook his head.

"Agent Warren, "I said into my radio. "We're in the compound. Where are you?"

"By the fence. It's partially down."

"We just came through there. We've got more casualties inside here. It seems to be going toward the main building."

"It?" Warren said. "What are you talking about?"

I realized that I'd internalized Blackbear's theory about the *Wendigo*. It was too complicated to try and explain. We needed backup, and we were out of radio range for my base.

"Use your cellphone to call for assistance," I said.

I was about to tell them to come up to our location when I heard what sounded like three pistol shots from inside the building, followed by a scream.

"Shots fired inside," I said into the radio. "We're going in."

I jammed the radio back into its holder and looked at Blackbear.

His clenched teeth shone in the artificial lighting like a bone showing through a wound, and his dark eyes held a clear message: *no fear, only a warrior's heart.*

He nodded.

We gripped our weapons and took off at a trot toward the main building. When we got there, a set of metal double doors had been ripped from their hinges. The hallway beyond was well-lighted, and I saw a sign on the wall indicating the office was at the end of the hall. Blackbear took the left side and I stayed right. We advanced with caution, moving from each recessed doorway to the next, using them as cover positions. The door of the office lay in the middle of the hallway, discarded like an undesirable playing card.

As we approached the last room at the end of the hall we could hear a plaintive wailing sound. It was the voice of a man.

"Nooooo," the voice said. "Please. Nooooo."

Heavy, rasping breathes drowned out the wails, which transformed into a high-pitched scream.

Then silence.

I'd seen pictures of Ward Ellis in the newspapers and on television, but I barely recognized his bloody head as it came hurling out of the open door of the office. It rolled and bounced on the tiled floor like an errant bowling ball with distorted features frozen in an expression of sheer terror.

I leveled my AR at the vacant space between the door jamb. A shadow appeared on the wall, and then something immense burst forth. I fired at the dark shape as I saw two glowing orbs, white against a swarthy leather-like face. A huge maw opened displaying two rows of sharp, dagger-sized teeth. The head reared back as I fired more rounds and I saw twin horns curling upward from each temple.

The bolt of my rifle locked back and I dropped the magazine, pulled out the fresh one, and slammed it home. The monster seemed to swell in size, doubling itself in mere seconds, after fully emerging into the hallway. My hearing was gone, which I counted as a blessing because it meant that I couldn't hear myself scream. Across the hallway, Blackbear was firing his M-1, the fire-spitting weapon expertly controlled by his strong hands. The creature turned toward him, advancing. Blackbear didn't move. He just kept firing. I took careful aim and acquired target acquisition on the rear of the now barrel-sized head.

Kill the brain, the body will die, I silently repeated to myself, over and over.

I squeezed the trigger and repeated the motion, minimizing each recoil, as the hot brass was being rhythmically expelled through the ejection port in a steady stream.

The monstrous beast turned, glared my way, and began lumbering toward me.

It looked as big as a tank now. The floor shook with each step.

I pulled the trigger again, but nothing happened.

Out of ammo.

The cold shadow settled over me like a black shroud.

Blackbear's words came floating back.

P'Cate Wendigo. The black devil that devours.

I felt a tremendous impact, then darkness invaded, and consciousness fled.

When I awoke, Blackbear was cradling my head in his hands and chanting. Warren and Vickers stood about thirty feet away.

I managed to take two deep breaths.

Blackbear stopped chanting and grunted.

"Glad you've come back," he said. "The Great Spirit has seen fit to spare you because you are noble of heart."

I took in another deep breath and struggled to sit up. My whole body ached.

"Where is it?" I asked.

Blackbear shifted his upper torso and I saw a man lying a few feet away, a pool of crimson surrounding his body like a small lake.

Charlie Whitefeather.

"No," I said. "The *Wendigo.* Where did it go."

Blackbear shook his head.

Warren and Vickers called out to me. "We've got an ambulance on the way, sheriff," one of them said. Neither of them moved closer.

I canted my head to acknowledge, and it hurt.

I managed to sit up completely and stared at Blackbear, who was now smiling.

"It was...Charlie?" I whispered.

He gave a fractional nod.

"Sometimes the *P'Cate Wendigo's* spirit channels itself through a man," he said. "To set things right, in accordance with the ways of our ancestors."

I felt a wave of revulsion. "This was setting things right?"

Blackbear shrugged. "I told you there would be much death."

"But why was I spared?"

He shook his head slightly. "No one knows the way of the *Wendigo*. Perhaps it had completed what it had set out to do."

As he said that I caught a glimpse of Ward Ellis's decapitated head a few feet away, the vacuous eyes staring upward.

"I guess it did. But what happened to it?" I gripped his arm. "It was here. It was so big. Where did it go?"

"After it fell on you," he said, "I ran over and started banging it with my rifle. Suddenly, the shape changed."

"Changed? How?"

"It left Charlie's body," he said. "He was only its vessel for vengeance and retribution. Once that had been attained, it fled."

"Fled?"

"Yes," Blackbear said. "In the form of seven ravens."

FEAR TO TREAD

Patrick Thomas

PAUL OPENED HIS EYES TO CRIMSON-STAINED CONCRETE. HE ADMIRED THE morbid beauty of the spattering until his mind whispered that the pigment for this reddened rendering drew from his life's blood.

The bloody sidewalk artists stood over him, grinning like the violent idiots they were, obviously proud of their handiwork. Deciding to add some footwork to the mix, they kicked Paul's ribs repeatedly with steel-toed boots and smashed his cell phone to circuits.

They were talking or maybe screaming at him. Paul couldn't tell over the roaring of the hundred angry seashells that filled his ears.

It sounded like they were intent on teaching him a lesson, but he never was an exceptional student. Then again, his teachers in school had never beaten him to the edge of unconsciousness like these two had. Paul realized with perfect clarity that they would continue until he plummeted over that edge into the waiting darkness, so he let himself fall in hopes it might somehow save him.

A limp and unmoving victim wasn't as much fun for the brutes as one writhing and convulsing, so they left him lying in a pool of his own bodily fluids. Between the vomit and the blood, there was a wonderful, disgusting collage on the sidewalk.

Paul's personal darkness was pushed aside by a tunnel of light, blinding to his eyes. The afterlife was nothing like he had imagined it to be. There was no sense of majesty, no feeling of floating — only extreme, all-encompassing pain. Death was supposed to be the end of pain, the great release. If he hurt this much, Paul realized he must still be alive. The sight of the cop shining the flashlight in his face confirmed it.

"Get up and move it along. Sleep it off somewhere else," demanded the blue-clad officer of the peace. Piece of shit is more like it.

"I was just mugged," Paul moaned, rubbing his sore head and squinting against the light. The light and the cop were not impressed.

"We all have problems," the cop replied, already walking away and paying Paul even less attention than the lamppost he had just passed.

"I just told you I was mugged," Paul grumbled, fighting off a headache and the indignity and losing on both fronts.

"So? What do you want me to do about it?"

"Your job, maybe even catch them," Paul said, his voice dripping with sarcasm.

"Fill out the paperwork and we'll keep an eye out for them," he said, emphasizing his lack of sincerity with a phony smile.

"That's it!?"

"Watch it. I don't think I like your tone," the cop warned, raising his night stick. "With all those bruises you are sporting, nobody would notice a few more. Move along."

Paul realized there was no point in arguing and spending yet another night in the city jail, so he headed toward home instead. It wasn't far, just an eternity measured in torturous minutes and painful footsteps, each chiseling their niche in his soul. Halfway home he stopped off to drown his sorrow and pain, just a block shy of meeting his destiny.

That destiny was pulling a half-eaten tuna sandwich out of a dumpster. He shared it with a kitten, despite the look of hunger that stared out from his own blazing eyes. Digits, daring to peek out from gloves with no fingers, patted a matted gray beard, not quite so much filthy as lived in. He smiled as the young feline ate its fill. The half-gloved hands reached down to scratch behind the kitten's ears and were rewarded with a contented purr. The man looked up to the dusky sky and again smiled. The kitten climbed up into his lap and the pair drifted off to the land of dreams, leaving their bodies behind in the land of alleys and trash cans. After a literal cat nap, the pair parted company, the kitten going back to the alleys and the man to the streets.

A song without words graced his lips. A dance without steps embellished his walk. A thought without reason spanned his mind.

"The fallen are in the sky," he whispered, but he would not avert his eyes from the heavens.

A light rain dripped from the sky and politely ignored him. The people he passed on the street did the same.

A young woman, forgetting the law of the jungle and the rules of the city, made eye contact. She found herself returning a smile and humming a song without words for the rest of the day, never quite knowing the reason why.

As he traveled the concrete canyons, a bar called to him. It took him a moment to hear the words carried on the winds, but eventually, the whisper reached his ears. Looking up, he stared at the bar door, and he knew what lay inside.

His mission. The enemy. And something else.

First, he chuckled, then winked at the sky. The enemy didn't frighten him. Perhaps this would be the one, the deed that earned him his reward. Not that reward was the reason for the deed, but it would be nice to finally be recognized. And to have them on his shoulders.

Inside the bar, Paul nursed a watered-down beer and silently cursed himself because he didn't even have the guts to let go and get drunk, despite his physical pain.

The bartender felt the same way. Paul could tell by the looks he kept giving him after he only tipped a quarter.

Those looks were nothing compared to the stare he gave the guy with the fingerless gloves who walked in the door. As far as Paul was concerned, he was just some goofy, sweet, old guy. The bartender disagreed and said so.

"We don't want your kind in here," the bartender growled through gritted teeth.

The old guy answered, smiling all the while. "I don't want your kind anywhere, but we can't always have what we want, can we?"

"Leave now," the bartender demanded.

"Or you'll what?" the old man asked, subduing his grin. "I have every right to be here. You can't stop me."

The bartender grumbled and walked away. The old guy sat down across from Paul and offered his hand.

"Pleased to finally make your acquaintance," he said. "I'm Jim."

The man acts like he knows me, Paul thought. *Poor guy.* Paul accepted the proffered handshake. "Name's Paul."

"I know," the old guy said, still grinning. *Probably the father of one of my neighbors,* guessed Paul.

"You don't seem too popular with the bartender," Paul observed, making small talk. It beat staring at his battered reflection in the mirror.

"Never had the stomach for demons," Jim replied.

"He wasn't that bad," Paul said, defending the bartender.

"They never are. Until it is too late. Without something appealing, people wouldn't consort with the hellspawn."

"You think he's a demon?" Paul asked, realized the old guy was not talking figuratively. He was unsure of whether to leave quickly or get some kicks listening to the man ramble. Afraid to offend, Paul remained in his seat.

"I have no doubt. And he's not alone. You can find them easily enough. Squint and look at them out of the corner of your eye. The horns and a hellfire halo are unmistakable."

Paul started to do as he suggested before catching himself. "How do you know this? Are you a demon hunter?"

Jim chuckled. "No, I'm no hunter. More of a gatherer. I work for the other side," he said, in a conspiring tone. Seeing Paul's confusion, he added, "I go with only what's on my back. I fight but by resistance and strengthening others, not by violence. I'm on the side of the angels. In fact, I am one."

"Of course." Paul decided the best course was to humor the old loon. "I should have known by the halo and wings."

Jim stopped smiling. It was as if his face had gone and died. "I have no wings."

"Why not? Haven't you earned them yet?" Paul asked, willing to take it as far as Jim was.

"Something like that."

"So, are you here to fight the demon? Stop him from watering down the drinks? Because if you are, I'm behind you all the way."

"That is a false legend. We do not battle demons. Not directly, at any rate. That must be done by people. Human people, like yourself."

"I'm no fighter."

"But you are. Or were. And can be again. But there are different ways of fighting. As angels, we try to shield our charges against the forces of Hell, whenever appropriate. Unfortunately, they seem to outnumber us at the moment. A more attractive recruitment package, at least at first. Leaves our side incredibly overworked. If only we had a better PR department. I can't blame anyone else for your predicament. I fear I've neglected you too much of late and I apologize."

"Wait a second. You're telling me you're my guardian angel?"

"Yes."

"What a load of crap. The next thing you'll be telling me is we have to listen for bells ringing to see if any of your comrades in arms have earned their wings."

"That legend is true. But enough of stories for now. It's you I've come to see."

"Why? I'm not even religious."

"But you are. You try to do good and be fair to others."

"Maybe, but I don't believe in God."

"Sure, you do. You're just angry at Him because you feel He has abandoned you, that He let you become unhappy. You keep fighting for your ideals, even when you know there is no hope of winning."

"Bull. I don't give a damn about nobody."

"Really?" Jim asked with a sly smile. "Then why did you step in to help that girl earlier tonight?"

"Those men were going to rape her."

"So? Did you know her?"

"No."

"Did she mean anything to you?"

"No." But even as Paul said it, he knew it was a lie. So did Jim.

"Sure. That's why you risked your own safety and took the beating of your life. To help someone you cared nothing about. Pretty boneheaded. Didn't accomplish much."

"She got away, didn't she?"

"Why yes, she did. Why should you care?"

"I don't."

"Bullshit!"

"I didn't know angels were allowed to curse."

"You cared about her because she was a person and you believe everyone should have someone who cares about them. Just like you wish you had someone to care about you."

"People care about me."

"True, they have. Unfortunately, not the way you want to be cared about. Unconditionally. There is someone who does you know."

"Who? You? I don't swing that way."

"Not me. I was talking about someone else," Jim said, discretely pointing up at the ceiling.

"You mean God?"

"Yep."

"I've heard all this before."

"But have you ever listened?"

Paul started to answer, then really considered the question. "No. But how do I do it? Which church or religion do I turn to?"

"Makes no difference. Don't look to others for your salvation. Most religions are the same. They all worship the Supreme Being, the Creator. They all say be nice to each other in some way, shape, or form. Things get screwed up when someone in the organization presumes to be speaking for God and instead sticks in their own views and demands. God's not such a stickler on rules or where you pray from. He answers just as easily to Yahweh as He does to Jesus or to Allah. She even answers to Shirley."

"God is a woman?"

"Yes. No. He is both and She is neither."

"Well, that clears that up."

"Good."

"But if the religion doesn't matter, how do I talk to God?"

"I never said religion doesn't matter. It just doesn't make a difference which, as long as you live a good life. That is the important thing. Of course, I can tell you how to communicate with God," Jim said, then paused in silence.

Paul kicked himself for being taken in so easily. "All right, how much of a donation do you want?"

"Angels ask for no donations. I was hoping you already knew the answer to your question. Just open up your heart and listen."

"Does he talk back to you?"

"Yes, but not the way you think. I get urges and feelings that let me know what I must do. Messages come to me in dreams and in the waking world."

"Uh-huh."

"You try to be cynical, but part of you wants to believe me."

"Can you prove it to me?"

"No," Jim said. "Only you can prove it to yourself."

"I see." Paul sighed sadly. It was then he realized what Jim was. Was he a nice guy? Oh, yes. Was he deluded? Most definitely. Was he an angel? Sadly, no. Paul paid his tab and walked Jim outside. The bartender stared daggers at the pair the whole time. *Not a friendly guy, but not a demon either,* Paul thought. *Probably pissed because I only left him another quarter.*

The pair stepped out of the bar and straight into an ambush from his attackers from earlier. This time one of them had a knife.

"We told you to never show your face around here again," the smaller of the pair said.

Jim stepped between Paul and the hoodlums.

"Gentlemen, violence never solved anything," Jim said.

"Sez you, gramps. Out of the way. We're gonna cut the punching bag a new throat."

"I believe Paul is quite happy with the one he has, aren't you, Paul?" Jim asked. Paul nodded dumbly, looking for somewhere to run. The problem was Jim wasn't moving. He was the picture of calm. And insanity.

"Don't matter. He's getting one whether he wants it or not. Step aside or we cut you up too."

"No," Jim said. He did not raise his voice. He did not threaten with tone or gesture. He was calm, gentle even. Paul watched, too terrified to speak, to move. He was convinced they were going to die.

"What? Are you gonna stop us? You gonna beat us down?" mocked the shorter hood.

Jim smiled and put his hands out to his side. "No. I will not lift a hand against you."

"Then we're gonna gut you," the shrimp said.

"I suppose you will," Jim answered, with the serenity only madness brings.

The big guy spoke up. "You don't need to be hurt, old man. We got no beef with you."

"I will not let you hurt Paul."

"Then we hurt you," the big guy answered.

"What will be, will be," Jim answered, shrugging his shoulders as if they had asked him whether it was going to rain.

"Hey, Skull," said the bigger guy to the shrimp. "Maybe we should leave them alone. They aren't hurting anybody."

"Cause of the punching bag, I'm still horny. Can't let that slide," said Skull. "You was warned." With that, Skull stabbed Jim in the gut. Jim let him, did not even flinch. Fear forgotten, Paul jumped forward to rush Skull, but Jim held out a hand, holding him back. Skull tried to pull the knife out, but Jim wrapped his hands around it, sheathing it in his own body.

"Shit. Give me the knife! I still got to slice punching bag boy here," Skull demanded.

"Not a chance," Jim said and damn it all, he was still smiling as he collapsed to the sidewalk. Choosing the better part of valor, Skull spilt, running down the street. His large companion looked down at the river of crimson pouring out the poor, brave lunatic then his glaze reluctantly drifted toward the wounded madman's eyes. The big hoddlum's face was pale and limp.

"I'm sorry, old man. I tried to stop him."

"I know," Jim said smiling. "You stand at a crossroads. Be careful which path you follow from this point forward."

The big guy was confused. "Aren't you angry at me? Don't you hate me?"

"No. Go in peace but remember, Vincent, this is your last chance," Jim said.

"How do you know my old name?" the big man asked. Jim just kept smiling.

Shaking his head, the big man ran off after Skull, then stopped. His head swiveled between where Skull had gone and Paul cradling bloody Jim on the sidewalk.

"Screw it," Vincent said and sprinted in the opposite direction.

"He made the right choice," Jim said, smiling. His eyes were beginning to glaze over and roll back in his head.

"Shush, Jim. rest. You lost a lot of blood. I'm sure someone called for an ambulance," Paul said, trying to stop the red currents by pressing his jacket against the wound. A finger in a damn would have had more effect.

"So, you think 911 has been flooded with calls over our little drama? And you say you aren't an optimist," Jim laughed.

"Why the hell did you do that?" Paul asked through the tears in his eyes. Jim may have been a lunatic who Paul had only known for forty-five minutes, but he laid his life on the line for him. No greater love has any man.

Paul's insides were tearing up. "I don't deserve this."

"Nonsense. You deserve it and more. This was not the reason I came to you. I came to offer you a job."

"I already have one."

"Which you despise. I offer you the stardust halo. I ask you to join the side of the angels, officially."

"What?"

"Which word didn't you understand?"

"I understood. I'm just not sure I'm buying any of it."

"You believe, but fear keeps you from acting."

"You're bleeding. Angels don't bleed."

"Angels bleed. Angels weep. Angels give a shit. Promise me you will do this. We are so few, the fallen so many."

"I... can't. I promise to think about it."

"Fair enough," Jim coughed up red mucus. "I'll take what I can get."

Jim started to fade. Paul remembered hearing somewhere that you had to keep injured people talking and awake.

"How do I accept the job? Is there a hotline?"

"In a way. Just open your heart. The Boss will do the rest. Watch out for the demons regardless."

"Was Skull a demon?"

"No, just a man. Remember you can tell by squinting and looking out of the corner of your eye. Besides a demon couldn't harm me. Not directly. Tell me, do you hear any bells?"

"No. Do you?"

"Unfortunately, no. I was hoping this would be the one."

The one where he got his wings. The old man was crazy, but Paul owed him big time, the ultimate debt. Paul could see Jim was knocking at death's door. If the Grim Reaper had a doorbell, Jim would have already been gone. Then he looked up at the pole he was leaning against. It was one of the old-fashioned fire alarm call boxes.

Paul reached for it and pulled his hand back. The sign said pulling it if there wasn't a fire meant a thousand dollar fine and up to ninety days in the slammer. The fear had him again. Or rather it tried before it was beaten badly by something freshly dug up from the pit of his soul. Paul's hand shot up faster than he imagined possible. A klaxon of alarms and bells sounded.

"You hear that Jim? Major bells. Must be one killer set of wings they got waiting for you."

His eyes, clear again and full of hope, looked up. "You didn't pull it?"

"Nope."

"Are you sure?"

"Would a prospective angel lie?"

"Absolutely," he said laughing. "Wouldn't be much of a candidate if he wouldn't. But thanks regardless."

Just then a church bell rang in the distance. Jim smiled contentedly, laid back his head and died. Paul held him and silently cried until the EMT pried Jim's body out of his hands. The knife was still sticking morbidly out from his abdomen.

Jim was pronounced DOA at the hospital.

Paul could not walk away from the paperwork this time. Jim had no next of kin so Paul made the funeral arrangements, but a funny thing happened on the way to the morgue. They lost the body. Without a trace. No one had a clue as to what happened. All Paul's demands for an investigation were ignored. Seems he had the right to bury him but not to do anything about their screw-up. Not even an angel could fight city hall.

Jim still deserved a service. Stopping at the corner grocery store Paul picked up two things. One was a rose. Then he returned to the corner where Jim had saved his life at the price of his own. There was a police line, ordering him not to cross. Paul ignored it. On the sidewalk, a chalk outline was drawn where Jim had fallen. Not entirely accurate as they had moved Paul out the way to make the picture.

Paul took the second item out, bent down on hands and knees to add two things to the outline. A pair of huge chalk-white wings. Only then did Paul place the rose over his heart. Standing, he bowed my head.

"Jim, no words will ever be enough to thank you. Not only did you save my life, you gave it back to me. I quit my job this morning. Suddenly paying the bills doesn't seem so important. I would consider the job you offered, but I need more. I need a sign."

The bartender from the night before stepped out of the pub to scowl at the memorial service Paul was giving. Truth be told, at first Paul paid him very little mind, seeing him only out of the corner of his eye. That was enough to make out the hellfire and the horns as he squinted against the tears.

Paul stared, first with disbelief and finally with realization.

Turning, he walked slowly away to get his affairs in order. Nobody was going to believe this one. Except Paul. And for the first time in far too long, he was happy. Really happy. Perhaps Jim's insanity was contagious, but Paul knew it was more than that.

And so he went with only what was on his back to do what needed to be done, smiling as his "sign" grimaced back at him. Paul tossed a quarter at his feet, smiling as the bartender bent to pick it up.

"See you around," Paul promised as his ears perked up, listening for the sound of bells ringing.

THE BIONIC MERMAID VS. THE SEA DEMONS

Hildy Silverman

THESSALONIKE FELT THE HEAT OF COMMANDER SUMMER JAMES'S GLARE from across the sizable conference room. "I *know* you must have an excellent reason for interrupting this highly sensitive meeting, agent."

The delegation from the United Nations and Oceans Security Council had recently arrived in Okinawa for a high-level meeting on possible illegal whaling activity. Japan had signed onto the Treaty of Triton with the mer — Thessalonike's people, although they no longer acknowledged her as such — later than many other surface nations due to the stipulation that all whaling cease. However, they had adhered to the terms for a decade, which made their caginess over a recent mer sighting of a trawler hauling a whale aboard worthy of a face-to-face.

Thessa chafed at being scolded. "Commander, my apologies, but this could not wait. We have intel regarding a disturbance from the fault known as the Pacific Ring of Fire."

The senior Japanese official, Minister Yamato, exclaimed, "If this is so, then why are my people not the ones reporting it?"

Thessa shrugged. "Perhaps U.N.O.S.C. monitoring is superior to yours." He bristled and she quickly added, "Or maybe they do not believe there is cause for alarm."

James's eyes narrowed. "But *you* do."

"Commander, if I may?" Oliver Martinez, another U.N.O.S.C. agent assigned to the whaling investigation, held up an electronic tablet. Upon James's nod, he joined her at the head of the table and pointed to the screen. "This is a graph of the seismic activity detected. It doesn't match what a tectonic shift would produce."

The delegates around the long cherrywood table began muttering. "Clarify, please," said James.

"This activity indicates something *really* large has erupted from the depths of the trench." He ran his forefinger across the tablet. "It looks to be coming right for us."

James pinched the bridge of her nose. "These readings don't make sense, Agent Martinez."

"Yeah. I know." He shrugged.

Surface-dwellers. As long as she'd lived among them, Thessa doubted she would ever understand them fully. Why did unfamiliarity keep them from accepting facts? Instead, they tried to deny them or force them into conforming to their known science. *Yet what they actually know about this world would not fill a clamshell.*

Now was the time for action, not debate. Thessa said, "Commander James, our immediate concern is that whatever has risen from the trench is heading for Okinawa rapidly. We must evacuate the populace."

The chatter around the table grew louder. "Are you mad?" Yamato stared as though Thessa had just transformed her bionic legs into a tail. "How are we supposed to do that with scarcely any notice and no clear explanation why?"

Martinez abruptly turned away with his finger pressed against the commlink in his right ear. When he looked back, his dark brown eyes were wide. "Commander, a U.N.O.S.C. drone has a visual on the anomaly. It… *Díos*, I don't even know what… hold on." He hastily linked his tablet to the conference room projector. A minute later, the drone feed appeared on the front wall.

Several people gasped. All eyes shifted to the commander and Yamato.

The minister snatched a cellphone out of his pocket and began hastily relaying what Thessa hoped were mass evacuation orders.

"Agents, thank you," said James curtly. "The team here will assist our Japanese hosts with making all necessary arrangements. I trust the two of you to coordinate the frontline response. Dismissed."

Thessa saluted and joined Martinez in a hasty exit. As they hurried through the conference center, she wondered briefly when walking had become so natural for her that she barely noticed doing it anymore. Brushing the extraneous thought aside, she said, "The drone image was blurry, but I was able to make out the shape of what swims this way." A childhood memory stirred. "I believe I have seen this creature before.

Not with my own eyes, but as an illustration in a... what would you call it? An educational papyrus."

"You mean a mer textbook?"

"Close enough. But this creature should not exist, not anymore. If it does—" She twined a strand of orchid-colored hair around her index finger.

"Uh, oh." Martinez twirled his forefinger. "You're doing that thing you do with your hair when you're really anxious. This *is* bad."

She was too absorbed by the potential threat to express annoyance at his overly attentive, yet accurate observation. "If memory serves, yes."

"What do you think it is?" Martinez asked. "Because it sure as hell looked like a giant sea serpent with several spare heads."

"If I am correct, it is a demon."

He stopped abruptly. "A *what* now?"

She met his wide-eyed gaze. "A demon. An ancient creature that serves dark and dangerous gods. And, if mer lore is accurate, there may be more."

"H-how many?"

She frowned. "That is but one answer we urgently require."

A seven-headed sea demon the size of a mid-rise skyscraper rose off Okinawa mere hours later, sending a wall of water crashing over the peninsula's coast. The tsunami warning siren had sounded, but the short timing hadn't allowed for a full evacuation, so most of Okinawa's citizens fled to designated local shelters. Unfortunately, judging by the panic Thessa observed in the streets, not everyone would reach safety before the demon came ashore.

The U.N.O.S.C. delegation was woefully short of field personnel, having come unprepared for more than boardroom negotiations. She and Martinez did their best with who they had—establishing a perimeter in partnership with local law enforcers based on where they expected the demon to surface. When the beast rose from the shallows bellowing from all seven throats, they opened fire.

Two heads snaked down and rose with four screaming Okinawan officers in their jaws. A moment later, blood sprayed, and the screaming ceased. The demon continued wading north along the peninsula's coast.

"*Jesucristo!*" Martinez clapped a hand against his forehead. "What are we supposed to do against this thing?"

"Focus, agent." Thessa squeezed his shoulder briefly. "What is its trajectory?"

He consulted his tablet. "Motobu, a klick north of us."

"Then we follow and keep it from advancing further onshore."

She relayed orders to the joint response teams to fall back. Their weapons were ineffective, so there was no point wasting ammo or sacrificing more lives. All they could do was follow and observe.

When the demon reached Motobu, it stopped in front of a reddish-hued building near the coastline. One head reared back and spat something black onto the roof, which began to bubble and dissolve.

"What is that place?" Thessa asked.

"The Oceanic Culture Institute." Martinez shook his head. "What could a sea monster want from a museum?"

"I do not know but I find it doubtful that this is a random target." The creature plunged more heads into the now-gaping hole in the roof. "It seems to be searching for something within." She twisted her hair around her forefinger. "Which confirms that it is not acting of its own accord."

"Why is that?"

"Demons are not particularly intelligent, according to the lore. They are described as servants to powerful beings." The sea demon spat a second bellyful of caustic substance onto the roof. "If it were uncontrolled, it would simply rampage."

"So, we should just sit back and let it get whatever for whoever and it will leave?" Martinez sounded hopeful.

She shook her head. "I suggest that whoever has the power to control this demon should not get what they want."

"I was afraid you'd say that."

Two free heads bellowed in what sounded disconcertingly like triumph. The demon withdrew its other five heads, which dragged something about half its size from the ruined building.

"Is that... a *whale*?" Martinez blinked. "Why would it leave an ocean full of whales if it just wanted dinner?"

"Because that is not a whale." Thessa tilted her head to the left, then the right. "It appears to be an enormous leg. Covered in... scales?"

With the limb clamped firmly between multiple jaws, the demon turned and retreated toward the open ocean. A voice in Thessa's commlink asked, "Team Leader, do we pursue?"

Ideally, she knew they should stop the demon from delivering the huge leg to whoever commanded it, but that wasn't feasible given their limited firepower. "Negative. Refocus efforts on crowd control and mobilizing emergency services."

Martinez looked relieved. "So, what now?"

"We assess the damage, report back, and figure out who sent the demon and what they might want with that leg." She surveyed the wreckage of the Oceanic Institute and scowled. "Clearly, the mer were in error thinking the trawler stole a whale from the sea. The crew must have discovered the leg and brought it to the Institute, which in turn failed to properly notify the mer authorities."

Martinez wagged his index finger. "No wonder Yamato was so reluctant to discuss the incident. Probably didn't want the mer to claim the find as theirs."

"I wonder if it is. A massive human-like leg but covered in scales? We need answers, which means…" Her heart sank. "Curse it to Hades!"

She pivoted and began jogging back to the conference center. She had a lot to accomplish quickly, including arranging an emergency flight to U.N.O.S.C. headquarters.

Martinez caught up to her, panting. "Wh-what's wrong? I mean, besides the obvious."

"I must return home to consult with someone." She hesitated. "My childhood home."

"Oh-h-h." He knew her well enough to understand the implication. "I know that won't be easy, but given the circumstances, surely they'll be willing to talk to you, even though you're, uh, not their favorite person."

"That is a kind way to say I am dead to them." She sighed. "Regardless, it must be done. One demon has wreaked havoc already and others may follow."

"Who are you going to see? In the sea?" His full lips quirked into a grin.

She rolled her eyes at his attempted humor. "An expert in ancient mer history and legend. My mother."

Thessa approached the coral gates of her family's Atlantic Ocean grove and immediately drew the attention of their personal guard. The male with pale-green hair stared past her even as he raised his spear.

She attempted diplomacy. "Greetings, noble guardian. I am here as a representative of U.N.O.S.C. on a high-priority mission. I must speak to my... to Dorea immediately."

Still gazing past her, he said, "This ghost will depart."

"I understand you are obeying orders, but those only apply to the exiled daughter of Dorea and Eldoris," Thessa said through gritted teeth. "I am here as a U.N.O.S.C. agent and bear the authority of one who upholds the Treaty of Triton." She swam forward only to be met by the guard's spear, now pointed at her chest. Long-suppressed grief and rage bubbled forth. "I have no time for this nonsense!"

"The dead are unwelcome here." The guard feinted toward her. "Begone!"

Thessalonike grabbed the spear under the head. She sheared the shaft in two with the razor-sharp edge of her tailfin and caught the upper part in her right hand. Pointing it at the guard, she said, "I am *not* dead. However, you may not be able to say the same if you do not *get out of my way*."

"As soon as I heard the disturbance, I knew it was you." Thessa looked past the gawping guard to see a woman with silver-streaked orchid-colored hair swept into a bun glide through the gates. "Greetings," Dorea swallowed visibly, "daughter. Kindly do not kill Pasha. Decent guards are challenging to retain."

Thessa let the top of the spear drift away, pressed her palms together, and bowed. "Greetings, honored Dorea. I am here..." Realization struck. "Wait. You *acknowledge* me?"

Dorea waved her hand. "The world is under siege, or about to be. I assume that is what brings you home?"

"Y-yes." Thessa struggled to focus. "So, you are aware of the demon attack. I need to know everything—why it appeared, about the enormous leg it stole, how many more to expect. Any information could be vital."

"Indeed." Dorea glanced over her shoulder. "Not here though. Your father... we are not of the same mind with regards to you."

"Fortunately, I do not require anything from him." Her tone was sharper than intended.

Dorea gestured toward a grotto. "We will have privacy in there." Her gaze shifted to the guard. "Pasha, we will meet later to discuss the difference between enforcement and excessive force."

Pasha cringed but turned it into a bow. "As you say, mistress."

They swam over into the grotto. Once settled, Dorea steepled her fingertips beneath her chin. "How much do you remember of our prehistory?"

"Some. The mer as we appear today are not the earliest iteration of ocean-dwellers. Just as modern *homo sapiens* were preceded by earlier human-like species."

"Correct. Our few surviving scrolls refer to them as godlings—the spawn of Tiamat, goddess of the salted seas, and Abzu, god of the land-bound freshwaters. A great war broke out because Abzu feared their children would overthrow him to rule the lands as well as the seas. These proto-mer posed a threat because they could function equally well in either environment. They are depicted as having had scales, but with web-toed human legs and fins." Dorea's gaze slid down to Thessa's tail briefly. "They prevailed and slew Abzu. In her fury, Tiamat utilized her mythical power source called the Tablet of Destinies to asexually spawn demons, which annihilated their half-siblings.

"Tiamat sought to conquer the landbound next so she could rule Abzu's former domain unchallenged. It took a Mesopotamian king, Marduk, to defeat Tiamat by stealing the Tablet, but even with it, he was unable to slay her. Instead, he divided her parts and hid them throughout the world."

Thessa's thoughts churned. "How many demons did Tiamat birth?"

"Eleven are mentioned by name. You have seen the rise of one—Musmahhu, the Exalted Serpent. They all fell dormant after their mother's defeat and vanished." Half to herself, Dorea mused, "So why, after millennia, are they returning?"

Thessa swam from one side of the grotto to the other. "Something is awakening them, or rather some*one*. Who has that kind of power and wants the pieces of Tiamat?"

"More concerning is what they want them *for*." Dorea frowned. "What little we know is a tangle of myths and actual history. That said, there is one version of the lore involving a loyal child of Tiamat and Abzu—Kingu. He tried to save his father but, failing that, sided with his mother and served as her general, leading the demons against the proto-mer. Tiamat designated him the one true heir to Abzu."

"What became of him?"

Dorea shook her head. "Again, the lore conflicts. Some versions say he was slain by Marduk, others that he slunk off into self-exile."

"That does not sound like the reaction of a crown prince-god to defeat." She stopped pacing and twisted her hair. "Most stories depict gods as immortal. What if Kingu survived? Biding his time for generations of swims until a Japanese trawler accidentally retrieved his mother's leg."

Dorea swam closer. "Stop, you will tangle it." She gently pulled Thessa's hand away from her hair. "The Tablet of Destinies has also been recovered."

"When was this?" Thessa exclaimed.

"During a recent archaeological excavation of Marduk's tomb along the border between Iran and Iraq. Among the items recovered was a tablet with cuneiform-like writing that no expert could decipher."

"And you know this... how?"

Dorea flared her gills. "I keep up with archaeological finds made below *and* above the waters, like any respectable scholar. Which is why I also know the Tablet, along with the Danish archaeologist who discovered Marduk's tomb, were being transported to a museum when the vehicles bearing them vanished without a trace."

Thessa massaged her temples. "So it is possible Kingu has the Tablet and is using it to control his demonic half-siblings with the goal of reassembling their mother."

Dorea nodded. "That is reasonable, if horrifying. Tiamat sought to destroy all life on this world she considered disloyal, including her own children. I doubt the time she has spent severed and scattered has improved her disposition." She squeezed Thessa's hand. "Your organization *must* find and stop Kingu, but I fear the risk you face will be... significant."

Feeling her mother's touch again after so long, gazing into eyes that not only acknowledged her but shone with affection, suddenly became overwhelming. Thessa embraced her. "I have missed you so, Mother."

"And I you," Dorea murmured.

Warmth suffused Thessa from the top of her head to where her waist fused to the bionic tail. The moment was heady and surreal, and she did not wish it to end.

Dorea pulled away gently, nodded at Thessa's tail. "You have the same ability as the ancients to swim and walk. Perhaps that is the source of our modern prejudice—jealousy over what we lost to a different evolutionary stream." Her lower lip trembled. "One could argue you should be revered, not reviled."

Thessa shook her head in wonder. "What has changed, Mother? You were never one to defy custom. Yet here you are, speaking to the dead."

Dorea's expression turned wistful. "I have learned in the most painful way that it is easier to shun a child as dead knowing, factually, she still lives when you have not experienced the agony of having one truly die."

"Aegeon." Thessa whispered her late brother's name. "Mother, I—"

Dorea pressed a fingertip to Thessa's lips. "No. You were not to blame." She lowered her hand and clenched it into a fist. "The Sea Witch destroyed my son. What you did... were forced to do, was mercy." She cleared her throat. "Regardless, I can no longer maintain such an awful pretense when it comes to you."

"But Father—"

"Will hopefully realize the same during a swim to come. Until he does, we must keep any further association private. Assuming you wish for more?" Dorea regarded her expectantly.

Unable to speak around the sensation of having swallowed jagged coral, Thessa nodded.

Martinez's voice shattered the moment. He had returned with her to headquarters and was overseeing global monitoring for additional demonic activity. "Thessa, are you there? We have multiple sightings. Over."

She raised a forefinger to her mother. Swallowing hard, she tapped her commlink. "Report, over."

"A—I can't even believe I'm saying this — half-man, half-scorpion the size of a locomotive just came out of the Black Sea and started digging near Georgia. Just outside Lesotho, a mammoth snake monster is drilling through what used to be a village. We've got reports of quakes and tidal waves from other locales, but whatever creatures are causing those haven't surfaced yet. All available U.N.O.S.C. field personnel have been deployed, but so far nothing we've hit the demons with made a dent." He paused for breath. "You should know one of the largest masses we're monitoring is moving along the floor of the Atlantic Ocean toward the Florida coast. Over."

That was too close to U.N.O.S.C. headquarters for comfort or coincidence. "Understood. I have completed gathering the necessary intel and will have eyes on the source of the latter directly. Over and out." Addressing Dorea, she said, "Apologies, but I must leave immediately."

"Understood." Her mother smiled. "Swim fast, daughter, and return soon." She offered a wry grin. "I promise Pasha's future duties will *not* include the front gate."

Thessa clasped her hands and bowed. "Until then. Thank you again for... everything."

Thessa observed the phalanxes of proto-mer moving through the depths in awe. Speaking softly, she informed Martinez, "These are not demons." She had shared her mother's intel during the swim to her current location. "It appears Kingu has utilized the Tablet of Destinies to reanimate his slaughtered brethren."

"And they're definitely marching toward headquarters?" Martinez's voice shook.

"Yes. Prepare a defense. Muster whatever armed forces you can, ocean and surface-based."

"But," Martinez sputtered, "surface military action against any mer violates the Treaty. There are protocols and red tape up the wazoo—"

"None of which we have time for!" She forced herself to remain calm despite the tremendous number of proto-mer moving past the coral reef behind which she hid. "These are not any mer with whom your people have a treaty. This is an invading force, capable of fighting just as well on land as in water and have doubtless been tasked with destroying U.N.O.S.C. as their greatest impediment to conquering the surface." Realization struck. "Which means the one commanding them must be nearby directing his legions into battle."

"That man-scorpion thing pulled a big arm out of the ground a few minutes ago. For the record? This dismembered goddess scavenger hunt is *really* gross."

She sighed. "Duly noted, agent. Over and out."

Thessa refocused her attention on the beings marching past, scarcely believing the evidence of her eyes. Up close, the proto-mer were re-pulsive—rotting things draped in seaweed. Gaps in their wasted flesh revealed gristle and bone. Yet she took note of the iridescent scales that covered them from scalp to webbed feet, and thought, *in life, they must have been magnificent.*

Steeling herself, she slid out from behind the reef to assess their threat level. She slipped behind one at the back of a phalanx, split her bionic tail into legs, and wrapped them around its waist. Then she triggered the shift back to the tail, severing her target into halves. Organs drifted out but little to no blood. As the torso and lower extremities floated their separate ways, she noticed both were still moving, as if unaware they no longer formed a single being. Her flesh crawled.

Thessa flipped upside-down to slam her tailfins into another's jaw. The impact launched it like a torpedo above the waves. It splashed down several yards away and immediately dove down to join another phalanx.

She continued battling her way through, occasionally shuddering with disgust. Their eyes were devoid of intellect, their bodies mere animated shells. She could render them harmless by dismemberment or beheading, but they would not truly die. As individuals they posed scant threat—they would not even defend one another. However, she suspected that once they reached their designated target, they would become extremely deadly, if only through sheer force of numbers.

Thessa broke off her forays and relayed her assessment to Martinez, hoping it would at least help the combined forces of surface and ocean stave them off. She just needed enough time to reach her target.

Again sheltering behind the reef, Thessa gathered seaweed strands and swathed herself head to tail. Since she couldn't sprout scales on her upper body, the camouflage would have to suffice. She shifted her tail into legs to further help her blend in.

She joined the undead in moving along the ocean floor, copying their same slow, jilted movements. She gazed straight ahead as they did, trusting her peripheral vision to alert her if they suddenly reacted to her unfamiliar presence and attacked.

Fortunately, their relentless but mindless obedience worked in her favor. Ignored, she followed first one group then another, zigzagging along until she spied the base of a rocky outcropping overhead. Gliding upward, she peered through the waves at a small landmass just large enough for someone to stand upon.

And someone was, but he was not at all what she'd expected. Instead of a god, she saw a man—a very ordinary one at that. He appeared middle-aged with a receding hairline and soft waist.

She drew closer cautiously. He cradled a massive rectangular stone that looked far heavier than a man with his build could heft, yet he did so with ease. He scanned the tablet while chanting in an unfamiliar language, in a timbre so resonant it seemed to issue from more than one throat. His eyes blazed with a greenish-gold light. She recalled her mother's account of the archeologist who had vanished along with Marduk's treasures and realized what his mortal flesh must now contain: *Kingu.*

She ducked beneath the waves, contacted Martinez, and relayed her theory. "It is unfortunate, but he must be stopped," she concluded.

"You can't just kill that poor guy," said Martinez.

"I do not have a choice," she snapped. "He is clearly controlling the proto-mer, and already sent demons ravaging throughout the world. All of this is mere prelude to what will happen if he succeeds in restoring Tiamat!"

"Just… try to come up with an alternative to executing an innocent man, okay?"

"I cannot promise." She groaned at his impractical softness. "But I shall try. Out."

Thessa swam to the back of the tiny island, slipped out of the water, and crept up behind the possessed human while plotting non-fatal ways to disable him.

"Good. You have arrived." One head, the archaeologist's, continued looking down and reading from the Tablet in a now-ordinary voice. At the same time, a superimposed translucent head with glowing eyes spoke in a sonorous tone as it swiveled to face her. "Come closer, little goddess. We are pleased to meet you."

She made herself stride forward despite the instinct to flee. "I am no goddess," she said with only a slight tremor in her voice.

The god's face smiled. Though barely substantial, Thessa made out his heavy brow and aquiline nose—features entirely different from the human face it overlapped. "In Our time, you would have been. Perhaps you still can be. Only prove your loyalty to Mother Tiamat, and when We are finished with Our great work, there may be a role for you in the perfected world to come."

Pulse thrumming in her ears, Thessa strove to keep her expression neutral. "Then you *are* Kingu?"

The ghostly head bobbed. "We are. Only loyal child of Tiamat and Abzu, rightful heir to land and sea, imprisoned by accursed Marduk, and freed by Our blessed vessel, doctorjanstryger."

It took her a moment to parse the name. "Doctor Jan Stryger, the archeologist. You possessed him."

"We had need of a casement for Our spirit once it was released from the Tablet."

So Marduk had trapped Kingu within the Tablet of Destinies itself. She wondered what Stryger had done to release the god-prince's spirit but discarded the thought. What mattered was stopping Kingu's army and ending his efforts to reassemble Tiamat. "Is there any point in my asking you to spare the peoples of this world?"

"None."

She nodded. "And if I destroy this body you wear. What would happen?"

"You might succeed." A predatory smile spread across the phantom face. "We have observed your activities this day and are impressed. We would enjoy inhabiting a more powerful form than doctorjanstryger."

There it was. Even if she killed Stryger, Kingu's spirit would survive and move into the nearest convenient vessel—her.

"Accept Us as your king and Our mother as your Goddess. Do so as yourself or as Us. This is your only choice." The mist head swiveled back to merge with the man's as their voices melded once more into a single, booming chant.

Thessa fought down despair. Kingu clearly had abilities so far beyond her comprehension she might as well be a guppy attempting to stop a rocket launch. Could she take the risk he was exaggerating his power to survive Stryger's death? No, there had to be an alternative. *Think! You cannot overpower or kill him. So what can you do?*

An answer came to her in a rush: *What Marduk did.*

He had used the Tablet to entrap Kingu's spirit, but she had no idea how. Still, it had to be the answer. Kingu was using it—apparently *had* to use it—to control the proto-mer and the demons. Her mother had said it was Tiamat's source of power. *Remove the Tablet and I remove the threat. Theoretically.*

Thessa launched herself into a somersault. She caught a glimpse of Kingu's phantom face tilting up to watch her with an expression of bemusement... until he realized he wasn't her target.

She drove her right foot into the Tablet clutched in Kingu's hands. Between the strength of his grip and the power behind her bionic leg, the thick stone split.

She landed and immediately pivoted, expecting a retaliatory strike. But Kingu merely stared in shock at the two halves of the Tablet he now held. The glow from his eyes faded until only Doctor Stryger's pale blue irises remained.

"What have you done?" Kingu/Stryger boggled at her. "This... it cannot be!"

Thessa saw his arms trembling as he struggled to fit the pieces back together. She kicked one half out of his left hand. As it came down, she roundhouse kicked it to pieces. He dropped the right half as though it suddenly weighed too much, and she stomped it into dust.

Kingu's spirit blazed out in streams of green-gold light from Stryger's eyes, nose, and mouth. Shrinking back, Thessa shielded her face with her arms, but the god-prince's essence didn't approach. Instead, it rose into the air and dissipated in the sunlight. Stryger slumped to the rocky beach and lay moaning, but alive.

That will please Martinez, she thought.

As if he'd head her, Martinez spoke through her commlink. "Thessa, what did you do?" He sounded half-accusing, half-relieved. "The zombie not-mer... they made it to shore and just... evaporated!"

She drew a satisfied breath. "Stryger lives. I was able to find an alternative to killing him."

"Good on you!"

"Thank you. What of the demons?"

"We're still getting reports, but it seems like they've also vanished. Except—"

Her shoulders tensed. "What?"

"Well, they left giant, scaly goddess bits lying around." Martinez sounded like he had swallowed something unpleasant.

Thessa rolled her eyes. "I suppose it was too much to hope that those would vanish too."

"Yeah, so what should we do about them?"

"Send teams to collect the parts and take them to new sites for burial—as far apart from each other as possible. No individual or team should know where all the pieces are distributed."

"Yuck, but acknowledged."

Thessa glanced at Doctor Stryger, who sat up and cradled his head gingerly. "Tablet," he muttered. "Kingu means to…"

"It is no longer a concern, doctor." To Martinez, Thessa said, "Send a rescue boat to my location to pick up the archeologist. He requires medical attention."

"Shall do. You on your way back to headquarters?"

Thessa started to affirm but reconsidered. "I shall return tomorrow, unless that is problematic?"

"No, the situation's under control," said Martinez. "Where are you going?"

"Home." She liked the feel of the word in her mouth. "This time simply to visit."

"Well, that's a thing." He sounded surprised. "I'm happy for you, Thessa."

She imagined her mother's expression when she told her about foiling Kingu's plans and smiled. "As am I. Over and out."

D⊻AL!TY

John G. Hartness

A Quincy Harker, Demon Hunter Short Story

"Oh, *Hell* no!" I shouted from the balcony, not caring even a little that my language was unbefitting an angel.

"Are you barking mad, Harker?" yelled the demon from where he stood pouring a drink.

"No more than normal," replied the smirking Quincy Harker from where he sat on his sofa swathed in bandages. He leaned back against the white leather and winced as something under his loose-fitting black dress shirt pulled, or maybe it was just the pressure on his wounds. I wasn't inclined to care at that moment.

I walked back into the room, my strides strong and my countenance locked in a scowl. At least, that's what I thought I looked like, anyway. It was certainly my intention to look both determined and no-nonsense, but every once in a while the form I chose when I manifested on Earth a dozen years or so ago gets in the way of being taken seriously. Humans, especially men, just don't give blondes the respect they — *we* — deserve. I stood on the rug in front of my charge, kinda boss, and probably best friend, put my hands on my hips, and glared down at him.

And my scowl was immediately undone as a big floofy curl of blonde hair sprang loose from my scrunchie and dropped right in the center of my face. I blew it out of the way with an exasperated huff, and said, "Jonathan Quincy Abraham Holmwood Harker, you have absolutely lost your mind."

Q stretched his arms across the back of the sofa and grinned at me. "What do you want me to do, Glory? I'm obviously too injured to investigate anything more dangerous than high-stakes kitten wrestling, and so is Luke. Becks is knee-deep in paperwork at the cop shop, and Jo has some kind of parent-teacher thing. To be honest, I kinda didn't listen to what she said she had going on, but I think it's a kid thing. That leaves you two. I'm not sending you out there without backup, and there is no way I'm sending Faustus off to deal with a possible demon infestation on his own."

I looked at my newly-assigned partner and sighed. Harker was right. Faustus was on the lower end of evil, as demons went, but he was still a demon. Obsidian-black skin, pointed teeth, yellow eyes, the whole deal. And he might not have been the *Father* of Lies, but he was damn sure the Weird Uncle of Lies. No matter what Goethe said, the demon in that story was the one named Faustus, and he was currently standing in Harker's living room on the top floor of a condo building in Charlotte, NC, drinking expensive bourbon at ten in the morning. He'd saved our asses more than once since deciding to work on the side of the angels, pun completely intended, but I still didn't trust him any further than I could throw a Buick. Well, I'm pretty strong, so maybe no further than I could throw a tank.

Faustus sat on the sofa facing Harker across a glass-topped coffee table. "Harker, buddy, pal, friend-o-mine, there's got to be some way I can handle this without you putting the white knight of albatrosses around my neck. I'll go take a little mountain holiday and figure out if whatever's happening in the hills is something we need to worry about, no problem, but I *cannot* roll up on one of my brothers with a flippin' Guardian Angel as my sidekick! I've got a reputation to maintain, man!"

Oh, that was *it*. I hopped over the back of the couch and perched on the arm, my glare now having a whole new target. "What in the world makes you think I'd ever be your sidekick, demon? Or don't you remember which side came out on top the last time you and your buddies tangled with angels?"

Faustus barely spared me a glance. He just cocked his head to the side and said, "Glory, my dear, as long as you're picking that particular form to manifest, you can be on top anytime you like." Then he turned back to Harker as I counted to ten in English, then Latin, then Enochian, then Sumerian, Aramaic, Russian, seven different regional variants of Chinese, and eight dead languages that don't even have names anymore. When I was better than half sure I wasn't going to manifest my soulblade and chop Faustus's head off in Harker's living room, I reached out with one foot and kicked him behind the ear.

"Ow! What the—"

"Swear jar," came a voice from the kitchen, freezing Faustus's curse on his lips. Cassandra Skyler had us all firmly under her thumb when it came to profanity, and I'm pretty sure Harker and Faustus had already contributed enough to her granddaughter's college fund via the swear jar that Ginnie could afford the best Ivy League education. I'm sure I wasn't the only one who took great pleasure in watching my more profane friends contort themselves into all kinds of weird pretzels self-censoring any time Cassie was within earshot. They'd even cut down on the profanity they used when she wasn't around, albeit only marginally. Technically, I owed a dollar for my "Hell no," but if Cassie wasn't going to call me out, I wasn't going to remind her.

I smiled and slid down the arm to sit on the couch next to Faustus. I put one arm around my new sleuthing partner and grinned over at Harker. "I've changed my mind, Q. This is a great idea. It'll give us a chance to bond and become more productive members of the team. I'm in."

Harker wrinkled his brow. "You know I don't trust you when you agree with me, right?"

"You don't trust anyone, Harker," I replied. "That's what makes it fun to push your suspicion buttons."

"I'm Count Dracula's nephew, I work for a secret division of the federal government, and one of my best friends is a demon who literally coined a term for getting screwed over in a deal. Of *course*, I don't trust anyone. Especially angels. I've met too many of you. Y'all might not lie, but neither do the Fae, and that's never stopped them from being scary as..."

"Swear jar," came the singsong voice from the kitchen. "And you owe a dollar for that s-word."

"Heck," Harker finished. He tossed an iPad at Faustus and a set of car keys at me. "Here are the details. Try not to drive my truck off a mountain. I just got new tires."

Three hours later we pulled up in front of a small clapboard building badly in need of a paint job with a sign that proclaimed it the "Evangelical Temple of Jesus Christ the Redeemer of All Mankind

Ministry." I hopped out of Harker's Chevy Colorado and stretched my arms toward the blue Appalachian sky, working the kinks out of my neck. The truck was a decent ride, but after a couple of hours, it still rode like a pickup, which is to say it was built for utility, not comfort.

My partner closed his door and looked at the church. "What a shithole," he said, taking a toothpick out of his mouth and flicking it to the gravel parking lot. Faustus had changed into something less panic-inducing for the investigation, so at least he now appeared human. Handsome, too, if I'm being honest. When the demon decided to put on a human suit, he knew how to pick them. He stood about six feet tall, about one-ninety, with wavy brown hair, a strong jawline, and just enough stubble to make it look like he didn't care how he looked. And then he bent down and fixed his hair in the truck's side mirror, reminding me yet again that vanity was just one of his favorite deadly sins.

"Come on, pretty boy, let's see what we can see around this place," I said, walking toward the church. According to the reports we'd received, the vandalism was all inside, so I climbed the steps and tried the knob. It was unlocked so I pushed the door open and called out to anyone inside.

"Hello?"

"In here!" came a friendly voice. I walked toward the sound of it and found a smiling man with a bountiful white beard and enough twinkle in his eyes to make him the perfect mall Santa walking toward me in a paint-spattered tie-dyed t-shirt and worn denim overalls. He had a paint roller in one hand, a red bandanna sticking out of the bib of his overalls, and a streak of white paint curving across his forehead in a mirror image of the grin he wore.

"Howdy!" he said as he reached the back of the dozen rows of pews. He held out a hand, then looked at the paint on it and pulled it back. "We can just wave for now. I'm Pastor Dino Hicks. Welcome to the Redeemer Ministry. Sorry about the mess, we had a peck of trouble the other night and I'm just now getting around to cleaning it up. What can I do for y'all?"

The kindness radiated off this man in waves, almost strong enough to push Faustus completely back out the door. No matter what else was going on in this ramshackle building, this was a *good* person.

"Well, Pastor Hicks, we're here about your...'peck of trouble,' actually," I said. "Can we walk to the front of the church?" He turned and led us back up the aisle toward the pulpit, where I really just wanted to get him over a drop cloth before he dripped any more white paint on his carpet. "I'm Agent Rubim and this is..."

"Agent Goethe," Faustus said, holding out his hand. The pastor shook without thinking, then looked down at the demon's immaculate palm.

"Well, ain't that something? I reckon the paint on my hand must have dried faster than I thought."

That, or the paint saved my partner from bursting into flames at the touch of a decent human being, I thought. "Pastor Hicks—" I started.

"Please, call me Dino. Or if you have to be all formal, you can call me Pastor Dino. Anytime somebody starts using my last name, I have to look around to make sure they ain't talking about my daddy. And he's been dead these twenty years!" His whole face lit up as he smiled at his own joke, and I couldn't help but do the same.

"Pastor Dino, then," I said. "We're with the Department of Homeland Security's Paranormal Division, and our Regional Director asked us to come take a look at the vandalism here, just to make sure that it really is some silly kids, and not something worse."

His bushy white eyebrows almost touched as he turned my words over in his head. "You think this might be some kind of terrorist thing? That's what Homeland Security is all about, ain't it?"

"We work to defend the country from domestic and foreign threats that can strike at the very framework of our nation. Attacks upon our religious freedoms absolutely fall under that umbrella, as the right to worship as we choose is one of the most important rights granted to us by the Founding Fathers." Faustus actually put his hand over his heart as he invoked the Founding Fathers. I had to give it to the crafty little bastard, he was *good*.

He went on. "We specifically investigate any church vandalism that seems to invoke a supernatural, paranormal, or otherworldly element, in an effort to ensure that something like the Satanic Panic of the 1980s never happens again. You remember what that was like."

Pastor Dino's face darkened. "Oh, I do indeed. It's only been in the past five years that I've been able to get a small role-playing game club set up here at the church for our local teens." He gave us a slightly bashful grin. "I'm a huge geek as well a minister. I love all kinds of science fiction and fantasy stuff. That whole mess back then was just silly."

"Yes, it was," Faustus agreed. "But it could also be used to under-mine the public's faith in our religious institutions, and from there, our government. So, we take any kind of church vandalism very seriously, be it a hate crime or some type of occult symbology."

"Oh," Pastor Dino said, looking crestfallen. "Well, I've already put a solid coat of paint over everything they did in here and was just getting started on a second coat. Some of the red was hard to cover over. So, I think I might have screwed up your evidence. I'm sorry."

"That's okay," I said. "Did you happen to get any pictures of the symbols before you painted over them?"

"Well, of course," he said. "Let me just put down this roller before I drip all over everything, and I'll get my phone. But the sheriff's department took a bunch of pictures, too. Didn't they send them to you?"

Faustus and I looked at each other. Coordinating with local law enforcement wasn't exactly DHS's strong suit on its best day, and neither of us had any idea of how to go about that. Fortunately, my partner had literally millennia of experience coming up with lies at the drop of a hat. "We clued them in as to our interest in the case, but often the locals get a little bent out of shape when they think the feds are stick-ing their nose in where it doesn't belong, regardless of jurisdiction. So, we try to get any evidence we can independently of them, just to make sure we get an unbiased version."

"That makes sense. Terrell Landis is a good man, but he can get a little xenophobic, if you ask me. Took him a long time to warm up to the idea of a gay preacher who quotes *Lord of the Rings* from the pulpit, let me tell you." Pastor Dino favored us with another one of those room-melting smiles, and I swore that I would rain all the fires of heaven down on anyone who threatened to hurt this sweet, sweet man.

Pastor Dino returned a minute later sans paint spatter and held out either a small tablet computer or the biggest damn cell phone I'd ever seen.

He chuckled when I raised an eyebrow. "Just you wait, young lady. One of these days you'll start getting older, too. Then all the teeny tiny print will be just so many scratch marks on paper and you'll be leaving your reading glasses behind in every room and trying to find a bigger screen, too."

"Oh, she's older than she looks, pastor," Faustus said, earning himself an elbow in the ribs. He was right, though. I'd seen the sun set on more than one millennium and had little doubt that I'd see many more before my work was done.

"Here's what I found when I opened up the church yesterday morning. We lock the building from midnight to six in the morning, but any other time, the doors are open to all."

He flicked through a series of images showing the typical faux-Satanist graffiti — inverted crosses, pentacles with the point facing down, profanity, squiggles that look like the symbols off the fourth Led Zeppelin album, and one really good goat's head painting. The vandal must have taken his time with that one. I defaulted to thinking about whoever painted the church as male because they usually are, and because of some of the more...salacious paintings found on the walls had nothing to do with religion, and everything to do with a teenaged boy's fascination with breasts. Come to think of it, over all my time on earth, I've noticed that human males never really lose that fascination, no matter how old they are.

"Can you zoom in on that one?" Faustus's words shattered my reverie, which was just as well. The minds of men are unknowable, even to angels. That's what makes humanity interesting. That, and their eternal development of new things to deep fry.

Pastor Dino stretched his fingers apart on the screen, making the center of the image larger. This was why we were here. The picture was a triangle, with writing on all three sides. Triangles are at least as magically powerful as circles, with three being the number of the Trinity and all, and they are often components of some high-level casting or binding rituals. This wasn't one of those, though. This was more like a calling card. A very specific calling card that made my blood run cold, and from the bead of sweat rolling down Faustus's temple, had the same effect on him.

The words written along the outside of the shape, running along each leg of the triangle in neatly printed Enochian, were a battle cry announcing the coming of Byleth, one of the Kings of Hell and one of the most evil of Lucifer's minions. This was, in a word, not good.

I stepped back from the iPad, my hands trembling a little. I had met Byleth once, in battle during the War on Heaven. It didn't go well for me. He's powerful, far more powerful than any creature I could vanquish or banish, and if he really had found a way out of Hell onto this little mountain, then Western North Carolina was in for a really bad couple of nights.

"Th-thank you, Pastor Dino. That image in particular is very useful. It looks like some others..." My voice trailed off. I'm not great at the whole cover story thing in the first place, and this had me too rattled to come up with even a crappy one.

Fortunately, I had one of history's greatest liars standing by my left elbow. "It resembles the symbology we've seen in a string of church vandalizations throughout the Southeast," Faustus continued smoothly. "We would like to come back later and spend the night in the church, just in case our vandal happens to return. We'd like to have a few words with him." The grin Faustus gave made *me* shiver, and I'm practically immortal.

"Of course," Pastor Dino said, taking a big step back from the grinning demon. "It gets dark around eight this time of year. If y'all want to park up the hill at my house and walk down, won't nobody see your truck that way. I've got a nice little path leading to the side door. Paved it with local stones myself."

"Thank you, pastor," I said, shaking the gentle man's hand. "We'll be back tonight. For now, we're going to head into town and do a little research."

"Alright," he replied. "If you get hungry, check out Bella's Bagels on Main Street. They'll put about anything you want on a bagel and call it a sandwich."

The pastor was right about the bagel place, they would put literally any arrangement of meat, veggies, and toppings on a bagel, a policy Faustus tested with his barbecue pork, avocado slice, bacon, lettuce, and honey Dijon mustard bagel. I had to admit, the expression on the server's face when she watched him take a bite and rave about the blend of flavors was hilarious.

But the only thing we found out about the church or its members in the local newspaper records going back eighty years was one parishioner going to jail for embezzlement from his workplace and a father-and-daughter team of bootleggers who donated heavily to the church as well as to every other charity in the county, earning themselves a sterling reputation among the locals before being sent away for a tax-evasion charge that would have made Capone jealous.

There was one thing that I wanted to chat with Pastor Dino about. The man who built a house next door to the church three years ago had filed a string of noise complaints against the church, one every Wednesday night for the past eighteen months. It seemed like he had a serious objection to the praise band playing during evening services, and he wasn't shy about letting the sheriff's department know about his displeasure.

"That guy's nothing but a massive Chad," Faustus said as we drove back to the church with the sun setting on the horizon."

"A Chad?" I asked. "I'm not sure I get it."

"Like a Karen, but the male version. You know, the guy in the pastel golf shirt with an opinion on everything, always an uneducated one at that. He's the guy who berates his barista for spelling his name wrong on his cup, then asks to see the manager anytime his food is five degrees too hot, or too cold, or comes to the table too fast, or too slow, or…you get the picture."

"So, a douchebag?" I asked.

"Yeah, pretty much, but the kind of exclusively middle-manager-white-dude douchebag that's cropped up since the rise of *Yelp!* and other internet review sites. He's the guy who files a dispute with his credit card company if the set of golf clubs he sniped on eBay is a day late in shipping, then never releases the funds back to the buyer when the shipment arrives. He pulls at the threads of society, hastening the unraveling of the social contracts humans enter into with each other to be…well, not douchebags."

"That sounds like exactly the kind of thing you and your kind do all the time," I pointed out as I turned the truck into the church parking lot.

"Exactly!" he said. "The Chads and Karens of the world are making it almost impossible to corrupt anyone, because they spread the kind of minor shittiness that we count on to make our soul quota. They get all the low-hanging fruit to be nasty to everyone, and then hard-working demons like myself…well, not like *me*, since of course I don't collect souls anymore because that's *wrong*, but other demons get left with the hard cases."

"Of course." I tried to hide my smile, but I was glad it was getting dark out because I'm pretty sure I sucked at it.

"When humans are awful like that, it takes away opportunities for corruption by demonkind. If people like this Neighbor Chad are always out there setting such a sterling example of assholery, then how can a poor demon get someone to be just casually nasty to everyone and end up damned for all eternity? Let me tell you, people like Neighbor Chad do nothing but escalate evil in the world. They take over all the petty badness, and then demons have to go for worse and worse behavior to get souls, and before you know it, the world is full of assholes. And all because some dickweed was told he was the most precious little baby boy *ever* by his over-prescribed helicopter mommy, and he believed it."

"Lemme get this straight," I said, putting the truck into park and sitting back to contemplate what he'd just said. "You're upset because when humans are terrible to each other, it makes demons have to work harder to get people to consign their souls to Hell. Is that it?"

I saw him nod out of the corner of my eye. "In a nutshell, yes. Let's face it, Glory. Demons are pretty lazy by nature. If it was in us to put in an honest day's work, we would have been angels. But we're not. We're demons. We're indolent, shifty, untrustworthy, corrupt, jealous backstabbers that exist for no other reason than to condemn as many humans to the eternal fires of damnation as possible."

"And yet you wondered why I insisted we get separate hotel rooms for this trip," I said.

"I was really wondering why you even agreed to stay in the same hotel as me," Faustus replied, opening his door. "But for now, follow me. I just saw somebody go in the side door of the church, and unless he's lost about eighty pounds in the last six hours, it wasn't Pastor Dino."

I followed him to the front door, which was locked. At least, it was locked until Faustus put his hand on it, closed his eyes for a second, and whispered something in Latin. "Did you just use a spell to unlock the door?" I asked. I knew that Faustus was innately magical, just like me, but I never knew he could use human ritual magic. I'd never known of any demon, or angel for that matter, with that ability.

"You didn't know we could do that, did you?" He asked with a saucy grin.

"No," I admitted. "I mean, I've never tried, because I've never been in a situation where I needed to cast a spell, but no, I didn't."

"Magic works for us the same way it works for mortals, only we can channel more power than they can without burning ourselves to a cinder from the inside out. I learned it back during what I call 'the Goethe incident,' because he wanted to learn ritual magic, and I'd never tried it. Turned out he had no aptitude for it, but I did. Most of the time we have better solutions to a problem, and it can give away our presence if we're not careful, because people with power tend to notice when someone else uses magic, and then they use their Sight, and then they see what we really are, and then it's a whole thing...you get it."

"Yeah, I get it. Now are you going to go inside, or you just gonna stand out here pontificating about the nature of magic all night?" My snark was to hide the fact that I didn't get it, and that bugged me more than I wanted to let Faustus see. He'd proven a solid ally, but he was still a demon. I didn't feel comfortable with him knowing how much it bugged me to learn about my abilities from him. And why hadn't anyone in the Host ever mentioned this to me before? Or to anyone that I was aware of? I pulled my attention from the metaphysical to the physical and followed Faustus inside.

The vestibule was dark, but that didn't slow either of us down at all, since we could see just as well in pitch black as we could at noon. The sanctuary lights were on, but low, and just over the pews. The pulpit area remained dark, and a broad-shouldered figure in a hoodie knelt in front of the communion table.

I motioned for Faustus to hang back and walked up the center aisle of the church. I sat down next to the person, who I could now see was a rangy young man with just the lightest dusting of peach fuzz on his upper lip as his hormones worked on transitioning to adulthood.

"Hi," I said, breaking the silence that lay over us like a warm blanket.

By the way he jumped sky-high, I was the only one that found the darkened sanctuary a comforting place that night. The boy was on his feet in an instant, spinning around and taking a big step back to give himself a little fight-or-flight room. His instincts were good, but the furtive look on his face told me a lot more than the fact that he was uncomfortable in the church at night. This was a young man who'd been in some fights, most likely ones that he couldn't escape from, and he didn't want to be in that situation again.

I stayed seated, holding up my hands so he could see they were empty. "Easy, son. I didn't mean to startle you."

"You didn't," he said, straightening his hoodie and squaring his shoulders. He was at that age where it wasn't acceptable to be scared or caught off guard, where he had to be disaffected and blasé about everything. In some humans, that phase lasts a few years. In some, like Quincy Harker, it lasts a hundred and twenty or so. And counting.

"What are you doing here?" he asked, trying to assert some control over his environment.

"I think I might ask you the same question," I replied. "But we'll get to that. I'm Agent Rubim of the Department of Homeland Security's Paranormal Division. I'm looking into the vandalism here, and Pastor Dino said we could come back tonight and keep an eye on things."

"He didn't tell me anything about that," the boy protested.

"Does he usually keep you informed about his interactions with federal agents?" I asked.

He shifted back and forth on his feet and looked away. He wasn't the most open book of any human I'd ever seen, but he was in the Top Ten, for sure. A large part of me hoped that he could hang on to that, and that he would remain a crappy liar for the rest of his life. It might make his life a little tougher, but it would probably make for a pretty good afterlife.

Finally, he met my eyes. "He tells me about most things. He's my dad. Adopted dad," he corrected. "I mean, not that gay dudes can't have kids, and like, not that there's—"

"Anything wrong with that?" I finished, smiling so he could see that I was teasing him for being awkward, not really mocking.

"Heh. Yeah. He fostered me for a while, and we got the adoption final last year. It's not the easiest thing to do in North Carolina, but we finally got it done." He sat back down on the pew beside me and turned so we could look at each other. It was a little awkward, but he managed to throw one arm over the wooden back of the seat and twist his legs around to make it work. "Are you...do you think whoever did it might come back and try again?"

"Maybe," I said. "Or maybe admire their handiwork, if they didn't know Pastor Dino had painted over everything already. Or do it all over again. That would be the best case for me," I said, then continued as his confusion was evident. "If I caught someone walking in with a couple of spray cans of red and black paint, I could close my case before they ever did anything. If I walked in and someone was just sitting quietly on a pew, I don't really have anything, do I? I mean, it's possible they were getting themselves psyched up to do more damage..." I let my voice trail off as I watched what I was saying sink in.

"But maybe they just wanted to pray, and they liked the way the moonlight looked through the stained glass over the choir loft," he said, raising an arm and pointing at the rose window that lined up perfectly behind the pulpit.

"I'm pretty sure that's a streetlight," I said, smiling. "But you're not our guy."

"How do you know?"

"Because you don't have any paint on your clothes, or your hands, and there aren't any paint cans at your feet or sticking out of your hoodie pocket. If you're the vandal coming back to do more work, you're the least prepared tagger I've ever seen. Literally, the only thing you got right was the black hoodie. And you don't look like any of the people I've known who are fluent in Enochian."

"Eno-what?"

Shit. That might have tipped my hand a little more than I wanted to. Note to self—try not to mention ancient angelic languages to civilians unless you're certain they already know such languages exist. "Some of the symbols in the graffiti matched up with an ancient language that some people think is angelic in nature. I'm sure you're a bright boy, but they don't even teach Latin anymore, much less million-year-old angel writings."

He nodded. "Yeah...I'm barely getting a C in Spanish. So, I guess I'm off the hook." He laughed, but there was a hollow quality to it. He might not have been responsible for the vandalism, but he knew who was, and he had a hand in what happened here. I just needed to find out what that was, and how he got roped into this mess.

"You're right, I don't think you're the person I'm looking for, but you might know who is. Mind if I ask you a few questions?"

"Um...should I have Dino here? Or a lawyer?"

"You're not under arrest. I just need your help finding out who I should arrest. I'm sorry, what was your name?"

"Jason," he replied. "Jason Chavez. I know. I don't look Mexican."

"I...wasn't going to comment on your name," I said. "It's a little too dark in here for me to see what kind of heritage you look like, and a lot of people have so many different bits and bobs of culture mixed up in them that they look nothing like what their last name sounds like. I work with a guy that unless he told you, you'd *never* guess where his family was from."

Admittedly, Faustus is from *Hell*, and that's not something humans usually even consider as an option, but no need to muddy the waters with that tidbit.

"Sorry. It's just...something I hear a lot. It's a small town, you know?"

"I get it. A lot of people need to put things in mental boxes, and anything that doesn't fit gets labeled as weird, or even scary."

"Yeah." He was quiet for a moment, then said. "Okay."

"Okay?"

"Okay, you can ask me stuff. If I know anything, I'll tell you."

I felt like there was a lot behind those words, and it was going to take some pretty serious investigating to ask the right questions. Fortunately, I've been Quincy Harker's Guardian Angel for a while now, so I know something about humans who like to keep their motives vague, and their secrets close to the vest.

I decided to start with a softball, just to see exactly how forthcoming he wanted to be. "Do you know anyone who might have a grudge against the church?"

"Not really. I mean, there are some people who don't like Dad because he's gay, and some people who don't like the way he preaches, because he talks about how love is love, and how if you really want to follow Jesus, you'll take care of each other and be kind to people, and stuff like that. But I don't think any of that is, like, *personal* hate, if you get what I mean? It's more like...I don't know, not liking him on principle, because somebody told them they shouldn't like gay people, or that they should think God is all about sending people to Hell and stuff. But that's not what the Bible says, you know?"

I did know. I was around when it was written. I even remember the bits that got left out in various translations. "I get that. Jesus was all about love, and kindness, and forgiveness. A lot more about being kind to people as opposed to all the Old Testament turning people into pillars of salt and stuff."

Never actually happened, for the record. The salt thing. Lot's wife wasn't struck down for looking back on Sodom and Gomorrah. She was struck down, but it had a lot more to do with the demon she was banging behind Lot's back. But back in the day, dudes didn't want to admit their wives were unfaithful, even if they got seduced by a seriously powerful demon. So Lot made up a tale about his wife getting blasted for looking back on Sodom as they were leaving town, when really she died...while in the act, so to speak, with a demon who burst into flames at the moment of climax. Come to think of it, having God turn her into salt probably would have hurt less.

"Yeah, exactly. So there are some folks who write to the paper about Dad and his 'hippie church in the woods,' but I don't think any of them are devil worshippers or anything like that."

"It's been our experience that most of these cases don't actually involve any Satanic or demonic influences," I said. "It's more often than not been some kids acting out, trying to be cool, or maybe just doing it on a dare."

"Maybe that's what happened here," he said, and the hopeful tone in his voice was a little heartbreaking. He *really* wanted me to buy that, and leave, but the symbology was too accurate. This stuff didn't come off the back of a Slayer album, it had some real knowledge behind it.

"Unfortunately, I don't think so," I said, and watched his face fall. "Some of the symbols used in the graffiti are very old, and not the kind of thing we usually see outside of heavy-duty practitioners of magic. I know that there is a pretty strong Wiccan community in this part of the state. Maybe I should speak to the local coven leaders tomorrow."

"No!" he almost shouted, then scooted back from me a little as he realized how forceful he'd sounded. "I mean, I know a couple of those folks, and they wouldn't do anything like that."

"But how do you know for sure?" I pressed. I don't have any magic that could *make* him tell me, just the kind of pressure everyone knows how to exert on a scared teenager who's looking around for any way out of a conversation. "I don't want to run all over town interrogating people, but if there is a cult of some type operating in the area, we need to make sure they aren't into anything they can't handle."

Jason looked at me, confusion all over his face. "What do you mean, they can't handle? You're talking like all this stuff is real."

And that's when my partner made his ever-so-theatrical entrance, stepping out of the shadows so Jason could get a good look at him. The real him, not the human-suit version of him. Faustus wore his same clothes, but his skin was obsidian black, his eyes glowed a golden yellow in the dim light of the church, and his pointed teeth were particularly pronounced. "That's because all this stuff *is* real, Jason. It's as real as it gets. As real as I am."

"And as real as I am," I said, standing up and taking a step back. Then I manifested my wings, huge white feathered things stretching eight feet on either side of my shoulders. They unfurled and I floated up about six feet off the ground, summoning my gleaming white soulblade to my right hand, wreathed in purest flame.

After a few seconds of hovering, I decided that we'd probably rattled his cage enough for one night, and I let my sword and wings vanish as I dropped to the ground. "My name's Glory, or at least it is for now. This is my…partner, for the moment at least."

"Faustus," the demon said with a grand bow. "At your service."

"Holy shit," the boy said, in perhaps the most reasonable response to learning that angels and demons were real I'd ever seen.

"Yeah, that pretty much covers it," Faustus said, perching on the pew next to Jason. "So, kiddo. You wanna tell us why you painted magical symbols in the language of angels and demons all over the inside of your dad's church? Or do you just want Glory to cut you in half with her big shiny butter knife?" He grinned and flicked his tongue out over those pointed teeth as I shook my head. You can take the demon out of Hell, but you can't take the Hell out of the demon.

"I'm not going to cut anybody in half, Faustus," I said. "Except maybe you."

"Please don't," he replied in mock terror. "This is a new shirt."

Jason looked back and forth between us and said, "Is this for real? I mean, Asheville's too rinky-dink for anybody to be shooting one of those surprise TV shows, but are you guys making a movie?"

"I don't do that anymore," Faustus said. "Those people are too un-ethical even for me. Now I stick to more moral pursuits, like politics."

"No, we're not shooting a movie. Yes, we're really exactly what you think we are. And no, we're not going to hurt you or send you to Hell. But we do want to know where you saw those symbols, because there is no good reason for a preacher's kid in the mountains of North Carolina to even know the Enochian word for 'sacrifice,' much less be painting it on the walls of a church," I said.

"Sacrifice? Holy shit," he repeated.

"I wouldn't use the h-word for it, kiddo, but sacrifice is exactly what you were supposed to be," came a new voice from the back of the church. "But since my plan to make a willing offering of your soul to my Lord and Master seems to be blown up, I'll see what he thinks about the still-beating heart of the traitor Faustus instead."

I looked up the aisle to see the source of the sound, and sure enough, there was a Tempter Demon, all black leather and push-up bra, leaning on the doorframe grinning at the three of us. So much for a simple investigation that doesn't involve any bloodshed or combat. Guess I should have worn my other shoes.

"Alicia?" The boy asked, and I turned to see Jason gawking at the demon in the doorway. "That's...a new look, I guess."

"Pretty sure it's an old look, kiddo," I heard Faustus mutter.

"Oh, sweetie," the demon said as she strutted up the center aisle of the church. I've never understood how sex demons manage to strut with goat legs and hooves, but they're good at it. "You didn't *really* think I was a freshman anthropology major at UNC-Asheville, did you? That's precious."

"I mean, yeah," Jason replied. "Why would I think anything different?"

"The world is just chock-full of people who aren't what they seem to be, kid," Faustus said. "For example, I look like a demon, and she looks like a centerfold. But she's way more likely to rip out your eyeballs than I am. At least, she would be if Glory and I weren't here to stop her, that is."

"You want to actually *fight*, Faustus? Wow, everything I ever heard was that you were the fast talker, the one who never lifted a finger unless it was completely unavoidable, the conniving mastermind who would more likely convince two warring parties to kill each other than pick a side. Guess my information was way off."

"Nah, that's pretty much him," I said. "But spend a couple of years with the Reaper and you'd be amazed at what that can do to a person's baser instincts. Before you know it, all thoughts of self-preservation are thrown out the window, and you're just dropping f-bombs and starting fights at the slightest provocation." I watched to see if she reacted to the nickname most of demonkind used for Harker. There was a little flicker of something there. Maybe fear, maybe hatred, but definitely something. I decided to press my advantage.

"So why don't you just fuck right off back to the Pit you crawled out of, before I split you from nose to navel?" I manifested my soul-blade and stepped into the aisle, glaring at the demon.

"Guess you weren't kidding about the f-bombs, were you, Princess?" the Tempter said, but the sneer on her face had a slightly less arrogant cast to it.

"I wasn't kidding about the killing you part, either," I said. "Do you know what happens if I kill you with a soulblade? Even on this plane? You're dead, cupcake. Real dead. Not just poof out of existence and materialize back in Hell with a shameful story to tell Lucifer about how a Guardian Angel kicked your ass but gone forever. No reconstitution, no resurrection, nothing. Remember, we don't have souls. We are souls. So if I kill you, here, with this," I spun my blade around in a lazy circle, carving a trail of white fire in the air at my side. "You're done. And I've fought a lot of demons in my day. I flew with Michael in the Great War. I stood on the Fields of Heaven as we beat back your advances, and I have stood ankle-deep in the viscera of my fallen brothers and sisters. So, you want some? Come get some."

Now she looked rattled. It was complete bullshit, of course. My soulblade was no more lethal to her than anything else on this plane. I could chop her up into kibble and feed her to Carol Baskin's tigers (cut me some slack, Harker was watching it and I got sucked into the train wreck that is *Tiger King*) and all that would happen is her soul would get dropped back into Hell. But I was counting on her not knowing that. And judging by the fear on her face and the hesitation in her steps, she didn't.

"Or…" Faustus' voice slipped in between the two of us like fog, all cat feet and silky.

We both turned to look at him. "Or we could give you a slam dunk of a soul, ripe for the picking, and nobody needs to get their hands dirty."

"Or I could just kill her," I said, keeping my voice hard while inwardly hoping that whatever Faustus had up his sleeve was good. If she called my bluff and I beat her, then I'd never be able to use the BS about my blade destroying demons for good again. If she backed down, then the legend could grow stronger, and maybe eventually spread to more demons and become something really useful. Not to mention I didn't really want to destroy a demon in the middle of Pastor Dino's church. It wouldn't leave much of a mess, *per se*, but it would screw up the atmosphere of the sanctuary, and it would be a lot less comforting a place of worship. Demon battles are kinda scorched-earth affairs, typically.

"What did you have in mind, traitor?" The demon asked. "I'm not a legendary coward like you, but I would always rather talk — or…do other things — than fight…" The look she gave Jason sent the teen spinning around on the pew to look away from her in a flash. And probably to adjust his jeans at the same time. There was zero doubt as to what other things she was talking about, even if you weren't a teenaged boy.

"There's a guy living next door," Faustus said with a grin. "I call him 'Neighbor Chad.' I think he might be someone that you could...enjoy negotiating with..."

"So what's going to happen to Mr. Saperstein?" Jason asked about an hour later when Faustus came back into the church.

"Nothing he doesn't already want to happen," the demon replied. He wore his human suit again, and the smarmy smile he gave us would give a used-car salesman nightmares. "Elira — that's your friend Alicia's real name, by the way — will provide him with the opportunity to live out some of the things he's only ever seen on the internet. The kinds of things that most people can't bring up to someone they met in a bar. Well, depending on the bar, I guess. She'll take him down a few different rabbit holes of perversion before she's through, but eventually I'm sure the local constabulary will have cause to seize his hard drives and they'll find imagery that is very reminiscent of the Enochian used in the vandalism of the church on a website that Neighbor Chad runs. A website dedicated to...shall we say compromising drawings of anime girls with tentacles? If you get my meaning."

I was a little ashamed to admit that I knew exactly what he meant and surprised to see by the confusion on his face that Jason had *no* clue about hentai. Weird. I thought everybody had the internet by now. "So, what will that do?"

"Nothing, really," Faustus said. "Pastor Dino probably won't press charges, but it should take care of the noise complaints and the annoying calls to the police that Chad seems to love making."

"But he won't go to Hell, will he?" Jason asked.

"No idea," the demon replied. "Don't know, don't care."

"What he means is that Mr. Saperstein won't be damned for anything that Faustus does, or for anything Elira does to him. If he sins enough to end up in Hell, he'll end up in Hell. But it won't be because of anything we've done," I explained. I didn't want to get into the truth of the matter, that Hell is where people go if they think they're supposed to go there. If they think they need to be tormented until they've paid for their sins, then that's what happens. If they think they've lived a good life and deserve to have a pleasant afterlife, then they get a harp and a cloud. Or a beach and a never-ending blender of margaritas. It's really up to the person.

"Yeah, that," Faustus said.

"That doesn't seem like enough to get her to take her attention off Jason and Dino," I said. "They're pretty appealing targets for your old boss." Lucifer was still in the business of collecting souls. That part of the mythology was true. The purer the soul, the more power it gave his army. And Lucifer was still building an army with the intent to storm Heaven again. Because it worked out so well for him last time.

"It wasn't. I had to sweeten the pot a little," Faustus said.

I immediately became suspicious. Faustus is like a divorce attorney — if there is anything not in writing or completely outlined in your agreement, he's going to twist it to his advantage. "What did you offer her?" I asked.

"I gave her a Get-Out-of-Dead-Free Card. A one-time pass, good with you, me, Harker, or any of our people. She runs afoul of any of us in the future, she gets one out. One time she can use that pass and we won't kill her. Your little BS about killing her forever scared the *shit* out of her. She likes being alive. A lot. She's gotten accustomed to it over the millennia. So I told her I could give her a pass good for one shot at us not killing her, and she jumped at it."

"You know Harker will never go for that," I said. "If he runs into her, and she's in his way, he's going to incinerate her from the inside out."

"Yeah, I know." The blasé expression on his face was classic Faustus.

"And you'll forget about this deal you made by the time we get home," I said.

"It's already getting hazy in my memory."

"So basically, you convinced her to do what you want for an unenforceable promise for us not to do something we can't do in the first place," I said.

"Well, when you put it like that, it feels almost deceptive," Faustus said. He sketched out a rough bow in the air and turned away, heading for the truck and home.

I looked at Jason. "Your eyes have been opened a little, huh?"

"Yeah, for real."

"What do you think it means for you?"

"I dunno," he said, and I had to admire his honesty. "I mean, I can't unsee the stuff I saw tonight. But it doesn't really change anything, does it? I screwed up. I painted that stuff on the walls to impress a girl with how much of a rebel I was, and it almost took me down a dark path that could have gone someplace really bad."

"But it didn't," I said.

"Because of you."

"Because somebody gave a shit," I said. "Look, there are a lot of people in the world who'll try to take advantage of you. Try to get you to do things for them that you know are bad, or wrong. And sometimes you won't recognize them for what they are. They might not be demons. They probably won't be. Sometimes they'll just be assholes. But as long as you keep enough people in your life to pull you back and set you on the right path when they see you screwing up, you'll be okay."

"What if you're not there next time?"

"I probably won't be," I said. "I'm *a* Guardian Angel, but I'm not your Guardian Angel. But he'll be there. Because that's what fathers do." I pointed to where Pastor Dino stood in the doorway, watching us.

Jason got up and ran to the bushy-bearded preacher, wrapping his arms around the burly man. "I'm sorry, Dad. I'm so sorry."

Dino patted the boy's head and looked at me, kindness in every wrinkle at the corner of his eyes. "I know, son. I know. It's okay. I forgive you. And so does He." The preacher looked up at the stained-glass window, and for just a second, I could have sworn the light coming through it was too bright to be the moon. Then I blinked, and it was gone.

NEVERENDING

Christopher J. Burke

VALARON TENDED THE FLOWERS IN THE GARDEN OF THE ANCIENTS. HE didn't have power over the weather – whoever had was long gone – but it regulated itself nicely. Sun shone down on the gleaming faces of the statues of heroes – men and women, warriors and scholars who were immortalized long ago. The morning was quiet, except for a light breeze.

Then he heard a faint hum.

On the far end of the garden, a marble arch, decorated with alabaster sculptures and glass and crystal ornaments, rose up and disappeared into the clouds. It was the bridge that crossed the planar boundary and led to the Great Ring, the site where bridges and pathways from the other worlds beyond converged. For nearly a century, it sat as an obelisk whose purpose had been forgotten. The humming and the faint glow meant one thing: friend or foe, a visitor approached.

Valaron's heart lifted even as the hair on his skin stood. Before the klaxon had sounded, he'd left his plowshare, retrieved his sword, and taken to the sky. With wings spread at their fullest, he soared to meet the returning soldier or invading enemy. He touched down near the bridge's base, drew his sword in salute, and waited.

His hopes deflated when a scaly, three-horned creature lumbered down the ramp. As it shambled, its bare feet left a trail of dark, brimstone prints behind it, which evaporated into rising smoke clouds.

The angel's face fell. He lowered his blade to the pavestones before the thing reached the landing. Rupsgath!

The only traveler to come down the bridge in the past century had returned. The round, reddish-black demon had a bulbous face, and tattered wings folded behind its back. It carried nothing more than a bottle in its fist.

"Halo, Val!" The creature belched laughter that reeked of sulfur. "That never gets old."

Valaron sighed at Rupsgath's salutation. "Old? Your fetid attempt at humor is absolutely decrepit."

The demon feigned outrage. It placed its free, sinister hand over its barreled chest, where one might imagine a shredded, beaten heart. "You wound me, Val! Where's your hospitality? Do you realize that in all my visits to Clarita, you've never once given me a 'halo'!"

It roared so fiercely that flames shot from the three nostrils of its porcine nose. Several minutes passed before it reined in its mirth and composed itself.

"Rupsgath, why have you returned?"

It pointed a clawed finger, and bellowed, "I have come for you, Valaron!" Then it raised the bottle high. "To get you drunk!"

For just a moment, the angel contemplated his swift sword then planted it into the dirt. "Why will you not leave me be? Be gone from Clarita. Return no more."

The demon ignored the request. Instead, it sat heavily on a large stone. "Leave you be? It's been eighty years since I last came! Have you seen any other than me in all that time?"

Valaron stood silent.

"Didn't think so. But you keep the home fires burning every night, I'll bet."

It offered the bottle to its host. "Care to join me for a drink? I brought my own."

The lone sentry raised a hand and turned his head in disgust. "No," he replied, hoping the lack of a "thank you" was understood.

Rupsgath laughed and slapped a knee. "Of course. What was I thinking? You probably pass your days tending the fruit of the vines, trampling out your own vintage. Get a snootful of your own divine snifter. Let the grape shiraz be poured!"

The angel stood frozen, annoying his visitor.

"That was hell-arious. You need to get out more. Let your halo down."

"I have no cause for celebration, nor time for idle chatter."

"You never do, but fear not! I shall partake enough for the two of us." It belched again and held up the bottle in both paws. "Forgive me.

I got an early start. I've finished six bottles of wine and whiskey already. You won't have a problem if I break this seventh seal, will you?"

Valaron turned away to shield his disgust. When he had collected himself, he faced his unwanted intruder. "Your role as emissary prevents me from crushing you beneath my heel—"

"As if!"

"But you are still not welcome here." He pondered the bottle in the creature's hand. Loathed as he was to prolong this conversation, curiosity forced his hallowed hand.

"There are no vineyards in Guumpthus. No grains grow. Where do you acquire your foul spirits?"

"Foul? Ha! They're actually quite pleasant." It sank its teeth into the bottle's cork and pulled it free with a satisfying pop. "There are more liquor stores between the heavens and hells than you can dream of, Valaron."

Rupsgath tilted its head back, held the bottle above its maw, and poured itself a measure. "You should see the planes in the Midrealms I've visited. They've had vast empires filled with great men telling other people what to do. Then the people rose up and declared that they would decide what to do for themselves! Can you imagine? You would've liked it.

"But in the end, they always get bored with that. Soon they start telling all the other people what to say and do again. And what they can't say or do. Yeah, I just loved those guys!"

The beast burped. Then it offered the bottle to its host.

Valaron declined once more.

The demon shrugged and took a second swig. "You must realize by now that no one else is returning. The war is done. The combatants have all fallen. Either to their deaths, to some lower dimensions, or to planes so terrible even I wouldn't want to consider them. And yet, I've found myself sitting alone in a molten amphitheater doing just that."

The thing gave an audible shudder as its scales rattled.

"Only you and I are left. We remain behind to guard our domains against non-existent invaders."

Valaron scoffed. "There are others out there. They didn't all go to war. Some traveled the planes. Scholars, emissaries!"

"Are you trying to convince me or yourself?"

The angel pulled his sword from the dirt. "They'll return! And when they do, I shall be standing here to salute them, and welcome them home."

Rupsgath curled up its legs on the large stone upon which it sat. It placed the paw with the wine on one knee and rested its muzzle on the other, looking lost in deep thought.

Finally, Rupsgath addressed its heavenly host. "Valaron, have you ever just flapped your wings and flown high into the sky until the fields grew distant beneath your feet? In all this time, have you ever traversed your marmoreal bridge? Have you gone to this plane's edge just to enjoy the view? Have you set foot on the Great Ring of Bridges?"

The demon could guess the answer. It grinned and chortled. "You know, it's not even a ring. It's just a flat hunk of rock anchored in the ether by a dozen bridges. Bridges to other flat rocks."

It held out its arms. "Like this one. Clarita floats like a cloud, without moving anywhere. It's held immobile by this glorious arch and two more over yonder."

Valaron stiffened his back, squared his shoulders. "How do you know about that?"

The creature stood and turned in place. "I always knew there was more to this realm. Could this possibly be all there is to Clarita? The welcoming fields and your church? Guumpthus has its towers and pits. Your little paradise can't be different. Additional heavens in the rear, complete with bridges to more worlds beyond.

"Besides, you can see them from the Great Ring. Or is it just one of infinite Great Rings? Whichever it is, I've spied two bridges through the ether. There might be a third. But I always lose sight of them as I come down this ramp. My wings won't carry me, but if you flew up into the clouds here, I'd wager you could spot them in the distance. Fly high enough, and you should see the literal edge of your domain.

"Problem is that perspective is more deceiving than a pack of devils with a stack of contracts and quotas to meet. And it shifts within each reality."

"You've traveled to many realities, have you?"

Rupsgath looked back to the ramp. "No. I've only been to a few lower realms between here and my domain, so far. You have to cross a couple of bridges to get to Guumpthus. First, you need to descend to the Midrealms. After that, take the Road of Good Intentions."

The angel raised an eyebrow as the demon chuckled at its own joke.

"Just kidding. That's something I picked up down there, along with the liquor, and a few diseases. And hand baskets! You're supposed to bring hand baskets. Don't ask me why."

It stared at the black glass of the bottle in its fist. "It's not difficult for someone like you or me to find the wretched, scoria path. It's a foul-smelling, slag-covered road of putrid brown, darkening to deepest black. Coal would be jealous of its color. It's paved with felsic obsidian flows over welded dacite tuffs."

He pulled another drink. "I've become well-versed in the nature of feldspar over the past millennia. Not much else to think about. The old, condemned souls, locked within their own torments, have sunken to places beyond my reach. No devils collect new ones because they all went off to some astral plane to fight in a war no one remembers the start of.

"You can lower your sword, Valaron. The time has come to stand down."

The angel rose up, unfurled wings elevating him, as his fury built up within him. He quickly settled himself again to the path but pressed his position. "Bestill your wicked, lying tongue, demon! I will not stand down. I will remain here. I shall always be here. Someone must guard Clarita, lest it become defiled!"

The demon looked up, aware that the last rebuff was not only laced with revulsion but also borderline hateful. It found the remark almost flattering.

"The lone sentry. I know the job." Rupsgath belched, emitting a spark of hellfire and another wisp of smoke. "I handle that the way I deal with most things. Poorly."

"That much is obvious from the way you leave your post un-attended."

The fiend roared. "Who'd ever want to go there? Do you think I care if there's an invasion? I'd welcome them in. Set up lava huts for all to settle down. Roast s'mores over an open pit!"

It sat back down, shaking its head. "I've had enough of it already. That's why I'm here."

"To torment me further?"

The demon stood.

"No. To say 'Goodbye.' That's why I'm celebrating. I've had enough! Enough of the solitary life. Enough of sitting on rocks in the middle of lava pools, laughing at my own jokes. Enough of being alone with my chilling, rotting, cataclysmic thoughts. Those and the booze."

It looked at the angel squarely. "The longer I stay, the more my ruminations turn to annihilistic visions and nihilistic beliefs. That's over. I'm leaving. I'm going to walk the planes.

"Maybe I'll return in another hundred years, or maybe a thousand. Maybe not at all. But I'm finished watching over an empty demesne, protecting it from outsiders. Like any creature in the heavens or hells would want to call it home!"

Putting the near-empty bottle down on the ground, Rupsgath turned and stepped away. "You could come with me, Valaron. Or we could go separate ways. But there's no one left to fight off. Listen to an expert on Gluttony, Sloth, and Lust. Where has all this eternal vigilance gotten you? Don't let Pride be your undoing. Don't let it hold you back."

It let out a laugh. "If you stay, I believe the saying is that you can beat that sword into a plowshare. For that matter, you should rotate your crops. I noticed on the way down that the soil looks low on nutrients. It will suffer from more of the same."

Valaron raised his sword high and shook his fist. "If you're determined to leave, then do so, and never darken my radiant bridge again! I'll erect a fence around that defiled spot in your 'honor.'"

"As you desire." The demon walked to the bridge, its claws setting sparks on the pavestones. "If you ever do get tired of this place, visit Guumpthus. Take some holy water and sanctify a path. There'll be no infernal magic to counter it. Farewell."

The decrepit creature faded into the distance as the bridge crossed the planes.

Valaron thrust his sword into the dirt again. Crops needed tending, and the steeple needed to be shined. He glanced back at the empty bridge once more. Or maybe those things would wait until tomorrow.

Perhaps, he thought, *I may take one day off.*

ABOUT THE AUTHORS

JAMES CHAMBERS received the Bram Stoker Award® for the graphic novel, *Kolchak the Night Stalker: The Forgotten Lore of Edgar Allan Poe* and is a three-time Bram Stoker Award finalist. He is the author of the collections *On the Night Border*, described by *Booklist* as "a haunting exploration of the space where the real world and nightmares collide," and *Resurrection House* as well as the dark urban fantasy novella, *Three Chords of Chaos. Publisher's Weekly* gave his Lovecraftian collection, *The Engines of Sacrifice*, a starred review and called it "...chillingly evocative." He has authored several novellas, including *The Dead Bear Witness, Tears of Blood,* and *The Dead in Their Masses* in the Corpse Fauna novella series. He also wrote the illustrated story collection, *The Midnight Hour: Saint Lawn Hill and Other Tales*, created in collaboration with artist Jason Whitley. He co-edited *A New York State of Fright: Horror Stories from the Empire State* and edited the all-new anthology *Under Twin Suns: Alternate Histories of the Yellow Sign*. His stories have appeared in numerous anthologies and magazines, and he has written numerous comic books including *Leonard Nimoy's Primortals*, the critically acclaimed "The Revenant" in *Shadow House*. His website is: www.jameschambersonline.

JOHN L. FRENCH is a retired crime scene supervisor with forty years' experience. He has seen more than his share of murders, shootings, and serious assaults. As a break from the realities of his job, he started writing science fiction, pulp, horror, fantasy, and, of course, crime fiction.

John's first story "Past Sins" was published in Hardboiled Magazine and was cited as one of the best Hardboiled stories of 1993. More crime fiction followed, appearing in Alfred Hitchcock's Mystery Magazine, the Fading Shadows magazines and in collections by Barnes and Noble. Association with writers like James Chambers and the late, great C.J. Henderson led him to try horror fiction and to a still growing fascination with zombies and other undead things. His first horror story "The Right Solution" appeared in Marietta Publishing's *Lin Carter's Anton Zarnak*. Other horror stories followed in anthologies such as *The Dead Walk* and *Dark Furies*, both published by Die Monster Die books. It was in *Dark Furies* that his character Bianca Jones made her literary debut in "21 Doors," a story based on an old Baltimore legend and a creepy game his daughter used to play with her friends.

John's first book was *The Devil of Harbor City*, a novel done in the old pulp style. *Past Sins* and *Here There Be Monsters* followed. John was also consulting editor for Chelsea House's *Criminal Investigation* series. His other books include *The Assassins' Ball* (written with Patrick Thomas), *Souls on Fire, The Nightmare Strikes, Monsters Among Us, The Last Redhead, the Magic of Simon Tombs,* and *The Santa Heist* (written with Patrick Thomas). John is the editor of *To Hell in a Fast Car, Mermaids 13,* C. J. Henderson's *Challenge of the Unknown, Camelot 13* (with Patrick Thomas), and (with Greg Schauer) *With Great Power ...*

You can find John on Facebook or you can email him at him at jfrenchfam@aol.com.

For the past twenty-five years, ROBERT E. WATERS has served in the gaming industry, first as a Managing Editor at The Avalon Hill Game Company, and then as a producer, designer, and writer for several computer game studios. Robert has been publishing fiction professionally since 2003, with his first sale to *Weird Tales*, "The Assassin's Retirement Party." Since then, he has sold over 75 stories to various online and print magazines and anthologies, including the online magazine *The Grantville Gazette*, which publishes stories set in Baen Book's best-selling alternate history Ring of Fire series.

Over the years, Robert has contributed to many E-Spec Books anthologies, including their wildly popular Military SF series, Defending the Future. His latest is a collection of his DEVIL DANCERS mil-SF stories, which is now available on Amazon.

Robert currently lives in Baltimore, Maryland, with his wife Beth, their son Jason, and their two kittens Snow and Ash.

Check out his website at www.roberternestwaters.com.

JENIFER PURCELL ROSENBERG wrote her first story in the form of a children's book for her 3rd grade G&T teacher. She's been hooked on writing ever since. She wrote and illustrated the book Alligator's Friends, which is about a socially awkward reptile trying to make new pals in the animal world. Her short story credits include "The Power of Five" from the 2018 Brave New Girls anthology Tales of Heroines Who Hack, "Waking Things" from the Crazy 8 Press anthology They Keep Killing Glenn, "Night Path" from The Nature of Cities, Tales of Silver Green, and "Evening Sonnet" in Nisaba Journal 4, and "Outsider", in *Thrilling Adventure Yarns,* among others. Jenifer has also written for online publications, and for the tabletop RPG industry.

When she isn't writing, Jenifer keeps busy with excessive volunteering, organizing charitable events, teaching paint classes, getting involved with Pride events, and learning new languages. Her garden is outfitted with a miniature fairy village that she has carefully cultivated. She also makes wine with her friends, loves to cook, and has been gaming since she was wee. Jenifer lives in the wonderful City of New York with her family. She is thrilled to be a part of this project, and plans to write more paranormal fiction in the future.

CHRISTOPHER J. BURKE is an author, high school math teacher, and webcomic creator. He's also a gamer and fan of science fiction who has been telling stories since he was little. This combination ultimately led to his first professional sale, "Don't Kill the Messenger," in Autoduel Quarterly. This was followed by the creation of a fiction fanzine, Driving Tigers Magazine, with stories set in the Car Wars universe of Steve Jackson Games, which had a five-issue run. Thanks to his knowledge and love of that game, he was asked to co-author GURPS Autoduel, 2nd edition for Steve Jackson Games.

He took time off from writing when he switched careers and went back to school to become a teacher. But not before he completed a goal of having a humor piece published in MAD Magazine.

In 2007, he started the math-based webcomic *(x, why?)*, filled with the kind of geeky humor that makes his students groan when he includes them in the daily lesson. Christopher still updates the comic with new strips every week on his blog http://mrburkemath.blogspot.com.

After a chance meeting at a launch party in 2014, Christopher was once again bitten by the writing bug and started producing flash fiction. He won several monthly flash fiction contests on the eSpec Books blog, and appeared in their anthology, *In a Flash 2016* and *In a Flash 2021*.

Christopher lives in Brooklyn with his wife, Antoinette.

MICHELLE D. SONNIER writes dark urban fantasy, steampunk, and anything else that lets her combine the weird and the fantastic in unexpected ways. She even writes horror, although it took her a long time to admit that since she prefers the existential scare over blood and gore. She's published short stories in a variety of print and online venues and has upcoming projects with eSpec Books and Otter Libris. You can find her on Facebook (Michelle D. Sonnier, The Writer). She lives in Maryland with her husband, son, and a variable number of cats. The Clockwork Witch is her first full-length novel, followed by *Death's Embrace* and *An Unceasing Hunger*.

Award-winning author, editor, and publisher **DANIELLE ACKLEY-MCPHAIL** has worked both sides of the publishing industry for longer than she cares to admit. In 2014 she joined forces with husband Mike McPhail and friend Greg Schauer to form her own publishing house, eSpec Books (www.especbooks.com).

Her published works include seven novels, *Yesterday's Dreams, Tomorrow's Memories, Today's Promise, The Halfling's Court, The Redcaps' Queen, Daire's Devils,* and *Baba Ali and the Clockwork Djinn*, written with Day Al-Mohamed. She is also the author of the solo collections *Eternal Wanderings, A Legacy of Stars, Consigned to the Sea, Flash in the Can, Transcendence, Between Darkness and Light,* and the non-fiction writers' guides *The Literary Handyman* and *LH: Build-A-Book Workshop*. She is the senior editor of the *Bad-Ass Faeries* anthology series, *Gaslight & Grimm, Side of Good/Side of Evil, After Punk,* and *Footprints in the Stars*. Her short stories are included in numerous other anthologies and collections.

KEITH R.A. DeCANDIDO has been an author, editor, critic, TV personality, martial artist, museum curator, Census worker, musician, sportswriter, and podcaster over the course of the last three decades. He's best known for his fiction writing, with more than 50 novels, around a hundred works of short fiction, and a mess of comic books.

He's written fiction in more than thirty different licensed universes, based on TV shows (*Star Trek, Supernatural, Doctor Who, Farscape*), movies (*Alien, Cars, Kung Fu Panda, Resident Evil*), comic books (Spider-Man, Thor, X-Men, Hulk), and games (*Dungeons & Dragons, World of Warcraft, Command & Conquer, StarCraft*), and also in his own original universes, including fantastical police procedurals set in the fictional cities of Cliff's End (*Dragon Precinct* and its sequels) and Super City (the *Super City Cops* novels and novellas) and urban fantasy tales set in the somewhat real locales of New York (the Bram Gold Adventures) and Key West (tales of Cassie Zukav, weirdness magnet). Recent and upcoming work includes the *Alien* novel *Isolation* (based on both the movie series and the videogame), the collaborative novels *Animal* (with Munish K. Batra, MD) and *To Hell and Regroup* (with David Sherman), the next books in his ongoing series, *Phoenix Precinct* and *Feat of Clay*, the award-winning graphic novel *Icraus* (with Gregory A. Wilson and Áthila Fabbio), the *Systema Paradoxa* novella *All-the-Way House*, and short stories in the anthologies *Across the Universe: Tales of Alternative Beatles, Bad Ass Moms, Footprints in the Stars*, and *Brave New Girls: Adventures of Gals & Gizmos*). Keith has also been writing about pop culture for the award-winning webzine Tor.com since 2011, has been an editor of thirty years' standing (though he usually does it sitting down), is a third-degree black belt in karate, plays percussion professionally, and probably some other stuff he can't remember due to the lack of sleep. Find out less at his hilariously primitive web site at DeCandido.net.

RUSS COLCHAMIRO is the author of the rollicking time travel/space adventure, *Crossline*, the SF/F backpacking comedy series *Finders Keepers: The Definitive Edition, Genius de Milo*, and *Astropalooza*, editor of the SF mystery anthology *Love, Murder & Mayhem*, and co-author of the noir anthology *Murder in Montague Falls*, all with *Crazy 8 Press*.

His most recent novel, *Crackle and Fire*, is the first in a new scifi mystery series featuring his intergalactic private eye, Angela Hardwicke. He has also contributed short stories to more than a dozen anthologies, and is host of Russ's Rockin' Rollercoaster, a podcast featuring scifi, fantasy, mystery, and horror authors.

Russ lives in New Jersey with his wife, two ninjas, and puppy, Jinx.

For more on and Russ's books, visit www.russcolchamiro.com, follow him on Twitter @AuthorDudeRuss, and 'like' his Facebook author page www.facebook.com/RussColchamiroAuthor.

MICHAEL A. BLACK is the award winning author of forty books, most of which are in the mystery and thriller genres. He has also written in sci-fi, western, horror, and sports genres. A retired police officer, he has done everything from patrol to investigating homicides to conducting numerous SWAT operations. Black was awarded the Cook County Medal of Merit in 2010. He is also the author of over one hundred short stories and articles, and wrote two novels with television star, Richard Belzer (*Law & Order SVU*). Black is currently writing the Executioner series under the name Don Pendleton. His Executioner novel, *Fatal Prescription*, won the Best Original Novel Scribe Award given by the International Association of Media Tie-In Writers in 2018. His latest novels are *Trackdown: Devil's Dance* and *Legends of the West* (under his own name), *Dying Art* and *Cold Fury* (under Don Pendleton), and *Gunslinger: Killer's Ghost* (under the name A.W. Hart).

PATRICK THOMAS has had stories published in over three dozen magazines and more than fifty anthologies. He's written 30+ books including the fantasy humor series *Murphy's Lore*, urban fantasy spin offs *Fairy With A Gun, Fairy Rides The Lightning, Dead To Rites, Rites of Passage, Lore & Dysorder* and two more in the *Startenders* series. He co-writes the *Mystic Investigators* paranormal mystery series and *The Assassins' Ball*, a traditional mystery, co-authored with John L. French. His darkly humorous advice column *Dear Cthulhu* includes the collections *Cthulhu Knows Best, Have A Dark Day, Good Advice For Bad People,* and *Cthulhu Knows Best*. His latest collection is the Steampunk themed *As The Gears Turn*. A number of his books were part of the props department of the CSI television show and one was even thrown at a suspect. Fairy With A Gun was optioned by Laurence Fishburne's Cinema Gypsy Productions. Act of Contrition, a story featuring his *Soul For Hire* hitman is in development as a short film by Top Men Productions. Drop by www.patthomas.net to learn more.

HILDY SILVERMAN was the Editor-in-Chief of *Space and Time Magazine* for twelve years. She is a short fiction author whose recent publications include, "My Dear Wa'ats" (2018, *Baker Street Irregulars II: The Game's Afoot*, Ventrella & Maberry, eds.), "The Lady of the Lakes" (2018, *Camelot 13*, French and Thomas, eds.), "Sidekicked" (2019, *Release the Virgins*, Ventrella, ed.), and "Divided We Fell" (2020, *The Divided States of America, Bechtel, ed.*). Her nonfiction articles have appeared in numerous legal and medical professional journals and blogs. In the mundane world, she is the Digital Marketing Manager for Oticon Medical US.

JOHN G. HARTNESS is a teller of tales, a righter of wrong, defender of ladies' virtues, and some people call him Maurice, for he speaks of the pompatus of love. He is also the award-winning author of the urban fantasy series *The Black Knight Chronicles*, the *Bubba the Monster Hunter* comedic horror series, the *Quincy Harker, Demon Hunter* dark fantasy series, and many other projects. He is also a cast member of the role-playing podcast *Authors & Dragons*, where a group of comedy, fantasy, and horror writers play Dungeons & Dragons. Very poorly.

In 2016, John teamed up with several other publishing industry professionals to create Falstaff Books, a small press dedicated to publishing the best of genre fiction's "misfit toys." Falstaff Books has since published over 200 titles with authors ranging from first-timers to NY Times bestsellers, with no signs of slowing down any time soon. 2019 saw the launch of *Book Babble*, a YouTube show where John and Falstaff Books Associate Publisher Melissa McArthur interview professional writers about the books they love.

In his copious free time John enjoys long walks on the beach, rescuing kittens from trees, and playing *Magic: the Gathering*. John's pronouns are he/him.

OUR DIVINE SUPPORT

Adam H Zerance
Amanda Cavanagh
Anita Morris
Anne Frates
Annie Allen
Anonymous
Apotheosis Studios
April Walters
Ashley VanMeter
Aysha Rehm
Beth Sparks-Jacques
Beverly Bambury
Bradon Jurn
Butch Howard
C.A. Rowland
Carol Jones
Cat Hunter
Charissa D. Jones
Chris Cooke
Christopher J. Burke
Craig "Stevo" Stephenson
Curtis & Maryrita Steinhour
Dale A Russell
Dan Nolan
Daniel Lin
Danielle Ackley-McPhail
David Perkins

David Sherman
David Stolarz
Debbie Cairo
Debra Lieven
Dee Sauerwein
Dex Greenbright
Dino Hicks
Dr Douglas Vaughan
Ed Washburn
Eric S. Schaefer
Eric W. Stephenson
Felicia Browell
Gary Phillips
Gav
Gordon Horne
Greg Levick
H Lynnea Johnson
Howard J. Bampton
IndolentCin
Isaac 'Will It Work' Dansicker
Jakub Narębski
Jay Targaryen
JC Kang
JDN
Jeanne Talbourdet
Jenn Whitworth
Jennifer Della'Zanna

Jennifer L. Pierce
Jeremy Audet
Johanna Sachs
John Green
John Idlor
John L. French
John Monahan
Judith Waidlich
Julian White
Julie Giles Cooke
Keith R.A. DeCandido
Keith Rohrer
Ken Brandt
Kierin Fox
L.E. Custodio
Lark Cunningham
Leokii
Leon W Fairley
Lewis Phillips
Lisa1200
Lori B.
Lorraine Anderson
maileguy
Marc W.
Margaret Bumby
Margaret St. John
Margie Martinson-Brezina
Maria T
Maria V. Arnold
Mark Lukens
Megan Mackie
Melissa Phelps
Mia Naeyaert
Michael Brooker
Mishee Kearney
Museworthy Inc.
Nanci Moy & Dave Bean
Nina Amaya
Oren Truitt
Otter Libris

Paul May
Paul van Oven
Pete Niedzielski
Peter D Engebos
pjk
Rich Riley
Richard Clark
Rick Heinz
Rob in AUS
Robert C Flipse
Robert Claney
Robin Lynn
Russell Ventimeglia
Ryan Harron
Sasquatch
Scherrix
Scott Elson
Scott Schaper
Shane "Asharon" Sylvia
Shell S.
Shervyn
Sheryl R. Hayes
STEAMPUNK Chef James
Stephen Ballentine
Stephen Lesnik
Steve Locke
Tad L. J. Pierson
Taia Hartman
Tasha Turner
The Creative Fund
Thomas Karwacki
Tim DuBois
Tina Noe Good
Tom B.
ToniAnn Marini
Tony C
V Hartman DiSanto
Wil Bastion
Yes